SUMMER SECRETS
NOVELLAS 1 - 3

SUMMER SECRETS

Novellas 1 - 3

VANIA RHEAULT

To anyone who wants to read something a little naughty. Enjoy!

SUMMER SECRETS

Novellas 1 – 3

Published by Coffee and Kisses Press
This is a work of fiction. Names, characters, places, and incidents are the
product of the author's imagination or are used fictitiously. Any resemblance
to actual persons, living or dead, events, or locales is entirely coincidental.
Cover design by Vania Rheault

Picture purchased and used with permission from canstock.com Photo ID
csp31587255
Uploaded by Bialasiewicz
Cattail vector used with permission by Pixabay.com

Coffee and Kisses Press owned and operated by Vania Rheault and David
Willis
Printed in the United States of America

E-Reader ISBN-10 0-9977930-3-1
Paperback ISBN 978-0997793024

JANIE AND VINCE

"What the fuck you have in here? Bricks?"

Yes, because she always packed bricks to go the lake. Just in case she needed to slam her head against one. "I didn't ask you to carry it in here," Janie Davenport reminded him. She was perfectly capable of carrying her own suitcase.

"I'm trying to be nice," Vince Campbell muttered. "Ungrateful."

She thought she heard the last but wasn't sure. Vince scared the piss out of her so she wouldn't have confronted him about it anyway. Janie always tried to keep her distance from him, and for the most part, she was successful in the attainment of that goal. On occasion, she liked to ruffle his feathers, but only with other people around—she was smarter than that.

Janie looked around the familiar cabin. She couldn't remember if she'd stayed in this exact one; they were all the same.

Two bedrooms were located down a little hallway, which held one king bed each. The living room was furnished, too, with a large brown couch sitting under a huge picture window framing a magnificent view of the lake. Its matching love seat was positioned in the corner. A bookshelf holding a few books flanked a fireplace they wouldn't use. Two arm chairs completed the furnishings, but her dog would use them more than they would.

The kitchen was functional with a fridge, microwave, stove, and table. They would eat in there sometimes; usually one of them would want to be alone. A person could tolerate only so much togetherness.

Especially with this group.

"This isn't my fault," Janie felt compelled to point out.

Nope, it was entirely one-hundred percent not her fault. In fact, she wasn't the only one being ungrateful.

Vince snorted.

Janie shrugged. He might not be happy for their friends, but she was. It was romantic.

Shaking his head, Vince dropped her suitcase just inside the door.

She cringed at the sharp clatter of the little black wheels hitting the wooden floor.

"I'm going out." He didn't wait for a response.

Not that she would have given him one. Asshole.

Janie tucked a piece of her brown hair behind her ear and stretched. The drive from the city to Poplar Point was long, and sitting on the old bench of Vince's truck, a spring had poked her in the ass the entire way.

She grinned, determined not to let Vince's surliness get

her down. He'd abandoned her, which meant she had the first choice of bedrooms.

Leaving her suitcase where Vince dropped it, she ran down the hall to choose the softest bed.

🐾

Vince Campbell marched down a trail, that, if he followed the damn thing far enough, would eventually spit him into Canada, never to be seen again. Every summer they followed the trail for a day or two, made camp, then turned around. There was a clearing they always tried to find. Some years they did, some years they didn't go fast enough to make it. And some years they even went beyond it to the state park campground, just for the hell of it.

He doubted Chuck would do it with him this year.

Going alone didn't sound so bad either because God knew if he spent any time with Janie, he was going to wring her fucking neck.

There was something about her plain brown hair, her plain brown eyes. Her average height, average weight.

Average.

And it bothered the fucking shit right out of him.

A dog barking slowed him down and he waited as the flat-coated retriever bounded around the bend. Casey was Janie's dog, and Casey had bolted the minute Janie opened the truck's door.

"Won't he run?" Vince asked.

Janie rolled her eyes. "You've come with us every summer. Have you *ever* seen Casey run away?"

That she was right made him feel foolish, and he hadn't answered her.

But now Casey found him and sure as shit, the dog looked happy.

And he was already soaking wet.

Another fucking reason he hated bunking with Janie. He'd smell like wet dog for the next two weeks.

Fuck Chuck for talking him into going on this goddamned vacation when his business was going to shit. But what the fuck else was he going to do? He certainly wasn't working.

There he was now, sitting on the edge of the ridge, glowing, yeah, the motherfucker was *glowing*, taking in the view of Lake Harriet.

Chuck didn't push the wet dog away instead giving Casey a hearty neck rub and was rewarded with a slobbery tongue in his face.

"Hey," Vince greeted his friend, his lips twitching. "How was the drive?"

The resort had put up a fence of sorts to keep visitors a reasonable distance away from the edge, but Chuck had taken a seat beyond it and his feet dangled, the lake swirling beneath his tennis shoes.

Vince sat beside him.

Chuck was the happiest Vince had seen him in a long time, giving Vince a wide grin.

"Good!" Chuck exclaimed, slapping Vince on the back. "We actually drove up yesterday. You see the rest of the gang?"

Vince pet Casey's wet fur, and the dog lay down next to him. Yeah, he imagined having to explain to Janie her dog died flying off the ridge and drowning in the lake.

She would kill him with one of the bricks in her suitcase.

"No, but it's still early. I wanted to get the drive over with."

Chuck smirked. "She's not that bad. You won't even see her."

Vince prayed that was true. "Where's Kara?"

A shadow crossed Chuck's face and his grin disappeared. "She was on a phone call when I left. Said she had to tie up a few ends before she could really enjoy herself."

"You grab reinforcements yet?" Vince asked, thinking about beer.

"Nope."

Vince carefully stood. He didn't need to go flying off the cliff either, though the first summer he and his friends vacationed there, he had done exactly that from that very spot. "Then let's go."

※

Janie stepped out of the little wooden cabin, a towel wrapped around her waist, a new gold, black, and bronze bikini bottom under it, her hair shoved into a messy ponytail. A beach bag that held her phone, a bottle of water, and sunscreen, hung from the crook of her arm. She intended to bake her brains out.

The cabin, well, all the cabins, were near the water, the wide expanse of beach and a small section of grass the only things between them.

Janie wasn't worried about her dog, though she looked around briefly, scanning the beach. Casey was well trained and knew the area. It was more than likely he ran off to find Vince. He had made a friend of him long ago, though Vince would never admit to it.

Janie hated Vince, probably as much as he hated her, but she knew with all her heart he would never hurt her dog.

"Time to bake your brains out?" Kara St. John teased, making Janie jump at the unexpected hello. They always had the beach to themselves, the five cabins being the only ones on this section of the lake, and the group paid extra for the seclusion. The resort's office was a mile away; there were few people around their neck of the woods.

"Kara!" Janie greeted her friend happily as if she hadn't had lunch with her only two days ago. "You just get here?"

"No. Chuck and I came up yesterday. I called and pulled a few strings. I wanted him to myself for a bit."

"I don't blame you." Janie pulled her towel from her waist and dropped her beach bag on the smooth brown sand. She spread the towel out and sat, leaving room for Kara.

Kara looked lovely in a light green tank dress that complemented her eyes, and her blonde bob was freshly trimmed. The woman even wore a bit of makeup.

Janie usually didn't envy her friends—what was the point?—but sometimes she wished she had a bit of pizzazz. She swatted at a fly buzzing around her head, then pulled her water out of her bag.

They'd have to talk about food soon and decide who would run into Poplar Point to raid its only grocery store.

She usually loved the first night of their vacation. Everyone would be there and they would barbecue a whole cow's worth of beef. But bad things had happened recently, and now Janie wasn't sure how smoothly these two weeks would to go.

"How was the drive?" Kara asked, helping herself to a sip of Janie's water.

Janie looked away. She didn't need Kara's speculative look. Kara knew how the drive went.

"We didn't talk. Three hours of silence. It was peaceful. I mean, it would have been peaceful if I hadn't heard his teeth gnashing the whole way."

Kara laughed. "Why didn't you take separate vehicles?"

Janie threw up her hands. "You tell me!" she wailed. "It's not like I haven't driven up here a million times, but he told me I was riding with him and that was that."

Kara laughed again and stopped when Chuck and Vince stepped from the tree line.

"Food and booze," Chuck called to them, his hands cupped around his mouth.

Janie studied the two men standing side by side.

Chuck styled his brown hair into spikes and wore a blue and beige t-shirt, khaki shorts, and brown sandals.

Vince was his opposite, his long black hair pulled into a ponytail, his black t-shirt stretched across his chest, jeans hugging his hips and thighs. He wore black work boots. Vince looked like he just stepped out of his shop, and he was probably hotter than hell. The sun was intense; there wasn't a cloud in the sky. The temperature was close to ninety degrees Fahrenheit.

"Coming?" Kara asked, standing, smoothing her dress.

"Uh-huh." Like she wanted to spend even more time with Vince. "You know I like lots of Doritos and fizzy water. You have my money, right?"

Kara handled everyone's money for the cabin rent, food, and booze. It made things easier.

"Yep. See you later."

Janie spread out on her towel, knowing Vince wouldn't want her to go. If they took his truck instead of Kara's SUV, there wouldn't be room for her anyway.

She dozed and hoped it wouldn't take the others too long to join them.

❧

"Get the fuck up or you'll be redder than a lobster, and I'll have to run your ass to the clinic for sun poisoning."

"Mind your own business," Janie snapped, but without malice. This was the most relaxed she'd been in a long while and even Vince's piss and vinegar attitude couldn't snap her out of it.

The sound of the water caressing the packed sand . . . the hot sun soaking into her skin . . . the occasional buzz of a bug . . . not a million dogs barking, no phones ringing . . . heavenly.

Casey's wet nose nudged her cheek and she rubbed the dog's neck, not bothering to open her eyes or turn her head.

"Then get up and help with the food. Kara bought enough for an army."

They *were* an army. At least, a baseball team.

Ten of them. Every summer.

"Is everyone here finally?" Janie hoped. It would be nice if Vince had his friends to talk to so he'd have something else to focus on rather than give her a hard time. She must have fallen asleep because she hadn't heard anyone, and no one approached her to say hello.

"Yeah," he confirmed curtly but offered her nothing more.

Vince was standing in her sun. She might as well "get the fuck up" as he so politely put it, or she really would burn. She couldn't give him the satisfaction.

Sighing inwardly, Janie sat up and adjusted her bikini top. It had slid a little sideways, and half of her left boob was peeking out. She rubbed her eyes, squinting against the sunlight, then shoved her water bottle into her bag.

She stood, picked up the towel, shook it out, and draped it over her arm.

Vince watched her every movement, and his stare made her nervous.

Leaning over to hide her unease, she grabbed her bag by its straps. "Let's go."

Vince's dark sunglasses hid his eyes, and she had no idea what he was thinking. She probably didn't want to know.

"Stare much?" she bit out, unnerved. Damn, she hated the man.

Janie walked away, carefully picking her way over the rocks in the sand, pretending more resolve than she felt. She could feel his eyes boring into her back, and it gave her the chills.

In the cabin, Janie pulled shorts over her bikini, then she went to help Kara and Chuck put away the groceries they would eat for the next few days. She hoped Vince found something else to do.

Why hadn't he ever noticed Janie was so built? Holy shit. The baggy clothes she wore hid one fine body. Her breasts were the perfect size and he imagined how they would fill his palms. When she walked away, the bottom of her bikini tucked slightly into the crack of her ass; he wanted to pull the bottoms over her legs and feel it for himself.

Fuck.

He *knew* this vacation was going to be sex-free. They always were for him, and even if he could get a little on this vacation, the last woman he would want to get it from was little Plainee Janie Davenport. His lips quirked at the nickname she'd had since high school.

She was probably still a virgin, and he didn't want a taste of that.

Vince took a long pull of his beer and watched his friends. This summer vacation was fucked and not only for himself.

The only couple who looked remotely happy was Chuck and Kara. But every few hours she answered a phone call or shot off a text, and it drove Chuck nuts. Bailey and Cameron's marriage was strained, Alycia and Bryce acted like they were ready for a divorce, and Crystal and Nate looked like death warmed over.

Vince winced at the poorly chosen phrase. Shit. The funeral was still fresh, and he hadn't let anyone see the few tears he'd shed over that white casket.

Janie and Kara were talking with the other women, or trying to, while he and Chuck, Cam, Bryce, and Nate uncomfortably stood around the campfire. The sun was setting, the mosquitos out in full force. Everyone was covered in bug spray, but that didn't stop them from buzzing around hoping for a tasty snack.

Sometimes he wondered why he even bothered to come summer after summer, but the sun turning the sky pink and orange, the water lapping at the beach and dock making the boats bump against the weathered wood, and the crickets and frogs chatting their usual gossip, made his tension ease. It was always the right choice to come, and scanning his friends' faces over the fire, he knew his life could always be a lot fucking worse than it was.

"You gonna survive bunking with Janie?" Nate asked him, an eyebrow cocked.

Vince took the question for what it was: a distraction, noise to cover the sound of the silence. Men didn't do well with feelings. Hell, he hid from his more often than not, and of all the men standing around the bonfire, he was the one with the least at stake. So what if his little business went down the tubes permanently? He'd find something else to do. That was almost nothing compared to what caused the shadows in Nate's eyes.

Playing the part of a disgruntled friend, he snorted and rolled his eyes. This was one of the few nights they all sat and ate together. The meal was long over, and the group had moved on to the dessert portion of the evening. Chocolate cake and vanilla cheesecake sat on a picnic table behind them. The women sipped Sangria from red Solo cups. The men drank beer. They only had six different kinds to choose from; Vince had made sure of that earlier at the liquor store. There was no way he was going to suffer sharing a cabin with Janie without booze.

"Not much I can do about it. Couldn't afford to come alone," he replied honestly. Well, it was true, even if Chuck guiltily shifted his eyes. He wouldn't have been able to afford to come alone, and he never asked if Janie could either. "It's no big deal."

"I don't get what you don't like about her," Cam commented, throwing a glance over his shoulder at the women.

Just like that, the tension broke and they all focused on him and his dislike of Janie.

He didn't like being a betta fish in a little glass bowl, with everyone staring at him, but he would do it if it helped his friends take their minds off their troubles.

The problem was, he didn't know the answer to the non-question, and he rubbed the back of his neck with his free hand. Ever since they were kids he'd had a severe dislike of her, and he'd never been able to explain it—or hide it. "I don't know," he admitted, stealing a glimpse of her out of the corner of his eye. Her hair was pinned into a messy bun on the top of her head and little diamonds, they looked real anyway, twinkled in her earlobes. She was covered up with some gauzy white top, and he thought she wore denim shorts. He wasn't used to paying attention.

He wasn't used to thinking about her at all.

She had an arm around Crystal, and Vince was glad she was over there and he was over here.

"What's on the agenda tomorrow?" Chuck asked when Vince proved to be less than forthcoming.

They bickered over what they would do in the morning, and Vince opted out of any plans. He wasn't a morning person. Half the day would be gone before he poked his head out of his bedroom. In fact, turning in and spending the rest of the night watching reruns of the *X-Files* sounded damn good to him. The resort had awesome Wi-Fi, and he packed his tablet.

Vince excused himself and threw his beer bottle into a huge metal trash bin. The sun was winking out its last light, and he guessed the time to be around ten-thirty. Plenty late enough to call it a day and not look like a fucking wuss.

He left Janie with the other women, her hair glinting in the torches that were supposed to keep the mosquitos away and doing a piss-poor job of it.

Vince showered off the day and some of his irritation and slid into bed. He didn't care which bedroom he'd ended up with, and it didn't bother him Janie took the bedroom with the view of the beach. Through his window he could keep an eye on his truck. Last summer, or was it two summers ago, a raccoon crawled all over it and scratched his paint job.

He popped in earbuds and blissfully lost himself in his favorite show.

§♠

Janie was exhausted. The long tense ride to Poplar Point, then seeing all her friends and catching up with their troubles zapped her energy.

She said goodnight to Bailey and Cameron, Alycia and Bryce, Crystal and Nate. All of them going through personal issues she wouldn't wish on anyone.

Were they still awake, the appropriate bedtime come and gone, because they didn't want to spend any time alone?

Janie couldn't understand how, if you loved someone, you couldn't soldier through the problems, but she'd never loved anyone enough to know.

The door spring squeaked loudly in protest as she let herself into the cabin. She needed to take a shower. Janie didn't hear anything but Casey's panting, and she assumed Vince had gone to bed. Did men talk about their problems like women? She'd certainly gotten an earful after dinner, and Janie had never drank so much, trying to literally drown out her friends' pain.

Maybe a little drunk, she stumbled through the cabin in

the dark, though she could have flipped a switch. They were hardly roughing it at Poplar Point. The cabins were equipped with electricity, air conditioning, and a shower and bathtub. Janie had never run out of hot water any of the summers she stayed here, and in the past, she'd used her fair share.

Standing under the hot spray, she relaxed and washed her hair. She would shower in the morning, too, to shave her legs, but tonight she rinsed off the grime of the trip, the sand of the beach, and a thick layer of bug spray.

She turned off the light before opening the door so the light wouldn't wake up Vince, but she bumped into him in the hallway. Clutching the towel to her breasts, she squealed, her head spinning from the collision, then leaned against the wall so she wouldn't fall over. "What the hell?" she snapped.

Blinded by the dark, she glared in his direction, disoriented. The only light in the little hallway was the moonlight coming in her window because her bedroom door was open.

"Didn't know it was a crime to take a piss at midnight," Vince growled.

Water dripped from her hair down her shoulders, and Janie shivered. Vince hadn't turned on the air conditioner, but his glare cooled her off just as quickly, and the irritation in his voice sobered her. "It's not. Excuse me."

She dodged around him, thankful her towel was large enough to cover her ass. Janie resisted slamming the door in frustration. She didn't know what she had done in this life, or any other, that would cause someone to hate her so much, but she was more than happy to return the favor. She would make sure his hard chest, bronzed skin, and long black hair he'd let loose to hang down to his shoulders, didn't affect her.

Men like that had women, and she wouldn't want to be one of the hundreds of notches on his bedpost.

Holy fuck he was hard. Janie never made him feel like this before. They'd been on this trip a hundred times, okay, ten, every summer since their twenties, but the sight of Janie in a suit, or the feel of her body as he threw her into the lake to piss her off, had never made him ache.

The smell of her hair still clung to him, where her head bumped into his chest. Some kind of floral scent that would draw the bees.

And her breasts, holy shit. When she clutched the towel to her chest, she made her breasts swell above the edge of the towel, her skin glittering from wet and moonlight.

He stroked himself to relieve the pressure, but because he was thinking of her, the motion made it worse. What would she do if he found her in her room? Crawled into bed with her? Pinned her down against the mattress and took her? Nestled himself between those thighs, a little burned from lying in the sun most of the afternoon? Yeah, he noticed. He noticed her nose was burned too.

Stupid.

His anger calmed him down. Vince didn't want her. He could have any number of women. He could even have brought his own woman on this trip but that would have left Janie high and dry, and that's not the way it was done. If he ever got married, he would skip these vacations.

Just as Crystal and Nate had planned to before . . .

Well.

His cell phone told him it was after one in the morning, so he put his tablet aside and stuffed a pillow under his head.

His window was open but there was nothing except the occasional frog croaking.

Rock hard, the unrelieved pressure making his stomach churn, Vince fell asleep to the breeze shaking leaves in the trees and dreamed of Janie's lips on his.

❧

Vince slept through breakfast and lunch. He stumbled into the kitchen in search of caffeine. Janie was leaning against the counter, her head lying on her arms, waiting for the coffee to brew.

This was the first time he'd bunked with her; he had always shared a cabin with Chuck, and he had no idea of Janie's habits. He was more than a little surprised she was a night owl too.

Her tiny pajama bottoms barely covered her rear end, and a matching tank with thin straps that rested on her sunburned shoulders.

Her plain brown hair was a tangle.

Her slim legs made his morning wood even harder, and he wanted to push behind her, make her feel how hard he was against her little ass. He wanted to kiss her lips to find out if they were as soft as they'd felt in his dreams.

Before he could carry out that fantasy, she pulled a mug from the cabinet, filled it with coffee, and pushed it aside.

"Here," she offered before a yawn.

"Where is everyone?" Vince asked, adjusting himself through the thin cotton shorts he slept in and pushing the erotic dream from his mind. He took the coffee and sipped it black, watching her fill her mug with milk and coffee.

Janie rubbed her eyes and sat at the kitchen table. "They took food out on the pontoon. It's just us until dinner tonight. Brats and hot dogs."

The usual fare.

Well, shit. Part of sleeping half the day away. No problem. There would be plenty of time to do that kind of thing with his friends later.

"You got plans?" he reluctantly asked. He didn't particularly want to hang out with her, and he'd been hoping to find some time to talk to Chuck.

Janie wasn't Chuck, but he wouldn't be alone. Being alone

didn't sound that appealing and spending the afternoon with Janie was better than nothing.

She scowled. "Yeah. Beach."

"Let's go fishing. If we catch some walleye, we can grill it with the brats and dogs."

She didn't answer.

"Come on," he cajoled. "Casey likes going out on the water." He looked around for the dog, hoping for support.

Janie smirked. "Chuck beat you to it. Casey's on the pontoon."

Vince shrugged. Maybe it would be better to be alone anyway; he could think about what the fuck he was going to do. "Whatever," he replied and went to change. He wouldn't beg her.

"Let me shower," Janie called after him.

Relief rolled through him, and it made him pissed. He was fine being alone. "I'll get the boat ready."

Janie didn't know what the fuck. Vince never asked her to go anywhere. In fact, she clearly remembered two summers ago he actually backed out of an overnight camping trip to one of the smaller islands when he found out she was going. She hadn't cared about going camping. She'd just wanted to piss him off—and it worked.

Why did she agree to go? That was even more what the fuck. She'd never cared how he felt, but there was some kind of weird tension while he waited for her to answer. And he'd seemed almost disappointed when he turned away.

The relief in his voice after she told him she wanted to shower was laughable. What did he care?

She packed a bag, depending, perhaps unwisely, on him to bring food. She brought sunscreen, a book (the cause of why her suitcase was so heavy; she always packed plenty to read), bug spray, and a towel in case she wanted to jump in to cool off.

Janie wore her bikini and pulled on a pair of denim shorts over the bottoms.

Vince was dropping poles in the aluminum boat when she stepped onto the porch. It was a smaller boat, and for the two of them, it was fine. A mound of life vests rested at the bottom between two of the benches.

He probably had worms with him.

"That didn't take long," he observed as she neared the dock.

Janie didn't do anything but shower to shave her legs. She left her hair loose so it would dry in the sun, but she wore an elastic band around her wrist in case she wanted to pull it away from her face.

She carefully jumped in, the boat rocking slightly, took a seat on the bench farthest away from the motor, and flipped her sunglasses over her eyes. Janie didn't want him to guess how weirded out she was by the whole thing.

Kara would tease her relentlessly when she found out she spent the day with Vince. At his request, no less.

She hoped she wouldn't regret it.

Vince pushed them away from the dock with his hand, then used a paddle to guide them into deeper water.

Janie's stomach lurched. It always took a few minutes for her sea legs to return.

After turning them around, Vince started the old motor with one vicious pull, then slowly cranked it to full speed.

Her hair whipped around her face, the sun toasted her skin, seagulls flew in the bright blue cloudless sky. She straddled the bench and sighed in contentment. There weren't any waves and the ride was smooth.

Vince handled the boat like he'd grown up on the lake, though the first time he'd come out with them he hadn't known a thing about fishing.

His hair was pulled back into his customary ponytail, and he wore his usual black muscle tee with blue denim shorts instead of jeans, and black flip-flops. He sat in stony silence, concentrating on navigating them around a few boats zigzagging across the water. Vince motored them to the shore of a little island that, to her knowledge, didn't have a name, but an island she'd explored a time or two with the girls.

One summer they had all camped there and brought lots of booze and food to drink and eat around a campfire.

After Vince cut the engine, there was nothing.

He didn't drop an anchor; he would let them drift, which was fine with her.

The water slapped the sides of the boat, and the crisp wind chilled her skin in a delicious juxtaposition to the heat of the sun.

Vince didn't say anything to her, and she enjoyed the silence.

Janie dug the sunscreen out of her bag and took off her shorts. Propping her feet on the edge of the boat, she smoothed lotion over both legs. She rubbed the white coconut scented cream onto her face, neck, and arms. "Will you do my back?"

It wasn't the best idea. Actually, the thought of his touch made her skin crawl, but she couldn't let herself burn out of sheer stubbornness.

She took his grunt as a yes, scooted across the boat, and gave him the bottle.

The rough palm of his hand made her shiver, his callouses scratching her skin.

Janie pulled her hair back so the ends wouldn't hang in the lotion and briefly he rested his hand between her shoulder blades. He was probably wishing he could break her neck and toss her over.

"There," he muttered, and he shoved the brown bottle into her hands.

"Thanks." She was glad her sunglasses hid her eyes, but he wasn't wearing any and hostility blazed in his ice blue irises plain as day.

Eager to get away from him, Janie spread the life jackets on the boat's bottom as a type of mattress and lay down, hooking her knees over the edge, her feet in the air. Her silver toe ring caught the sunlight, and she took a moment to admire the sweet find she'd made when she'd shopped Poplar Point's Main Street with Kara a couple years ago.

"What the fuck are you doing?" Vince snarled when she tugged her book out of her bag.

"I'm going to read. What of it?"

He didn't think she was going to . . . fish, did he?

"I brought you a pole."

Apparently, he did.

"I never fish."

His eyes drilled into her, but she ignored him, even though he scared her. He was such a *man*. All brawn. But he did have brains. She knew he did.

What kind of women did he date? Biker chicks, probably. She opened her book. She wasn't jealous. Not of those women. Leather and a hella lot of black eyeliner.

That wasn't her style.

T-shirts and dog hair.

That was about right.

"What are you so pissy for anyway?" She didn't expect him to answer, and his silence proved her right. She read half a page when he responded, surprising her.

"My business is in the shitter, that's what."

Janie tipped her pink sunglass down her nose and stared at him over the rims in surprise.

His jaw made a sharp angle like he was gritting his teeth, his eyes were narrowed against the bright sun, and . . . were his hands shaking? He dropped the hook into the water.

If he was going for walleye, he wasn't going to pull any up that way.

"Why?" she asked, though she didn't know how to help him. She didn't understand that type of business. Vince fixed motorcycles, rebuilt them and sold them. Sometimes he fixed cars. That was the extent of her knowledge. She hadn't even visited his shop because if she needed something done, her dad did it, and there was no way Vince would have shown her around just for the hell of it.

He dry-washed his face, holding the fishing rod between his knees. "You know where my shop is?"

"Sure. Ventura Boulevard."

Vince nodded. "Right. Light traffic, easy to get to. Okay, well, six months ago, another shop opened across the street. Real, ah . . ." he searched for the word, looping his hand in the air in small circles. "Not classy but . . ."

"Sophisticated?" Janie tried.

"Kind of. Yeah. Swanky. They serve cappuccino while you wait, have a big screen TV in their waiting room."

"And you have none of those things?" Janie guessed. "Don't you have any customer loyalty?" She did. She had tons of customers, and they always came back.

Vince snorted. "Plainee Janie, when I fix something, it lasts."

Janie stuck her tongue out at him for using the nickname that haunted her for her whole fucking life. "So wait for the novelty to wear off. Your customers, sorry, your *new* customers, will hear you're good. You must have a good reputation."

Vince stared stonily across the lake. They'd floated a bit away from the island's shore.

Janie turned back to her book, but the words blurred when he spoke.

"I can't afford to wait anymore. It's been six months. I've barely been able to make rent on the space."

That was a lot for him to tell her. In fact, he'd told her more in the past two hours than he had in five years.

It made him almost . . . human.

"Fancy up your shop then. Serve cookies and coffee, buy a new couch and magazines, offer free Wi-Fi, whatever the hell. Gotta be competitive, right?"

"I am competitive. I'm the cheapest guy in town because I don't have to up my prices to pay for those kinds of frills."

Janie waved it off. "Write them off as a business expense. I do."

She upgraded her equipment constantly. It was safer for the dogs.

"I don't need the hassle."

Mentally she rolled her eyes. Cam was an accountant; there wouldn't be a hassle if Vince hired him to do his business taxes, but whatever. He didn't want to compete that way for business. That was his prerogative.

What would *she* do? A dog groomer moved in next door, served the dogs fancy food on a silver platter, maybe chopped steak.

She could see not wanting to deal.

What would she do then?

Janie read a couple lines of her romance, wiggled when a life vest buckle dug into her back. Her grooming place wasn't anywhere near other groomers, but that was just luck. The building she rented was cheap, and the only thing she'd been able to afford at the time. She needed a larger space for the kennels.

"Look for a place away from other shops. That'll help."

When he didn't say anything, she continued, "Find a nice space, then throw a grand re-opening party, actually advertise you're open for business. Sure, you don't want to kiss ass, I get that. But you have customers. You have to treat them like *people*."

She emphasized the last word because besides Chuck, he

probably didn't treat anyone like anyone.

Vince sat quietly and fished, and Janie dozed, forgetting their conversation with the soothing rocking of the boat.

She didn't know how much time passed when he suggested they go ashore and eat, but she readily agreed. They both slept through breakfast and lunch; she was famished.

The island sloped and contained a bit of sand. Nothing they could swim from, but it was enough for Vince to push the boat onto the shore so it wouldn't drift away.

After she pulled on her shorts, he led her to a patch of flat rock, and barefoot, she carefully picked her way across the island.

She waited impatiently while he searched through the cooler and handed her a thick sandwich and a family-sized bag of Doritos.

Janie dug into both.

"How the fuck do you eat so much and not get fat?"

Crass, that's what he was. How did he keep customers? Ugh, he probably dealt with men as equally as crass as he was.

"This is my first meal of the day," she defended herself. "Fuck off."

Vince went back to eating his own sandwich, and she guzzled a diet Pepsi.

This wasn't so bad. A lot less tension radiated from him; maybe he'd needed to dump on someone.

Janie shoved her garbage into the cooler, and at the same time, so did Vince. His hands landed on hers and she jerked them away, the electricity of his touch zipping up her arms.

Oh, that was bad.

She refused to meet his eyes and she stood, brushing the little rocks and sticks off her shorts.

Vince drank his soda, but Janie knew he was watching her poke around the island.

"What about you?" he called to her.

"What about me?"

"What about your business?"

Janie's business was perfect. In fact, she hired an apprentice to start after she returned from vacation. She needed the help, and she was going to have to think about how big she wanted to grow because it seemed her grooming service and kenneling business gained new clients every day.

Soon *she* would be looking for a new space.

But she didn't want to tell him that. She had tact, unlike some people.

"Fine." She left it at that, and he didn't question her further.

She hid behind a tree to pee, the morning coffee getting the better of her, then they were back in the boat.

Vince didn't ask her any more questions, and she took the time to read and catnap.

"Let's head back. Fish aren't biting."

Janie smothered a smile.

When they reached the cabins, she helped him tie the boat to the dock and abandoned him. She was unsettled from the time she'd spent with him and needed the break.

Taking her book and towel to the beach, she intended to enjoy the time alone.

Vince was so fucking pissed, he wanted to slam his phone into the wall and watch it explode into a million black little pieces. But he needed the goddamned thing because he needed to call the real estate agent who had facilitated the rental of the shop he was using.

It looked like he was moving. He was so fucking pissed he hadn't thought of Janie's idea himself. What a fucking easy solution.

"Hey! You wanna help with dinner?" Chuck hollered through the screen door of his and Janie's cabin.

Vince had lost track of time. How long had he been sitting on the sofa stewing? Long enough for the pontoon boat to come back in.

"Vince?" Chuck said his name, amused.

"Yeah, yeah," he agreed, standing. "How was the pontoon?"

Chuck clucked in dismay, and Vince suppressed a laugh.

"That great?"

"Alycia and Bryce are fucked."

Alycia was a looker and Bryce was a prick. Chuck's conclusion wasn't a surprise.

But . . . how it would feel to be with the same person for twenty years? Would he get bored and do something stupid like Bryce?

Janie was throwing a Frisbee across the beach for Casey when Vince stepped onto the small porch. Her breasts swayed with every swing of her arm, her smile at her dog's simple joy lighting her face.

The light burn was turning into a golden brown, and gold highlights made her hair shine.

She screamed, not in anger, but in amusement, when Casey shook water all over her.

Absently, he smiled.

"What's this? Kara said you spent the day with Janie in the boat?" Chuck eyed him speculatively.

Vince's smile morphed into a scowl.

He wasn't going to try to explain about this morning.

Vince brushed off his friend's question and kept to himself through dinner.

He skipped the bonfire and the s'mores for dessert, made himself a fresh pot of coffee, and started in on the research he needed to put his moving plans in place.

His tablet read midnight when he heard Janie open the

cabin door and pad her way to her room.

His door was open and his tablet light made his room glow, but she didn't pay attention to him, only shutting the door to her bedroom with a soft click.

Vince waited a couple minutes then lightly knocked on the door.

Janie was sitting in bed wearing her shorts and tank top pajamas and reading the same book she'd been in the boat. Yeah, he'd noticed. He was starting to notice more about her than he'd ever admit.

The small lamp on her bedside table cast her skin in a gorgeous sheen.

"What?"

Vince stepped into the room and quietly closed the door behind him, even though the cabin was empty but for them and Casey who slept on the couch. Closing the door felt right. He didn't have a plan, but he knew if he didn't do something he was going to explode.

He sat on the edge of her bed still wearing the shorts and muscle tee he wore earlier.

Alarmed, she scooted to the head of the bed, her back pressed against the cheap wooden headboard.

"What?" she asked again, her voice quivering.

She was sitting on top of the blankets. It was too hot for blankets, even a sheet. The window was open but her blinds were shut.

Good.

He ran a hand up her leg and her eyes widened.

But she didn't move.

Good.

"Thank you," he said simply, resting a hand on her knee.

"F-for what?" Her voice came out in a whisper.

He wanted her to whisper like that in his ear, to tell him she wanted him.

Because for some fucked up reason, he wanted her.

Her hair was loose, and he was tempted to run his fingers through it. She wasn't wearing any makeup, as usual, but this close, he realized she didn't need it. Her face was a pretty tan, her cheeks pink. The pupils in her brown eyes were dilated in . . . what he hoped was desire.

He inched his hand up her thigh.

Vince wanted to feel between her legs, to discover if she wanted him as much as he wanted her, but he needed to take his time or she would bolt. Maybe even get a ride back to the city.

He couldn't have that.

"For the idea." He rubbed his thumb over her skin, her hair starting to grow in from her shave.

Her book slipped off her lap. "The idea?"

"To move my shop," he murmured, sliding closer.

She hadn't taken a shower, and she smelled of water, dog, and a scent that only belonged to her. It was intoxicating, and Vince took a deep breath.

He didn't know what it was about her now, this summer, this month, this day. He blocked her in with one arm and brought his other hand to her face, rubbing his thumb over her lush lips. She never wore lipstick, never wore lipgloss. He would never need to worry about smearing it if he wanted a quick kiss. He would never need to taste some vile, sparkling goop.

"Oh."

She said the word, but it didn't sound like anything to Vince but a sigh.

They'd hated each other for years. He, because he detested the plainness that disguised the real beauty he was only now discovering.

And her? Well, he'd given her plenty of reason to return the feeling. She may not even have her own.

"Let me," he requested because he would never coerce a woman, no matter how much he wanted her.

With barely a nod, she did.

Janie was wary when she heard the knock on her door. She figured he wanted to yell at her about something, rake her over the bonfire coals, but instead of rage, there had been a heat all right, of a different sort.

Now he wanted . . . to kiss her, or more? And she had given him permission.

It was a habit to cringe away; her primary reaction anytime he was near her, looked at her, spoke to her. Now she was trapped, her head braced against the fake wood of the headboard.

Janie resisted the urge to close her eyes and instead stared directly into his. They were always icy, but they were like dry ice now, smoky and hot. He dipped his head to press his lips to hers and they were warm, soft. He smelled like coffee and lake water.

He leaned in, and she had nowhere to go.

Vince nudged her lips with his tongue, and she cautiously opened her mouth. He feasted, moving his hand from her jaw to the back of her head, trapping her, devouring her.

Giving in, she wrapped her arms around his neck, and taking that as her acquiescence, he pulled her closer, almost into his lap. His tongue glided along her teeth and danced with hers.

Until he pulled away.

Desire and disappointment parried in her heart until he warned her, "Stop me now if you don't want to do this. This is the only time I'll ask."

Janie nodded dumbly. She didn't know what the repercussions would be, come morning, but she didn't want to stop tonight. "Please," she whimpered and thanked God he took that to mean more.

He yanked his sleeveless t-shirt over his head and threw it onto the floor. Vince pulled her into his arms again and claimed her mouth, running his fingertips over one of her breasts, his thumb flicking her nipple through her thin top.

Her nipples hardened instantly and heat pooled between her legs.

She pushed herself into his body for one moment then tugged her own tank top over her head, baring her breasts to him. She knew she wasn't stacked, but she was proud of her girls.

Vince must have been impressed too because he murmured, "Holy fuck," before claiming a nipple with his mouth, sucking at her tender skin.

Janie arched her back and pushed his head closer into her breast. She wished he'd take the band out of his hair, but she forgot to ask him as his teeth nibbled the sensitive skin, and she squirmed, the sensation traveling to her core. How long had it been since she'd last had sex?

"Slow, baby," Vince whispered, then blew on her skin before turning his attention to her other breast.

Slow. It was easy for him to say. She throbbed for his touch.

"Tell me you want me," he demanded. "I want to hear you say it."

"Please," she moaned, her eyelids half-mast. She was swollen with need and want. Oh, yeah. She leaned closer, desperate for another kiss.

Vince caught her face in his hand. "No. I want to hear you say it."

He sounded angry, and she could only guess at why. Vince had hated her from day one, and now he wanted to fuck her. He probably *was* mad. At himself.

But Vince had taken her too far to say no now. "I want you, Vince." She said his name; she wanted him to hear her say it. Not in anger, or frustration, or even unease. She wanted him to hear her say his name with want, with need, with desire. She rose onto her knees offering herself to him. "Touch me, please."

She steadied herself with one hand on his shoulder; his skin was blazing hot. With the other, she cupped his jaw rough with whiskers and kissed him.

He nudged her legs apart, pushed aside the hem of her shorts and the crotch of her panties, and Janie groaned into his mouth.

"Baby," he breathed and slipped a finger inside her.

It was as if he broke a dam.

Vince pulled his finger out and drew her shorts and panties around her knees. She sat on the bed so he could pull them off, and he unbuttoned and unzipped his shorts.

He pushed them to the floor, and Janie didn't think she'd seen a bigger cock. It was huge, a large vein ran along its length, and a drop of pre-come already glistened at the tip.

She resisted the urge to cringe away. He wouldn't hurt her. He may have, time after time, with his glares and barbs, his blatant disapproval of her, but he wouldn't now, not this way.

Janie trusted him. It was a new feeling, a new concept. In the past she would always stiffen, back away, whenever she saw him, like prey keeping an eye on the hunter, never turning her back even for a second. But in that very moment, with the water brushing the beach, the hum of a motorboat taking a midnight cruise, the light of her reading lamp bathing them in a golden glow, she trusted him.

He sat next to her and leaned to kiss her.

She broke the kiss, sank back to rest her head on her pillow, and she let him spread her legs. Did he like what he saw? She kept minimal hair down there during their trip because she was always wearing a bikini. Now she realized it gave him full visual access. He ran his fingers over her folds and circled her opening with a fingertip.

"I want you, Jane."

"Yes," she replied, taken aback he said her name. Not Plainee Janie, not Janie, not Pain in the Ass. He called her Jane, and she loved the way it sounded. It sounded almost as good as his finger massaging her. Only, she didn't want his finger there. She wanted all of him, everywhere.

"I don't have a condom, Janie," Vince admitted.

She propped herself on her elbows and gave him a long kiss, running her tongue along his lips. "I'm on the pill." Janie had never been so glad. She didn't have any condoms either. This was the last thing she expected to be doing on her vacation.

He pulled her into his lap, and surprised, she laughed.

Vince laughed with her and nuzzled her neck with his lips. "Now, honey, I can't wait any longer." He lay back so he was positioned sideways at the foot of the bed and placed her over him, his hands on her ribs under her arms. She slowly pushed herself onto him, and he filled her, as she leaned back to take him as deeply as possible. He touched her very center.

"I'm almost there, baby, I need you with me."

Oh, yes, she was, the pressure and pleasure building gloriously under his finger as he helped bring her to her peak. "Yes," she hissed, but . . . she guided his hands to her breasts and encouraged him to squeeze her nipples. She touched herself between her legs, finding her clit as she moved. "I'm going to come," she moaned.

Taking his hands from her breasts and moving them to her hips to hold her steady, Vince thrust up, ramming into her.

The orgasm rocked through her, her clit pulsing as her finger slid over the slippery nub, and she rubbed herself through to the end, her muscles clutching with every wave.

Vince pulsated inside of her, and he grunted with his own pleasure, his fingers digging into her hips.

God. She'd never come so hard, and she collapsed onto his sweaty chest in sublime exhaustion.

"You like to play with yourself," Vince noted breathlessly,

his hands skimming the sensitive skin of her back.

"Yeah," she agreed, a little embarrassed. She had certain ways she was able to come and that was one.

"I get to next time," he told her, kissing the top of her head.

"Next time?"

"Honey, we're just getting started."

Vince slipped out of Janie's bed before dawn. They made love three more times, and he was worn out. He stumbled into his own room and crashed onto his bed, naked. He was sleeping in seconds.

When he woke the second time, his cell phone said it was two in the afternoon.

This was a better vacation than he'd anticipated. Sleeping in and some of the best sex he'd had in a long time. Who knew little Plainee Janie was such a firecracker in bed?

But he didn't feel like facing the morning after, the whole, "Where are we going?" talk, before coffee, even. And that's what he knew would happen if he woke up in her bed. He would bet his shop on it.

The cabin was empty, but Janie left coffee in the pot, and he gratefully heated some of the remaining brew in the microwave and took it outside to hunt up his friends.

No one was around but Chuck who was fishing off the dock's end.

"Where is everyone?" Vince asked, dropping down by Chuck's side and dipping his feet into the water. It was a scorcher of a day.

"The women went into town to buy more food. Bryce, Cam, and Nate took the boat out. I don't think they'll be back until tonight. That is a clusterfuck of problems, and I really don't want to get involved."

"How are Nate and Crystal?"

"I think being away from the city is doing them some good, and I think Crystal and Bailey are talking some." Chuck pulled a face. "Kara and Janie got stuck with Alycia. I can understand the bitterness, but . . ."

Vince knew what Chuck was trying to say. Shit or get off the pot. Work it out or cut him loose.

"She's turning the screws." Vince guessed.

Chuck grunted. "It's fucked."

Vince nodded in agreement. "Ah," he started, then took a sip of coffee to wet his dry mouth. "What did it feel like when you and Kara . . . made love for the first time?"

"You screwed Janie last night?" Chuck asked incredulously.

He ignored the shocked look on his friend's face. "What did you do?" Vince insisted.

"This isn't about me," Chuck deflected. "What the hell? Like your relationship wasn't fucked before? Excuse the pun."

Vince rubbed the back of his neck. "Yeah, I don't know. I took her out on the boat yesterday and we talked some, and the silences, they weren't hostile. Not like they used to be. Then last night I went to her room to thank her for something she'd said, and one thing led to the next."

Only part of that was a lie. He went to thank her and have sex. There was no leading anyone anywhere.

Chuck smirked. "Was she good? I've always wondered."

Vince bristled. "Then why did you choose Kara?"

"I've always loved Kara. You know that. Besides, you would've beat me to a bloody pulp if I would've tried."

"What do you mean? I've never liked Janie."

"You've never liked her," Chuck agreed. "Hated her in fact."

"Yeah."

Chuck pulled a quarter out of his shorts' pocket and

flicked it at Vince, who caught it deftly one handed. "What's the flip side of hate, my man?" he asked, before shoving the pole at Vince and walking away.

Annoyed, Vince bobbled the pole, and he quickly set his coffee mug aside, sloshing coffee over the rim before the fishing reel fell into the water.

With slitted eyes, he threw the coin into the murky water and watched as it sank.

Janie didn't let herself cry when she woke by herself. She knew she would, but seeing him sprawled naked on his own bed didn't help.

Like he couldn't face her.

Good news, though, they didn't have a great relationship to begin with, so him fucking her didn't make things any worse. She vowed to forget about it.

"You're awfully quiet," Kara said, pushing the cart along the grocery store aisle.

The grocery store was larger than it looked from the outside and actually contained a generous selection of fruits, vegetables, and meat. The butcher seemed pleasant and worked with Kara on numerous cuts of beef. It wasn't Whole Foods, but they always managed to find what they needed.

"I didn't get much sleep last night." That was true. She woke up with her heart pounding and looked for Vince, but of course he was gone.

Avoiding her.

She wouldn't bet on him asking where they were going, what they were doing, and Janie wouldn't be *that girl*. Because she already knew.

"Oh. Well. You can take a nap later." Kara pulled an assortment of chips from the shelf and flung them into the cart.

Janie flinched. She hoped they weren't crushed now.

"Yeah."

"Here's all the corn we forgot." Crystal rounded the corner, bumping into a display of ranch dip and holding a huge plastic bag of corn on the cob.

"Thanks for going back," Kara said, making room in the cart full of meat, snacks, and soda.

"What did I miss?"

"Janie and Vince slept together last night," Kara offered nonchalantly, pushing the cart into the next aisle, a squeaky wheel shrieking in protest.

"Ahhhh!" Janie squealed.

"You're not going to deny it, are you?" Kara admonished, bending to tug a case of single water bottles onto the lower half of the cart.

"Oh," Crystal breathed, some life sparkling in her light brown eyes. "Was he good?"

"How do you even know?" Janie groused. She didn't need this, even if it took Crystal's mind off her troubles for a while.

"There's only one person around who could have given you that hickey and all that whisker burn."

"Don't let Alycia and Bailey know. They're anti-man right now," Crystal advised, grabbing a small case of lemon-flavored Perrier.

"Where did they go anyway?" Janie frowned, irritated. Damn it. One of the downsides of not being vain. She hadn't even looked in the mirror this morning after her shower.

"The liquor store next door," Crystal said.

Kara pushed the cart to the check-out lane. "We didn't buy enough white wine the first time around, and we drank it all last night. Janie didn't answer the question, though."

"What question?" Janie asked, debating a candy bar at the checkout counter's display. She should have bought something in the candy aisle, but that was okay, she picked out plenty of cookies.

Crystal started putting their groceries onto the conveyor belt.

Kara pointed to a tabloid magazine with an alien on the cover. "Enquiring minds want to know. Was Vince good?"

Janie bit her lip and tried not to smile. "Yeah."

The cashier hooted, and the three women laughed.

&.

The great thing about vacation was there wasn't anything to do. The shitty thing about vacation was there wasn't anything to do.

Vince took the Jet Ski out, but it wasn't fun alone. Chuck was having a little evening delight with Kara and the other guys were with their wives. Earlier Vince heard a wail come from Alycia and Bryce's cabin. They were fighting, and Chuck was right, he wanted to stay far away from that mess. He wished they wouldn't have come. It was a shitty way to feel, but it was true.

Janie had taken off with Casey the minute they returned from Poplar Point. Vince wasn't able to catch her, and she refused to meet his eyes over the expanse of beach when he tried to get her attention.

She wanted to avoid him.

That kind of pissed him off. Did she regret what they did?

Probably.

He couldn't blame her. In all the years they'd known each other he'd never given her a reason to trust him.

He would let things cool off a bit and make a hiking trip alone. Give her space. That's what women were always saying they wanted, right? Space?

He was packing his hiking backpack when Chuck slammed out of his cabin next door, whistling and holding a bottle of beer.

Vince was happy for Chuck. What Chuck told him on the

dock was true. He'd been in love with Kara for a long time, and it was great to see them finally together.

"What's up?" Chuck sat on the bottom step of Vince's cabin stairs that led up to a narrow porch just big enough for a wooden swing. He popped the top off his bottle and took a long pull. His hair was messed up, and the man hadn't shaved since he arrived at the lake.

"Packing."

Chuck laughed. "No shit. You hiking tomorrow?"

"Yeah. I'm going on the trail for a couple days. I don't know when I'll be back."

"Nuh-uh. Not without me."

Vince blinked in surprise. "I didn't think you'd leave Kara behind for that long."

"I didn't say I would. She'll come, and Janie. The four of us. If Bryce and Cam and Nate want to go, we'll go with them next week, just the guys. Kara was talking about the women taking the pontoon out and sleeping on the water sometime anyway. It will work out. We have plenty of time."

Vince bit the inside of his cheek. He didn't know if he wanted to spend that much time with Janie. Even if Chuck and Kara would be with them. But before he could decline Chuck's offer, Janie came into view from behind the cabin and Chuck waved her over, his gold watch shining.

The dog bounded to them and happily licked Vince's face. The dog loved being at the lake.

"What?" Janie asked warily, chewing on a fingernail.

Uncomfortable, Vince continued to pack.

"Vince wants to hit the trail in the morning," Chuck said from the step. "Let's the four of us go."

Vince risked a glance at her. Mosquitos buzzed around, but she didn't seem to care. She was wearing a pink V-neck t-shirt and dark blue denim shorts with rips near the pockets and frayed hems. They were short, almost Daisy Dukes, and they made him remember her lean legs wrapped around his waist.

Their eyes met and she squinted at him, but he didn't know if it was in anger or puzzlement. She was probably plotting revenge.

"Okay," she agreed then abruptly went inside their cabin, slamming the door behind her.

"What was that?" Chuck asked.

Vince was truthful. "I haven't talked to her since last night."

"Nice," Chuck commented. "Better apologize or tomorrow's going to be real fun. What is it with this vacation this year?"

Zipping his backpack with a violent yank, Vince pointed out, "You're the one who invited yourself along."

"I didn't know you were being a prick. I should have, but I didn't."

"I'll fix it. Go pack."

Chuck stood. "Good luck, buddy. When are we taking off?"

"Eight sharp. No sleeping in."

Chuck snorted. "That's not my problem, it's yours."

Vince gave his pack a shove in annoyance then let himself into the cabin, Casey at his heels. He found Janie in her room packing her own bag.

"Tents?" she asked without looking at him.

"Yeah, I guess," Vince agreed. He hadn't thought of one for himself, but for the four of them, they would be more comfortable. Thinking about sharing a tent with Janie made his cock stiffen. "Look, I'm sorry about this morning," he blurted, hating her ignoring him.

"What about food?" she asked as if she didn't hear him.

"If you can carry the tent, I'll bring the food." He would need to add more to the pack for her, but that wouldn't be a big deal.

Janie nodded, her back still to him.

Vince stepped farther into the room and squatted next to her. Pushing on her shoulder, he made Janie finally turn to look at him. "I'm sorry." He hated apologizing because besides moving to his own bed, he didn't think he'd done anything wrong. She'd been out by the time he woke up and busy ever since. What was he supposed to do? Track her down to apologize? And what the hell for? The words came out of his mouth because she seemed to expect it.

With a flick of her fingers, she waved him off. "It's fine, whatever. We're not a couple; you don't owe me anything. Go to bed now if you want to be up so freaking early."

Relieved she was being adult about the whole thing, Vince went to his own room and fell onto the bed. He hadn't done anything wrong; he was glad she was being grown up enough to admit it. And she was right again— they weren't a couple . . . but how it would feel if they were?

♨

Apologized for screwing her, well, that was a new low, even for her. She'd never been apologized to before. Janie considered herself a decent lay. Vince seemed to think so too, fucking her four times that night.

Well, so the hell what? They were back where they started.

She woke early to make coffee, check her pack, and take a shower. No one told her how many days they would be gone, but they wouldn't be roughing it too badly. At their turnaround point, if they made it that far, they would shower at the state park's campsite. She made sure she had a few pairs of socks and underwear, in addition to her sturdy hiking clothes. Sunscreen, bug spray, food for Casey.

She wouldn't leave Casey behind; this was her dog's favorite part of the trip.

She was on the porch waiting when Vince found her.
"Morning."

"Hey."

They waited in tense silence and set off when Chuck and
Kara joined them both looking perky and already laughing.

Starting at an easy pace, Chuck told them silly stories of
special requests from guests at the hotel where he was the
general manager. Two concierges quit in six months' time
because of the odd requests and demands the hotel tried to
provide.

Janie tried not to feel used and enjoy the hike.

She also tried not to be bitter that this was the first time
she'd been invited along anywhere Vince was going and he
hadn't thrown a tantrum. This hike was Vince's baby, and he
never wanted her to go, though sometimes she insisted just to
piss him off.

She was surprised when he dropped back to talk with her.

"Hey."

"Hey."

Casey ran up ahead, and after Chuck and Kara disappeared around a bend in the trail, Vince and Janie were alone.

"I never thanked you for the idea to move my shop."

Janie looked at Vince full on. The man was gorgeous, there
was no question about that. His eyes blazed, his cheeks and
jaw smooth from his morning shave, and he wore a light
cotton hiking shirt and pants, the bottoms tucked into his
boots to discourage ticks. He worked out a lot, lifting weights,
and it showed in the ease of how he carried his pack.

With her tongue tucked into her cheek, she said, "I think
you did, but I, ah, just thought about what I would do in your
situation. Are you going to do it?" If he was willing to meet
her halfway, she would try. She didn't want to be a bitch
about it. It was new territory for them both.

"Yeah, that's what I wanted to talk to you about. Would
you help me? I mean, fix up the waiting room? Give me some

pointers? You told me I need to be competitive. I get that, even if I don't like it."

He wanted to see her after the trip? Janie rarely saw Vince outside of their vacation. Sometimes one of them would host a party where they would all get together, but Vince rarely talked to her during those events.

His attitude and change of heart confused her. She wasn't doing anything new, but Janie wouldn't ask because that was *exactly* the type of question he would expect. The last thing Janie wanted to be was typical.

"Sure, I guess." He was probably only being nice, and he would forget about it the minute they were back in the city.

They stopped for lunch—peanut butter and jelly sandwiches and chips.

Kara took a call and walked down the trail for privacy.

Chuck glared unhappily at her back. He fed Casey the crust of his sandwich as he watched Kara walk away.

"How do you take time off?" Vince asked Janie, popping a handful of Cheetos into his mouth.

"Mmmmm, my clients know I close, but it's getting more and more difficult to make sure there aren't any dogs being boarded while I want to be gone because a lot of people go on vacation this time of year, too. I'm training a new girl, so that will make three on my staff. I could stay open if we go next year."

It was a sobering thought. The rest of the group weren't doing too well.

Janie wished she could help, but their troubles seemed so out of her scope. "What about you?" she asked him.

"I wasn't getting any business anyway so I completely shut down. I think, depending how long it takes my real estate agent to find me a new place, I'll stay closed and do the grand opening thing you were talking about. I have a couple of special-order motorcycles that will get me through."

Janie nodded, but she didn't like the tightness around

Vince's eyes.

After lunch, Vince talked with Chuck, and Janie walked side by side with Kara, the path barely wide enough for both of them.

"Did it feel weird going from friends to more?" Janie asked after a few moments of quiet. The men were ignoring them, talking about baseball.

"It still feels weird," Kara murmured, then stuck her tongue out at Chuck's back. "Sometimes I don't think we're going to make it."

Janie sighed. "Why? You guys seem so happy."

"It's not that we're not happy . . . exactly. It's different backgrounds, life expectations. But let's not talk about me. What about you and Vince? Have you talked about you two doing the nasty?"

"Gross. I don't know why people call it that."

Kara laughed and took a swig from her water bottle.

"No, we haven't, and we probably won't. All he said was he's sorry. Sorry for having sex with me? Sorry for ignoring the hell out of me after? I can't see how his apology does anything. He hated me before that, and he hates me now." Janie tried to keep the hurt out of her voice. It was par for the course for them. But in some ways, sex changed things.

He'd been gentle with her, and he'd cared she got off as many times as he did. They didn't talk much but for the occasional, "lower," or "right there," instead, tenderly exploring each other when he wasn't plunged so deep inside her she could barely breathe.

He had a nice body and she'd enjoyed discovering every inch. Even thinking about it now made her panties wet.

When Kara changed the subject, Janie was relieved. No point in beating a dead horse.

They started talking about their other friends instead.

❦

The snippets of the women's words drifted to Chuck and Vince, and they both heard what Janie said.

"Maybe you better stay away from her," Chuck suggested.

Vince winced. "Yeah."

The idea sat like a lead ball in his stomach. He'd been fine all these years ignoring her, belittling her, and contrary to what Chuck said on the dock, Vince had never been in love with her. He'd simply had no interest in her.

Period.

Somehow that changed on the drive to the resort. When she'd been content to sit in the truck in silence, staring out the window as the scenery bled from city to country.

He'd studied her profile, her little nose, her delicate chin. The way she would pet Casey's rump because the dog's head rested in his lap.

He'd tried to hang on to the anger and dislike during their first day, but their time on the boat wore those feelings away and her advice, some simple advice, very likely saved him his business.

Advice she didn't have to give him. By rights, advice she *shouldn't* have given him.

He didn't deserve her help.

And thanking her, he used her for sex then ignored her. It hadn't seemed like that at the time, but it did now, and he felt like a guilty asshole. He gave her a quick look over his shoulder. She carried the backpack easily, laughing with Kara.

But maybe it wasn't about how he felt about her, but how she felt about him. Because it wouldn't do him a fucking bit of good if she gave as good as she got and hated him for the next ten years.

The path they were hiking on changed little from year to year. Perhaps some of the cabin's visitors didn't like to hike, or they only took small daily trips, because some of the trail was overgrown, and in one area two small trees knocked over in a storm blocked their way.

It was a beautiful walk with the lake occasionally making brief appearances through the trees. The day was hot, but the trees provided plenty of shade, and the droning of the bugs and the singing of the birds were the only sounds for miles.

They did little to soothe the turbulence in his mind and heart.

They set up camp in a field of wildflowers, the colors exploding against the green grass. Kara wandered around the area admiring the flowers, and Janie trotted to the water's edge with Casey for a well-deserved drink.

Vince gathered wood for the fire they would need to heat the stew ration Chuck brought. Afterward, Casey kept him company when he pitched his and Janie's tent. How would sharing a tent work? Conflicted, he almost asked if Chuck would share it with him instead, but Chuck had Kara backed up against a tree so he knew what that answer would be before he even bothered to ask.

Janie sank into the grass near the tent and used Casey as a pillow.

"You okay?" he asked, concerned. Resting on his haunches, he rearranged the wood for the fire.

"Yeah. I think I better step up my game at the gym, or maybe it's all this fresh air, but I'm beat." She yawned, covering her mouth with the back of her hand.

While Janie dozed, he and Chuck heated dinner, and Kara made phone calls and tried to send emails with the spotty internet connection.

"Cool it," Vince advised when Chuck grew agitated. "Who's running the hotel for you?"

"My assistant. She's good. I think she'll be ready to run her own hotel soon. She might already be looking." Chuck jabbed at the fire with a stick.

"Who runs things for Kara?" Vince tried to make Chuck understand. Kara's career was important to her and taking two weeks of vacation was impossible for most people.

Chuck pulled the tops off the stew cans and dumped the contents into a collapsible pot. "Her family's firm is behind her. She doesn't need to be on the phone now."

Vince didn't say anything; it sounded like there might be more going on than Kara's job, but he didn't think this was an appropriate time to get into it. He settled down beside Janie, watched her chest move slowly up and down in sleep, and resisted smoothing her hair. He would need to wake her soon so they could eat.

She hadn't said one negative thing about sharing a tent. Now Vince hoped she wouldn't, that she wouldn't speak to Kara about sharing.

He shook Janie's shoulder when the stew was bubbling, and after the meal he rinsed the dishes with her at the lake's edge, finding a break in the reeds and cattails growing in abundance. The lake glittered blue in the setting sun, the heating fading with the day, and a cool breeze blew off the water.

Maybe one day owning a lake cabin wouldn't be so bad. Perhaps something heated and insulated so he could stay in the winter too, and he could buy a snowmobile and ice fish. He and his kids—

Holy fuck. What kids? And with whom? Janie?

Yeah, right.

"What?"

Startled, Vince almost dropped a plastic bowl in the water. "What, what?"

"You groaned. Are you sore?" Janie eyed him.

Vince knew she was still skittish around him, and he had to give her points for her positive disposition and her lack of derision toward him. Nothing about their situation was conventional. "No. Just thinking."

"Oh. Well, I'm going to turn in. Night."

Vince watched her retreat, taking the pot and bowls with her. She'd left him the spoons.

Janie changed into her pajamas and lay on top of her sleeping bag. The temperature had dropped, making the evening pleasant, the wind keeping the bugs away. She would have liked to stay out on the water's edge with Vince, but something was changing and she didn't know if she liked it. He'd actively sought her out all day, voluntarily speaking with her, and it confused the hell out of her. How far did he want to go?

She wasn't ready for the answer.

So she hid from him, needing a few moments of peace before he too, turned in for the night.

Enemies, to lovers, to . . . friends?

Would they be friends when they returned to the city? Or would they go back to ignoring each other? Did she want Vince as a friend? Friends with benefits?

No. she didn't want that. She wanted something substantial.

It upset her to know Kara didn't think her relationship with Chuck would last. Their friendship wouldn't be the same if they broke up.

Janie rolled to her side and ignored Vince when he stumbled into the tent in the dark. She prayed he wouldn't make a move on her.

While he settled onto his sleeping bag, she balled the corner of hers into her mouth to blow out a relieved sigh. She hoped he didn't hear it. It was only after she heard his even breathing she let herself fall asleep too.

They hit the trail early, eating trail mix for breakfast. It was another sunny day, but there were clouds with a grey tinge to them drifting in the sky.

"Did you guys go at it again last night?" Kara asked, half a mile into their hike. Janie wasn't as familiar with the trail as the guys, but if she remembered correctly, they would spend one more night in the tents and arrive tomorrow at the campsite where they'd shower and grill on the outdoor barbecue pits. They'd buy steaks for dinner and restock their backpacks at the small general store. No one told her the plan, but there hadn't been talk of turning back so Janie assumed this was what they were doing. A shower would definitely be nice. Her prickly legs were already driving her crazy.

She could ask Vince, but she didn't want to talk to him if she could help it.

"No," Janie grumbled and shoved a handful of peanuts, raisins, and chocolate candies into her mouth.

Kara lifted an eyebrow.

"We didn't," Janie insisted, twigs snapping beneath her boots. "I don't know if I want to anyway. Things feel weird."

Vince and Chuck were ahead of them, but Janie couldn't hear what they were talking about. Maybe Vince was telling Chuck about what a bitch she was. She winced. That wasn't fair, and Janie hoped they were beyond that now. She was tired of going around in circles.

"How's work?" she asked Kara to get her mind off Vince and realized immediately it was a mistake.

Kara's face closed off, and she didn't say anything.

Well, that's crazy. Janie kicked a rock and didn't question Kara further.

The group stopped for a lunch of beef jerky and protein bars.

As she chewed her jerky, Janie studied Vince and tried not to get caught. Was Vince glad they went along or was he wishing he was alone? Well, he would have plenty of time to go alone, if he wanted. They still had all next week to enjoy Poplar Point.

Near dusk they set up camp, having made good time.

They chose a higher area to pitch their tents since it looked like rain. The clouds were darker, the wind cool and wild. Janie hoped it wouldn't storm tonight, but being she felt the wet in the air, it was a wasted wish.

Kara and Chuck retreated to their tent, bringing Casey with them. "You know I hate storms," Kara said, resting a hand on Casey's head. "He'll help me feel better if it gets too bad."

"Hey, what about me?" Chuck teased. They disappeared into the tent, Janie's dog close behind, without even a second glance at his mistress.

It was too early to go to bed, so she walked along the lake shore. She found a small beach and Janie dipped her toes in, surprised the water was warm. She searched for leeches, but she didn't find anything swimming in the murky water. Cold raindrops occasionally hit her on the top of her head.

She didn't know what Vince was doing so she felt safe and she took off her top and bra, her shorts and panties. Janie waded in, relieved to feel sand as she cautiously tip-toed farther into the lake. She was deep enough to tread water when she turned toward the beach and saw Vince watching her, a grin splitting his face.

"You naughty little girl," he called.

Janie blushed. She wasn't the type to skinny dip, but she thought she was alone.

She shouldn't be embarrassed though because Vince had already seen her bits and pieces. Even kissed some of those places. She also couldn't be angry at him for watching the show, for undoubtedly enjoying watching her ass as she waded into the water. She'd offered it up to him plenty of times the night he was in her bed.

Before she could shout a scathing remark, Vince pulled off his shirt and reached for the button of his hiking shorts.

The sky was darkening, the clouds churning, making the water pewter. Cold droplets still dripped onto her head, but the lake water was warm, caressing her breasts and the delicate skin between her legs.

Janie planted her feet at the bottom of the lake, some seaweed brushing her ankles making her shiver, and watched Vince take his shorts and briefs off. He left them in a pile near her clothes.

His eyes locked on hers as he waded to her. She touched herself between her legs. Yeah, she was wet. Janie pushed on the little bud of nerves making it surge at her touch.

Seeing Vince in the open, he was even larger than he looked in her dim bedroom. His cock pointed straight up, rubbing against his six-pack abs. He was groomed with very little hair around his balls, and she'd enjoyed playing with them. He had too, she laughed to herself. But her smiled faded as he stalked her, a predatory gleam in his eye.

Vince met her, and without a word, he claimed her lips with his.

Janie tore her mouth away, determined this would be her choice. "What if I don't want this?" she asked, placing a hand on his suntanned chest, testing him.

"Then we swim," he replied easily, but his stormy eyes belied his nonchalance.

Yeah. He wanted her, and walking away from her wouldn't be as easy as he made it sound.

She smirked.

Again, Vince crushed his mouth to hers, and he rammed his tongue between her teeth.

Janie skimmed her hand up and down his hardened length. He groaned into her mouth and grabbed a handful of her hair. With his other hand he reached between her legs, and Janie parted them, giving him better access. She gasped when he pushed a finger into her.

Thunder cracked and Janie pulled away. "It's not safe to be out here if there's lightning."

"It's not safe," Vince agreed. "For me. Janie," he growled

as he lifted her.

The water helped buoy her, and she clung to his shoulders and wrapped her legs around his waist.

Vince suckled the curve of her neck and started to push into her.

The water washed some of her lubrication away, and she moaned as his cock pulled on her delicate skin.

"Am I hurting you?" he asked, withdrawing slightly.

"No," she denied, tensing, stopping him. "No. Yes." She lowered herself onto him, slowly. "I like it, a little." She pressed her face into his shoulder, enjoying the sensation of her breasts crushed against his hot chest and his arms wrapped around her.

"Janie, Janie," Vince murmured into her ear, "aren't you just full of . . ." and he thrust up, at the same time gripping her hips, ". . . surprises?"

Janie groaned as he filled her, and she bit his neck.

He thrust into her with sharp, short jerks, and he stiffened as he came inside her, his arms like steel cables trapping her against him.

Vince gradually relaxed and held her, capturing her mouth in a kiss that was more sweet, tender, and gentle than any kiss she'd ever received.

Goosebumps crawled up and down her skin, and Janie wanted to head back to shore and dry off. She'd been ill-prepared for her skinny-dipping adventure, and she didn't have a towel with her. She would need to dress wet and dry off with the one she packed for the shower she would take at the campsite.

"You didn't come," Vince noted, not letting her go and not pulling out of her, either.

Another boom of thunder sounded, and uneasily Janie tilted her face toward the clouds that were growing grayer by the minute. "Is this a good time to talk about it?"

The mood was gone for her anyway. She wanted to be safe

and dry in her pajamas. It would be a long night, listening to the wind tear at the tent and trying to sleep through the pounding rain.

A streak of electric purple lightning lit the sky, and Vince let her go. "Come on," he said, pulling her hand. "We better get back."

Janie bit back a sarcastic retort. That's what she'd been saying all along.

Shivering, the water being warmer than the air now, she waded back to shore.

She was sore, but that was her fault and she didn't regret it. Vince pounding into her felt delicious, even if she hadn't come. Nothing was so good than being filled to the brim.

Vince followed her to the beach and picked up his clothes while she tried to pull her panties over her wet legs.

"Don't bother," he yelled over the wind. "Your feet are covered in sand. Come on." He held his clothes in a ball, and Janie grabbed at hers, giving up trying to dress.

She watched Vince's taut ass as they scurried back to their tent, and as Vince zipped the tent closed, the sky poured rain and thunder shook the ground.

Casey barked in the tent next to theirs. Her dog wasn't scared of storms, but he was probably wondering where she was.

"Here," Vince said and handed her a damp towel.

He'd dried off with it first.

Nice.

"Will Casey be okay?" Vince asked.

Janie dried off and regretted the sand she brushed off her feet. It couldn't be helped. She flicked Vince a glance and her jaw dropped. He was lying on his side, naked, his head propped on his hand, casual as you please. His hair was pulled into its usual ponytail, and he watched her dry off, desire smoldering in his eyes. Without breaking eye contact with her, he rubbed himself.

Instantly, Janie's insides pooled with heat. She dropped the towel and kneeled on her sleeping bag. "He'll be okay. He likes the rain."

"You didn't come," Vince reminded her.

They were warm and safe, even if the wind punching the sides of the canvas was a little unnerving. It sounded like the tent would be ripped from its poles at any second. She trusted Vince though, and she knew he pitched a tent well.

Both figuratively and literally.

Janie shrugged. "No big deal."

"You don't know me very well if that's what you think. Come here."

Janie debated how smart that was, but he'd already fucked her in the lake, so letting him do her in the tent wasn't much of a step-down. The harm was done, but this time he couldn't leave in the middle of the night to avoid her.

What would the morning after be like this time? She decided to find out.

The last thing Vince followed little Plainee Janie to the water was for her to strip and partake in some skinny dipping. He was only going to watch until she took off her panties. Her backside was a startling white in comparison to her tanned legs, and her tan lines made him ache. He hadn't a choice but to follow her into the water.

When she confessed she liked a little pain mixed with her sex, he took her with more force than was necessary, but he didn't stop. She'd felt so good with her legs wrapped around him, clinging to him, her hot body against his. He'd slammed into her, again and again, as hard as he dared. He was afraid he would rip her in two, but she hung on and he'd come in huge spurts. He'd never done it in the water. Buried inside Janie, the water licking at them, the storm brewing outside competed with the storm of his feelings waging inside him. It was the most erotic thing he'd ever experienced.

He felt like an ass when he realized she hadn't come, but he decided to remedy that situation now. Doubt flickered in her eyes, and he smiled when she crawled toward him. He would like to take her on her hands and knees sometime, but not now. Tonight, he had other plans for her.

Vince stroked his erection, his tip wet with come. Janie made him insatiable. He didn't know how and he didn't know why; all he knew was he wanted to fuck her every chance he had while they were at the lake.

She reached for him, but he stopped her. "It's my turn."

He kissed her, rubbing the come from his thumb along her jaw as he caressed her face. He leaned her backward without breaking the kiss, and he slid his tongue into her mouth as he pinched one of her nipples. She gasped, but he knew he didn't hurt her when she arched her back, asking for more.

Vince ran kisses from her mouth along her jaw. He spent a few moments nibbling her neck, then ran his tongue along her collarbone, warming when she giggled.

He paid her breasts particular attention, licking her nipples and grazing them with his teeth.

"Vince," she hissed, and he smiled at her impatience.

Vince drew her knees up and spread her legs. The tent was saturated with the smell of sex and desire. "Janie," he whispered.

"Yes?" she asked, watching him. It was barely light enough for him to see, but he took in her body lying on the sleeping bag. Her hair was spread out, her breasts creamy globes, her pink nipples sparkling. Her belly sloped and she was damp with desire. How had he ever thought her plain? Boring?

"You like a little bit of pain?"

Janie swallowed and nodded.

He hoped to hell she trusted him not to *really* hurt her.

Vince knew there was a difference between a little pain to enhance pleasure and truly hurting a woman. Something he would never, ever do.

"I like to watch."

"What?" she asked, confused.

Vince grinned. "I want to watch you play with yourself. Make yourself come for me, baby."

"Oh."

She lay there for so long, Vince wasn't sure she would do it. But she dipped the fingers of her right hand between the lips of her pussy. His cock surged as he watched her rub herself.

Pleasure moved across her face, her hips jerking, her body seeking release. He licked his fingers, but he knew he didn't need to. Janie was plenty wet. He teased her opening and grinned when Janie moaned. "I want to touch you."

"Aren't you?" she asked breathlessly.

Her soft voice made him harder. She didn't look at him, her eyes clenched tight while rubbing her clit, her sleeping bag clenched in her other hand.

"I meant, like this," he said and shoved his fore and middle fingers inside her, his knuckles pounding into her.

Janie gasped, but before he asked if it was too much, she widened her legs even farther and bore down, reveling in the pressure.

When her muscles contracted, he wished he was inside her instead. But this was her turn, and he fucked her with his fingers fast and hard. Her hips met him thrust for thrust, her fingers never stopping.

Suddenly she stilled, and Vince worried he'd been hurting her in a bad way after all. She stopped his hand and held it between her legs, keeping his fingers inside her. "I'm going to come," she whispered and opened her eyes.

Vince lost himself in the liquid depths of her brown irises.

She gave her clit a final touch and she came around his

fingers, wetness pouring out of her.

A soft moan filled the tent.

It was *his* moan. He'd never wanted another woman as much as he wanted Janie. Her smell filled the tent, desire with the salty tang of their sweat.

Slowly, he pulled his fingers out, figuring if she hadn't been sore by the poor lubrication caused by the lake, she would be now. He hadn't held back, though he would have, if she wouldn't have encouraged him as thoroughly as she had.

A deafening boom of thunder broke the intimacy of the moment, and Janie let out a self-conscious laugh. "Thanks," she murmured. "That was pretty amazing."

"You're not hurt?" Vince asked, concerned. He passed her the towel they'd dried off with and she cleaned herself, dabbing gently between her legs. He wanted to kiss her there, let his tongue soothe her raw skin, but it was too soon for that. He wanted to be inside her, but he had to pace himself —for her.

She threw the towel aside and sat up. "I'll be okay. It was good, Vince. Thank you." She kissed him on the cheek and he ran his fingers through her hair, surprised he enjoyed the closeness. He rarely stayed after sex. Tonight, he had no choice. Had he planned that? Had he wanted to be trapped in the small tent with nowhere to go but to lie in her arms and listen to the rain?

She tried to draw away, but he held her and pushed her back against the sleeping bags. Curling around her, he pushed his erection into her hip in an effort to ease some of the pressure. She lay languid in his arms, her breathing deep, satisfied, tired. She wasn't ready for anything more, even if he was.

They listened to the rain as it blew against the tent. It didn't seem she minded him holding her; she didn't try to pull away, and he was glad.

"Will the tent flood, do you think?" she asked.

He was pressed so close to her, her jaw moved against his nose as she spoke. "No. Chuck picked a high enough spot."

"Hmm," she answered.

Vince splayed a hand on her flat belly. She did have a nice body. Maybe a little on the bony side, but he'd fix that.

"Jane?" he asked tentatively. She probably wouldn't like what he had to ask her, but after their lovemaking he felt he had the right to ask.

"Hmmm?"

He better ask now before she fell asleep.

"Why don't you do anything with yourself? Why the plain clothes, the hair, no makeup?"

Janie tried to roll away from him, but he gripped her firmly in his embrace. "No. I'm not asking to be mean. I know we don't have the best history, so why would you believe me? But I'm honestly curious. I want to know."

She sighed, her chest moving with the deep breath, the bottoms of her breasts brushing the tops of his fingers.

Vince wanted to screw her again. To slowly nudge his fingers into her slick heat, to suck a nipple into his mouth. But while he waited for her to answer, he thought about the way she clung to him in the water, the way she pushed herself onto his cock, and he realized with dread being with her was slowly becoming more than a vacation lay.

"You've never met my mother," she finally said, rolling onto her side.

This time he let her, but he didn't allow her to put distance between them, instead adjusting to her new position by spooning her from behind.

Her crack caressed his cock now, and he groaned into her hair.

Her laughter reassured him; he didn't want her to shut him out. "No, I haven't," he agreed, answering her before she decided she didn't feel like talking.

Janie rested her cheek on the arm he tucked under her

head. "My mother is on her fifth husband and never leaves the house without a full face of makeup, her hair done, her nails painted. She's always on a diet, always dressed in the chicest clothes. She would never buy anything from Walmart. Since I was a little girl, she's told me no man would ever want me if I didn't do what she did. But I knew I didn't want her life, didn't want her husbands. She broke my father's heart. When a man falls in love with me, it will be because I'm pretty on the inside. Besides," she added lightly, "I'm around dogs all day. They don't care what I look like. They only care I don't hurt them and give them treats for being good." She laughed against his arm.

That sounded good to Vince, too. Someone who wouldn't hurt him and give him treats for being good.

Vince fell asleep with his arms wrapped around her. The first time staying after sex felt good.

And right.

Janie popped some ibuprofen with the instant coffee Chuck made them. She was sore, in a spectacular way, but they had a long way to hike to reach the campsite that night and she didn't want to slow them down. Her thighs ached, the skin between her legs was tender, and she was a little crampy like she was about to get her period, though she wasn't due for a couple of weeks.

Vince had taken her again, gently, in the middle of the night. The things he whispered to her worried her. The way he'd held her, kissed her, alarmed her.

"You can't tell me you two weren't up to something last night," Kara teased, sitting next to her. Luckily the men were tearing down the campsite, debating a baseball player's stats, too busy to listen to them.

"How do you look so fresh?" Janie grumbled, annoyed by

Kara's sunny disposition, fluffy hair . . . and was that lipgloss?

"You're avoiding the question."

"Yeah, we did a little something." Janie fed Casey breakfast, the dog chow in a collapsible bowl near her feet. She'd bring Casey for a drink at the little beach before they continued on for the day.

"Do you think it might turn into something?"

Janie heard the concern in Kara's voice, and she was nervous, too. Someway, somehow, last night Vince wasn't fucking her anymore. He was, quite possibly, making love to her. "No. Hello, he hates me, remember?" Kara might not, but she sure did.

"But—"

"Nuh-uh," Janie interrupted. "I don't want it, I don't need it."

"Right." Kara agreed, unconvinced.

Janie was thankful the ibuprofen kicked in, and she felt fine hiking the path.

Vince spoke with everyone equally, and when Janie was paired with Chuck on the trail, she remained quiet.

"He's a nice guy," Chuck tried.

Janie shot him a glance of disbelief. "Are you serious right now?"

Casey barked in response to his mistress's tone.

"He's hated me since we were kids. Now all of a sudden we're sleeping together and he's a nice guy?" Janie whispered furiously. She knew Vince and Chuck were good friends, better friends than with the other guys in their group, but she didn't think that gave Chuck the right to defend a lifetime of shitty behavior.

The rain stopped before dawn leaving the air crisp and clean. The sun was shining, and the trail was spotted with puddles. They were lucky it stopped raining; it would have been a miserable hike otherwise.

Chuck winced. "Overall he's a nice guy."

Janie heard Kara laugh at something Vince said. "He probably is, not that he's ever given me the chance to find out."

Chuck nodded. "I don't blame you."

"Blame me for what?"

"Taking things slow."

Janie didn't correct him. The fact was, she didn't know what she was doing. She didn't know what Vince was doing either, and in a week and a half, she wouldn't care. He'd be out of her life as he always was after their vacation.

They stopped for lunch along a scenic overlook. They had been slowly climbing and now the lake was spread out in front of them, sparkling a deep blue surrounded by evergreens and poplars.

Vince stood near her and dropped a kiss on the top of her head. His voluntary display of affection in front of Kara and Chuck annoyed her. What if she wanted to keep their relationship a secret? So when he brought her back into the city next week and dumped her on her ass she wouldn't be the laughingstock of their group.

"I'm sorry you're sore," he murmured.

She brushed him off. "I took some ibuprofen. No big deal," she said, stepping away. She didn't know what game he was playing, but she was thinking maybe she didn't want to play it. Or maybe she would take it for what it was and use *him* during their vacation. He was a good fuck, no doubt about it. And it had been a while since she'd had some and some that good.

But goddamn if she was going to talk to him about it. It *wasn't* a big deal. She would make sure of it.

She *did* know one thing—when she went home next week, she'd start dating. She would have more time when her new apprentice was trained. Maybe avoiding men wasn't the answer. Maybe she wouldn't have succumbed to Vince's advances so quickly if she hadn't been single for the past few years. Even she needed love, but she didn't need to use her mother's methods of finding it.

"Looking forward to camp?" Vince tried again. He looked good in his hiking shorts and t-shirt. He hadn't shaved and he had a Grizzly Adams look going on. It was damn sexy.

"Yeah," she said, relaxing. No need to be a bitch about anything. It took two to fuck and she had been right there with him. And what he was feeling about her, about what they were doing, well, she wouldn't let it be her problem. "It will be nice to shower. And a steak for dinner sounds good."

Vince nodded. "Yeah. It will be good to have a real meal and a beer." He paused. "Listen, Janie, you're not mad at me?"

She bet it took a lot for him to ask; men like Vince didn't apologize, were never wrong. "No, of course not. There isn't anything to be mad about." She didn't say more, even if she was dying to.

He leaned down to kiss her, brushing the strands of hair away from her face.

She pulled away, but not before Kara and Chuck started teasing them, making kissing sounds aimed in their direction.

Some of the tension eased during the last leg of their trip to the campground. The four of them joked, had serious talks about their other friends, and complained about how hungry they were for real food.

When they arrived, Kara took off with her phone, calling over her shoulder to Janie, "Meet you at the showers."

Chuck scowled and Vince pushed him toward the office. "Come on, let's go see what they have available."

Janie walked to the girls' shower room intending to take a long hot shower. She wanted to shave her legs and wash her hair.

She left Casey under a tree near the building to sleep off the days' hike.

Janie was washing her hair when Kara called out, "Janie?"

"Yeah. Are you okay?" she hollered in response, catching a note of sadness in Kara's voice.

"No."

Before Janie could ask what was wrong, Kara turned on the shower next to hers, the curtain screeching as it scraped across the rod when Kara pulled it closed.

Janie continued to wash up in silence.

Kara's impending bad news took the joy out of Janie's shower. She shaved, swearing when she nicked her ankle, and ran conditioner through her hair. She wasn't looking forward to drying off with her towel. Vince handed it to her last night, and she knew it was covered in their come.

It even smelled like sex when she brought it to her nose to sniff it, and the scent made her aroused. Would Vince try to make a move on her tonight? If he did, would she spread her legs for him?

She wanted to. She wanted him the way they had the first night in their cabin. Him on bottom, her on top, rocking, her fingers on her clit. She imagined him squeezing her nipples and they puckered under the towel's nubby material. Yeah, if he wanted to fuck her, she would let him.

Kara's shower was still running, and there was no one else around. She sat on the bench, spread her legs, and slid her fingers into the slick folds. Thinking of Vince's cock inside her made her wetter. She pushed her middle finger inside; she was still a little raw from the rough sex yesterday. She pulled her finger out and touched her clit. She rubbed, opening her legs farther, the air tickling her skin.

As her fingers glided over her sensitive spot, Janie imagined Vince's fingers fucking her, oh so hard, and how good that felt. He had taken her at her word, she liked a little pain, and he'd rammed his fingers into her over and over.

Stifling a moan, she came, her muscles clenching in the waves of her orgasm, and she dripped onto the concrete floor. She gasped, her heart pounding. She frequently played with herself; she had toys at home but she'd never made herself come so hard before. It must have to do with thinking about Vince and what he'd done to her with his fingers.

When she heard voices outside the shower shelter, Janie tensed, clutching the towel to her. She exhaled a huge sigh of relief when the voices faded as the campers walked by.

Kara's water stopped, and Janie quickly cleaned herself off and wiped the floor. She casually pulled on fresh panties, the crotch rubbing her tender skin, and was fastening her bra, her breasts heavy and her nipples tingling, when Kara stepped out of the shower stall.

"Are you okay?" Kara asked, staring at her. "Don't you feel good?"

Janie nodded, quickly thinking of an explanation for her flushed skin. "Yeah. I'm okay. It's just hot, you know? Maybe when we get back to the cabins I'll actually turn the AC on. Now," she had to pause as she pulled a red tank top over her head, "what's the matter? Why were you crying?"

Kara started drying herself off, her lips pressed against her tears. "My father wants me to move." Naked, she sank onto the bench beside Janie and covered her face with her towel.

"Oh no," Janie whispered, horrified. "Why?"

"To open another branch of the firm."

"Does Chuck know?"

Kara cried into the towel and shook her head.

Janie pulled on a pair of denim shorts and started to brush her hair before it dried in knots. "What are you going to do?"

Kara sucked in shuddery breaths, wiping her cheeks on her towel. "I don't know. Please don't tell Chuck. We're already having problems. This will kill us. I know it."

Janie rested a hand on Kara's bare shoulder. "Of course not," she murmured. No wonder Kara thought she and Chuck weren't going to make it. Not if she'd known her father had plans to send her to a different city.

Silently, Kara dressed quickly in shorts and a tank top, and they packed their travel-sized toiletries.

When they stepped outside, Janie scanned the campsite and found Casey with Vince and Chuck. They were finishing putting up the tents near a barbecue pit far across the campground.

"Feel better?" Vince called as they neared.

"Yeah, thanks."

"Everything okay? You were in there for a while."

"The shower felt good." Janie wouldn't tell him she pleasured herself too, or about Kara's secret.

"Hey," Chuck greeted Kara. Kara responded by giving Chuck a big kiss. Looking at them, no one would guess they were having problems. "It's our turn," Vince announced, hoisting his pack. "After our showers, we'll grab the steaks from the store."

Vince and Chuck headed toward the men's shower stalls

"Thanks for listening to me; you're a good friend," Kara whispered, though Vince and Chuck were well out of range of hearing her. "God, I am so tired. I'm going to go lie down before dinner." She threw Janie a feeble smile over her shoulder before letting herself into the tent.

Janie took Casey to explore the campground and brought her pocketbook to browse the small store to hopefully buy a cup of coffee and something chocolate. The campsite was quite large and the store well-stocked. It was part of a state park that housed RVs, providing hookups to fill water tanks and empty waste containers. The park contained a huge playground for children, and kids of all ages were running around with the candy they'd purchased from the store.

Janie bought a large coffee and dumped in several little cups of chocolate creamer. At the same time, she bought a Twix bar and shoved it into the waistband of her shorts. She didn't have enough hands to carry her pocketbook too, if she didn't want to spill her coffee.

Janie threw her wallet into her tent and walked around the campsite near the water, Casey by her side.

The lake shallowed into a bay, docks lining the shore. Many campers boated there as well, and Janie wondered if that was something they could try one year, though they paid for the cabins at the resort. Spending too much time away didn't make sense, financially.

The mosquitos weren't too terrible, she was pleased to notice, sipping her coffee.

Away from the busy docks, rocks peeked from the water, forming a point. Janie stood on one, watching minnows dart under the murky water. The bottom of the bay was a dull greenish-brown, the sunlight shining through the water swirling the colors.

She felt bad for Chuck and Kara and didn't know what Kara would do. Kara didn't tell her where her father wanted her to move, but Janie couldn't imagine living anywhere else.

Would Vince really want her to help him with his shop? It would probably be wise if she didn't. They had nothing in common and no reason to continue whatever it was they were doing. He'd been mean, cruel, and indifferent far too long for her to entertain the thought of ever having a true relationship with him.

It was still unsettling he was being as nice as he was. Maybe the trouble with his business gave him a reality check. Maybe he disentangled himself from a poor relationship with someone before their vacation, and he was using her to forget about his ex. She didn't know enough about him to even fathom an accurate guess. The way he held her last night, the things he told her while he was deep inside her confused her.

What did he mean when he said he cared about her, that he wanted to be with her? Be with her how, be with her when? Did he think she needed the platitudes while he was fucking her? She didn't. She was fucking him too, and she was enjoying it.

She wasn't falling for him. Maybe the vulnerability he showed her in the boat while they were talking about his tanking business touched her. But they'd been talking about his livelihood. If she didn't know where her next paycheck was coming from, she'd be nervous, too. She didn't hate him so much she would wish bankruptcy on him.

Perhaps if they hadn't needed to share a cabin he would have kept his distance. If Chuck were more available on this trip and not always with Kara, Vince wouldn't want to spend time with her. She was a convenience on this trip, an easy lay.

Nothing about what they were doing would transfer into their lives in the city.

Janie carefully pivoted on the rock and saw him watching her. Her heart did a little flip in her chest. He was handsome, for sure. But under the raven-black hair, the hot blue eyes, and the well-muscled body, he was nothing she wanted.

She was everything he wanted and it scared the hell out of him. He'd never felt this way about a woman. Sure, he'd used them for sex, maybe a little companionship, but he'd never been sad to say goodbye.

He didn't know what had gotten into him last night. He'd been gentle with her, knowing she had to be sore, and he took her in the missionary position, so he covered her completely, totally. He'd desperately wanted, needed, to be near her.

He rubbed his chest now, in unease. Short of telling her he loved her, he'd told her everything that was in his heart. Vince knew she wasn't ready, but he'd spilled his guts, whispered in her ear, his hands in her hair. He'd told her things he'd never told another woman. Things he didn't understand. Feelings he never, in a million lifetimes, thought he'd feel for the woman standing on a rock sipping coffee, watching the ducks.

She hadn't said anything back.

She'd turned her head and hadn't said anything back. Not even a muffled, "Me, too." Nothing. At first, he'd thought she was offering her neck, and he'd accepted, ravaging the delicate skin between her shoulder and her ear.

But when they'd both come, he'd tried to draw her into some conversation, to try to feel her out about where they were heading, and she'd turned away claiming she was tired and she fell asleep.

So not only had he been rebuffed, he'd fucking been *that man* wanting to know where their relationship was going.

The thing he'd fear she would do, he'd done to her instead. And the response? What he'd give her if she'd tried to pull that shit.

The thought rankled, and it pissed him off. He didn't like being used for sex. Even if he'd done it plenty of times.

Vince waved at her. She was beautiful, bathed in the orange glow of the sunset.

He was falling in love with her, and he knew asking for her help with his shop was a thinly veiled attempt to keep in touch with her after their vacation was over. Vince couldn't let her get away.

He was relieved when she raised a hand to return his greeting.

A large fish jumped out of the water, breaking the quiet moment, and he watched, horrified, as Janie jumped in surprise and lost her balance on the rock. She dropped her coffee into the water as her feet slid from beneath her.

Vince hoped she would catch her balance, but she didn't. She fell backward onto the other rocks behind her, attempting to break her fall with her hand.

As Janie cried out as she landed, he was already running across the grass to help her. Casey kept pace with him, barking furiously at his mistress's obvious distress.

Vince trudged into the water, not caring about his hiking

boots or his shorts. "Are you all right?" he asked her urgently, pulling her into his arms. Cradling her, he waded back to shore tripping over the rocks, breaking through the reeds and cattails, and trudging up the bank.

Clasping her left arm against her body, Janie cried into his shirt, and he didn't know if it was from shock or pain or both. Her cheek was scraped, as was the side of her other arm. One of her thighs was bleeding, and her shorts were dripping, running water down her legs.

He cuddled her to him, giving her time to catch her breath. While he held her, nothing existed in his world but Janie and the fact she was okay. Slowly she stopped crying, gasping, and hiccuping.

"We need to get you looked at."

"B-but—"

"No buts," Vince interrupted, setting her gently on her feet. "You're bleeding in a couple spots. Did you hurt your arm?" He studied her tear-stained face; her cheek was oozing blood. It scared the shit out of him watching her fall.

Janie grimaced. Her wrist was swelling, and the skin was turning bright pink.

"We have to make sure it's not broken. Come on." With more calm than he felt, he led her to the campsite office.

The young woman who checked them in was still there, readying to leave for the day. The campsite wasn't staffed during the night, but someone would open the office at six in the morning to check out campers who wanted to get an early start on the road. "Oh, no," she exclaimed, her bright blue eyes widening at Janie's injuries. "Are you all right?"

Vince answered even though the question was directed at Janie. "She landed on her wrist. We need a ride into Poplar Point so we can get her to Urgent Care. I think she needs x-rays and her scrapes need to be looked at."

"How will we get back?" Janie protested.

"We'll call one of the guys to pick us up."

"But—"

"You're not going to feel like hiking back. We wouldn't be able to anyway. Our boots are soaked," he reasoned.

The blonde woman's attention ping-ponged between Vince and Janie as they bickered.

"But Chuck and Kara—"

"Will have to hike back alone. I don't see the problem," he argued firmly. "You need to get your wrist looked at. If it's broken, maybe you'll want to go home." Vince didn't let disappointment seep into his voice at the idea.

Janie stopped objecting.

"Would you be able to take us into town?" Vince asked the woman.

"Sure. Are you staying at the resort? You hiked here?"

Vince left Janie to explain while he went to pack their tent and supplies. Finding a ride to the resort from town was the only option. Hiking would be impossible with wet boots, and they wouldn't dry out in a reasonable amount of time to wait.

Chuck and Kara were sitting at a picnic table eating chips and drinking sodas when he found them.

"Janie fell, and the woman in the office is going to take us into Poplar Point. Janie's arm needs an x-ray; her wrist might be broken." His heart twisted at the thought of her being hurt. If she'd hit her head, if he hadn't been around . . . the possibilities jumped around his brain, out of control. He clumsily dismantled the tent in his haste while Kara repacked Janie's things.

"We'll keep Casey with us," Kara offered, zipping Janie's pack. "They won't let him into the clinic anyway. Let me run and grab him and say goodbye to Janie." She took off toward the campsite office.

When she was out of sight, Vince dropped his guard. He sank onto his haunches in the grass and dry-washed his face.

"It's not that serious?" Chuck asked, taking over and

securing Vince's backpack because it was obvious Vince's mind was far from packing.

"No. No. Thank fucking God. But holy shit, Chuck, watching her fall in, knowing I couldn't do anything . . . fuck."

"You're really falling for her." Chuck shoved the backpack at him.

"Yeah."

"Too bad," Chuck replied without sympathy.

Vince narrowed his eyes at his friend. "Why do you say that?"

"Because you've been such a jackass to her all these years. You think a couple nights of sleeping with her is going to make her forgive you? I tried talking to her on the trail."

Vince drew his lips into a tight line.

"You're screwed," Chuck said gravely, shaking his head.

Vince was deathly afraid Chuck was right. Instead of admitting it, Vince asked, "Will you and Kara be all right, or do you want to go with us?"

Chuck blew out a breath. "We need the time alone. The hike back to the resort might do us some good."

"What's wrong?" Vince asked out of courtesy, but not any real interest. He was being a dick but Janie was in pain; they needed to get going. He'd apologize later.

Chuck shrugged.

"See you back at the resort then," Vince said in goodbye, grateful Chuck didn't want to talk.

Vince met Janie outside the campsite office. She was huddled with Kara, whispering. The office worker locked up, and she stood off to the side, patiently waiting.

"Take care of her," Kara told him.

Vince nodded and put his arm around Janie. "Ready to go?"

"Yeah." Janie's voice wavered, and she still held her wrist protectively against her ribs.

Kara waved goodbye, a worried frown marring her delicate features.

Vince and Janie followed the woman to her car, and he helped Janie into the back seat of the little compact and buckled her in.

"Thanks," she whispered.

She looked tired, fatigue pulling at the skin around her eyes and mouth; it had been a long day. They'd be grilling steaks and lounging by the barbecue grill if she hadn't fallen.

"You're welcome," he replied, pressing a kiss to her uninjured cheek. He stored their backpacks in the car's little trunk, the bulky bags using the entire space.

"I'll take you to the ER," the woman said, pulling out of the campsite's parking lot. "Poplar Point doesn't have an Urgent Care, and it's after hours. Sorry about that."

"It's fine," Vince said from the front passenger seat. "The ER will work."

He frequently looked over his shoulder at Janie who had her eyes closed and her head resting against the backrest. Her skin was pale, her face drawn.

Vince's heart sputtered in his chest.

She would probably want to go back to the city, then his time with her, to explore what they were doing, would be cut short.

Fuck.

The office worker let them out at Poplar Point Saint Mary's Hospital. A smaller hospital, it serviced the tiny towns surrounding Poplar Point that didn't have a hospital or a clinic.

"I hope you'll be okay," the woman said, popping the trunk for Vince as Janie maneuvered out of the car.

"Thanks, and thanks for the ride," Vince said, awkwardly unfolding himself from the tiny seat of the car. His knees had been pushed against the dashboard the entire way into town. He pulled their backpacks out of the trunk and after he slammed the lid shut, the office worker drove away.

Vince led Janie through the automatic doors to the check-in desk, and immediately, the smell of lemon cleaner met his nose.

A young woman holding a whimpering baby was the only person in the waiting room.

Janie kept her insurance card in her pocketbook, and Vince helped her find it and fill out forms.

They settled uncomfortably into the black plastic chairs to wait for Janie's turn to see the doctor. The TV on the wall was showing an episode of *Cheaters*.

"I should probably call one of the guys to pick us up."

Janie bit her lip.

"What?"

She shrugged. "I don't know. Do you know what their plans were while we were gone? Are they on the pontoon? Or camping on one of the islands?"

Vince shook his head. "Chuck and I have been giving them space."

That was the polite way of saying he was leaving them the fuck alone. "You'd know more—gossiping with the girls," he said.

"I don't know much more than you," she said. "Alycia and Bryce fight all the time. Bailey and Cameron are barely speaking to each other, which is almost better than Alycia's and Bryce's fighting, though not by much, and you know, Crystal and Nate."

The woman and her baby were called into an exam room by a friendly-looking nurse dressed in pink scrubs holding a green file folder.

"You ever think about kids?" Vince asked, pretending a casualness he didn't feel by propping his feet on his pack and crossing his arms over his chest.

Janie laughed bitterly. "No. I mean, well. No. I've never

been serious enough about a man long enough to consider it and after seeing what everyone is dealing with this summer, I'm rethinking relationships in general, much less having kids with someone."

Rattled by her response, Vince said nothing in reply and they waited in silence until the nurse called them into an exam room.

❦

Janie didn't know why Vince clung to her. She'd been to Urgent Care by herself. The time she thought she had strep. The time a new client's dog bit her. She didn't need him and was going to tell him so, but he hauled their backpacks off the floor and was at her side before she told him not to bother.

The nurse took her vitals and examined her scrapes. She asked Janie if she wanted to change into an exam gown and she declined. She figured her shorts and tank revealed enough skin, and she didn't need Vince seeing her in one, either.

Vince paced the little exam room while she waited on the cushioned examination table, the thin paper crinkling beneath her ass.

Back and forth, back and forth water making squishing sounds in his boots.

"What the fuck's your problem?" she asked, his pacing making her nervous.

"You could've died!" he exploded, stopping in front of her, his hands on his hips, glaring.

Janie leaned back, her elbows cushioned by the little flat pillow. Vince was a big guy, in every sense of the word, and his anger made her hair stand up on end. She knew he wouldn't hurt her, but it was instinct after all these years to pull away. "Maybe," she conceded.

"There's no maybe." He glowered. "If you would have hit

your head, if you would have been alone, you could've drowned. You were being stupid."

Janie sat up, outraged. "I was not. I was perfectly fine until I saw you staring at me. Then that stupid fish jumped and scared me. It's your fault. Why in the hell are you following me around anyway?"

"Because I think I'm in love with you! I can't seem to let you out of my sight."

Janie opened her mouth to tell him how fucked up that was when there was a knock on the door and a doctor let himself into the little room, his white bushy eyebrows raised and a faint frown on his lips.

She didn't say another word to Vince, though her mind was spinning out of control at his declaration. He thought he was in love with her. She was going to believe that like she would believe someone who told her she won the lottery. He'd hated her far too long to let a couple nights of sex change that.

Janie sat through the x-ray and was relieved to hear her wrist was only sprained. The doctor fit her with a splint and checked the rest of her body. He deemed her roughed up but fine saying she'd have a large bruise on her side come morning. "The nurse will see to your scratches. Here's a prescription for pain. You're going to be hurting for a while."

Janie nodded and watched the doctor leave the exam room. Only a second passed before the same nurse who had ushered them into the room returned.

"Will you wait in the waiting room, please?" she snapped at Vince, pulling pink rubber gloves over her hands.

Janie's eyes shot to Vince's in surprise. He was with her because, well, not because she'd asked, he'd barged his way in, but because she had no objection to it. Besides the bickering, his presence was kind of reassuring.

"That's not—" she began, but the nurse cut off her objections.

"It's policy to give the patient some privacy," the nurse interrupted, her eyes moving between the door and Vince in obvious invitation.

Another ER nurse stood in the hallway watching them, a stack of blue file folders in her arms, a stethoscope hanging around her neck.

Vince kissed the top of Janie's head, hefted their backpacks into his arms, then glared at the nurse before stomping out of the room toward the waiting area.

"That wasn't necessary," Janie told the nurse who busied herself with antiseptic and gauze pads.

When the nurse turned around, Janie was jolted by the kindness and compassion in her eyes. Softly dabbing her cheek, the nurse murmured, "Doctor heard him yelling at you." She met Janie's eyes. "We get a few domestic violence cases through here. Not a lot, mind you, but some." The woman took Janie's hand and squeezed. "You're safe here. We can get these scrapes cleaned up, and we'll call the police and a social worker. You don't have to leave with him. You have options."

Janie easily understood how their relationship could look to people who didn't know them. Vince's rough demeanor would scare anyone. "It's not like that."

"It isn't?" the nurse asked, applying antiseptic to the long scratches on Janie's thigh and peering at her through a disbelieving squint.

"You don't need to call anyone. It was an accident." Janie winced as the sting slithered through her nerve endings making her entire body tremble.

Huffing out a sigh, the nurse applied a protective coating to her skin. "We can't make you accept help but please know it's always available."

Because she knew the nurses were only doing their jobs and that they probably did help women who needed it, Janie thanked her.

The nurse finished tending her scrapes in silence.

It was nighttime when they left the ER with a prescription in Vince's hand for painkillers she didn't want.

Vince dropped their backpacks onto the sidewalk adjacent to the almost empty parking lot. "Why did the nurse kick me out? I wanted to stay with you."

Janie bit her nail. She didn't want to tell him what the nurse said, but Vince's stare wouldn't let her escape. "She thought you hurt me, and she offered to call the cops."

"I would never hurt you," Vince yelled, his voice bouncing off the buildings of Main Street.

Looking away, Janie mumbled, "Maybe not physically."

Vince spun toward her, his mouth agape, but Janie knew he couldn't argue with her.

Settling on his haunches in front of her, Vince rested his hands on her thighs, carefully avoiding her scrapes. "I don't know what I can say, I don't know what I can do, to erase the damage I've done all these years."

"Vince, you're going to have to give me time, that's all I can say. You want too much from me." Janie looked down at his hands resting on her legs. "Now isn't a good time to talk about it."

He looked away, shame in his eyes.

She hated the way he closed off, but she didn't want to lead him on or make him think this could be easier than it would be.

"Why don't you want your painkillers?" he asked quietly. "I hate seeing you in pain." He flinched. "I'm never going to be able to make this right, am I?"

Across the large empty parking lot and the quiet street, a small bar with neon signs in the windows was doing brisk business. Music poured through the door when a group of people stepped inside.

"Because they make me sick," she grumbled, pulling her attention away from the bar. "What do you want to do?" she asked instead, rather than fight. They needed to talk, but they had other things to worry about. She felt strange, even a little homeless. She didn't have her dog with her, no way back to the resort, no imminent place to sleep. Vince didn't seem bothered by any of it, staring sadly at the white paint of the parking spaces, sparkling in the streetlights.

"I know you don't want me to, but let me call Cam or Bryce. Nate. We can be back at the resort in a couple hours. Please. I want to get you back so you can rest."

Janie shrugged. "Try, then, but it won't do any good."

Vince pulled his phone out of his heavy backpack and punched in some numbers, walking in a tight circle as he waited for someone to answer.

The cool evening breeze chilled her skin. Her wet shorts and tank were drying, but she felt dirty and wanted a shower. At least her wrist wasn't broken. She wouldn't have been able to swim with a cast or use the hot tub, and she would have needed to shower carefully.

"No one is answering," Vince muttered, frustrated.

Janie wasn't surprised. They could be out on the pontoon, or camping, or even sitting in the bar across the street. More than likely they were drinking by the bonfire and their phones were inside their cabins.

Janie let out a sigh. She wanted to go somewhere with water or a cup of coffee to swallow some ibuprofen. Her wrist was bothering her, and she was tired, mentally as well as physically. She was trying not to think of the L word Vince lobbed at her, and it wasn't 'loathed.'

That, she'd have understood.

He looked worried and guilty, stealing glances at her out of the corner of his eye. What had he thought when she hadn't said she loved him back?

She didn't know what she felt for him. He'd hated her for so long, and he'd turned on a dime. What did he think she would do with that?

What did she *want* to do with that? He was a kind man—to everyone but her. He ran a good business and Chuck thought well of him. She'd given Chuck a hard time on the hike to the campground, but he was a good judge of character and she trusted his opinion.

Vince was good in the sack, but could she make a relationship work based on hot sex?

She was willing to spread her legs, but was she willing to share her life?

"Still no answer. They could be doing anything."

Janie resisted rolling her eyes. She'd already told him that.

"How's your wrist?" Vince asked, running a hand over her hair.

"It hurts," she admitted. Along with everything else—including her heart.

"Do you want—"

"No."

"Stubborn."

Suddenly, Janie laughed. Their situation was so dumb. They essentially had nowhere to go and she was starving. The thought of the steaks they'd missed made her stomach growl.

"Shit. You're hungry. So am I. I'm sorry." Vince rubbed his face in frustration.

"Come on," she said, still grinning. "Let's go to the bar and order burgers, then take a taxi to the resort. It will cost, but probably no more than getting a hotel room here, if there's even one available."

Poplar Point was a tourist town being located so close to Lake Harriet, the hotels filling every night. Unless they wanted to pitch their tent in the parking lot, they had no choice. They'd been standing around too long as it was, and soon the cops would give them tickets for loitering.

Vince picked up their bags. Janie was grateful he knew she wouldn't be able to carry hers.

Once they were tucked away in a corner booth and their

order given to the waitress, Vince took her hand. "I meant what I said, you know."

This far into the country, Janie couldn't expect Beyoncé's newest to be playing, and a slow country song by Tim McGraw didn't help her.

"No, you didn't," she immediately denied. "Vince—"

"Janie. I don't know how, I don't know when, but I am, I do." Vince skimmed his fingers over her hand. "I—" He stopped when a black-haired waitress set down huge mugs of beer then sashayed away, probably hoping for Vince's phone number. Or at least a big tip.

Because God knew the waitress was more Vince's type than she was.

She pulled her hand away and downed half her beer, grateful for the distraction. She was thirsty and she needed the liquid courage. Her blood started buzzing the moment the beer hit her stomach—she had such a low tolerance. "It wouldn't work. We've hated each other for far too long. Three words aren't going to erase a lifetime of that. You're good in bed, Vince, but it can't make us a couple, no matter what you think you feel for me."

Janie looked away and Vince bit back a foul, "Fuck."

She wasn't feeling what he was; she wasn't going to give him a chance. He loved her, he knew he did, but after the way he'd treated her all their lives, she wouldn't believe it. So he would spend the rest of his life trying to convince her.

At first, he'd been appalled and mortified when Janie told him what the nurse thought of him. There was no way in hell the thought would have entered his mind that Janie looked like a battered woman, not when he'd actually seen her fall. But now he studied her, and that's exactly what she looked like—a woman who'd maybe fallen down the stairs. Pair that with his angry disposition, his worry channeled into a livid haze, and it would be a forgone conclusion to a nurse who'd seen it all.

That he could be perceived as a man who assaulted his wife or girlfriend and brought her to the ER with a lie, instead of who he really was, a man in love with a woman who had fallen, shamed him. It wasn't any wonder Janie didn't believe him.

The waitress brought them their burger baskets and Vince indulged, letting himself stare at Janie while she inhaled her food.

When she pushed her basket away, he slid closer to her on the bench and rested his arm on the back of the booth. He relaxed when she didn't pull away. With his other hand, cold from cupping his icy mug, he ran his fingers up the smooth skin of her thigh.

She trembled under his touch.

If they had anything going for them, they were compatible in bed. Relationships were built on less, no matter what Janie said. Vince would start there. It was the only place he knew of that would give him an in—so to speak.

Casually, he played with the hem of her shorts. Thinking about fucking her made him rock hard. His fingers brushed over the button of her waistband, and he popped it open.

"What are you doing?" Janie hissed. "We're in a restaurant."

"We're in a bar," he corrected, nuzzling her ear with his lips. Janie had taken out her earrings for the hike, and he sucked her bare earlobe into his mouth, as he slid the zipper of her shorts down.

"People will see," Janie objected, but her voice was weaker this time. She wanted him. Vince smiled. He'd wear her down, make this work. He loved the hell out of her, and he would prove it.

His hand dipped inside her shorts, past the waistband of

her panties. "No one is looking. Relax. I want to please you." *I want to make you love me.*

Janie, to his surprise, listened to him. She sat back and spread her legs, giving his hand space.

The waitress approached their table and smirked when Vince winked at her. She veered off to give them privacy.

Luckily, Janie's head was tilted back resting on his arm and her eyes were closed. She would have been embarrassed and probably pissed at him. "I love you," he whispered in her ear as his fingers found her clit. He would tell her that every day for the rest of his goddamned life.

She moaned and widened her legs under the table.

"I'll do whatever I can to make you believe me, and one day, you may even love me back." He hoped. He hoped like hell.

Vince peppered kisses along her jaw.

She quivered under his touch, and he moved his fingers, dipping his middle and forefinger into her, as far as her position and shorts allowed.

Vince captured her mouth with his and she opened, inviting his tongue. He kissed her, trying to convey all his feelings, love, guilt, fear, into one single kiss.

His fingers slid back to her clit, circling, rubbing, her hips undulating under his touch.

Yeah, she was almost there.

"Tell me you'll give me a chance," he pleaded, as if his life depended on it. His heart was on the cusp of breaking.

Janie moaned; her eyelids fluttered.

Vince stopped, resting his fingertips on her sensitive nub.

"Vince," Janie groaned, moving her hips, urging him to continue.

"Tell me you'll give me a chance," he repeated lowly in her ear. "I love you. Give me a chance to show you." He sounded like a blubbering idiot, but his instincts told him if he gave her too much time to think about it, she would tell him to fuck off. He had to sneak under her defenses, make her promise, because he knew she would keep it and give their relationship a fair shot. That's all he could ask of her.

"Please," she whimpered, her eyes shut tight. "I'm so close."

He gave her a slight rub. Vince didn't want to make her come before she said the words he wanted to hear.

"Tell me," he growled. He caressed the sides of her clit, back and forth, but not the top. Not yet. A rub on the top would send her over the edge. That was how well he already knew her. But rubbing the sides tortured her.

Janie met his gaze. Her pupils were dilated in desire and need, and there was a faint sheen of tears glistening in her eyes. Her irises were molten, a deep brown like a pilsner glass of Guinness—almost black. "Vince," she whispered, and she blinked, a tear escaping to rest on her cheek.

He knew then he had her, but she still hadn't said the words. "Say it."

"Okay," she choked. "I'll give you a chance if it means that much to you."

Vince claimed her mouth in victory. She'd said yes. Not to *the* question, time enough for that, but it was a start.

He smoothed his fingers over her clit, but before she came, he pulled her hand from the table and pushed it into her lap. He shoved his fingers inside her, and she slid her fingers into her panties. She convulsed around his fingers as she finished herself off.

"You're a jerk," Janie said, smiling against his mouth.

"But I'm a jerk who will try to make you happy." He pulled his hand out of her shorts and resisted the urge to bring them to his mouth. He loved how she tasted. He would never grow tired of burying his face between her legs. "It's all I want now."

"Vince—" she started as she awkwardly zipped and buttoned her shorts one-handed.

He silenced her with a kiss. "No. No demands. I get it. I can totally see where you're coming from. Fucking for a couple days doesn't make a relationship or make us a couple, you're right. But all I'm asking for is a chance. A chance to be a better man, a chance to share your life, in whatever way you see fit to let me."

Janie drained the last of her beer. "Okay." She nuzzled his cheek with her nose and feathered a kiss over his lips. "Okay."

The look in Vince's blue eyes as he fingered Janie broke something inside her. He'd looked so sincere, so hopeful, so sad and lost, that even in a cloud of lust and beer, she knew if she turned him down she would break his heart. What would it hurt then, to give him a chance? There was no timetable, no pressure. She'd give him a couple of months, see what happened. She could do that much since it seemed so important to him.

After Vince paid, they waited outside the bar to wait for the taxi.

She stood on the cracked sidewalk with his arm around her, and occasionally he would press a kiss to the top of her head. Maybe this wouldn't be so bad. She would have to make sure he didn't crowd her. She didn't play nice with others when she felt pressured or trapped.

A yellow taxi sedan pulled up alongside them, its headlights cutting through the darkness. The minimal lights of the little town didn't do much to combat the dark summer night sky.

"Are you sure you don't want to fill the prescription?" Vince asked, concerned.

Janie shook her head. The beer had given her a pleasant

fizz and with the splint and ibuprofen, her pain had decreased to a dull throb.

They still had a few days of their vacation left—she could always ask Vince to drive her, if she changed or mind, or when they needed to make another food or booze run, she would be able to do it then. But now all she wanted was to get back to the resort. She also had a little something planned to pay Vince back for what he did to her in the bar. Vince said for the next ten years he'd prove to her how much he loved her; she'd use the next ten years to pay him back—in the most delicious ways she could think of.

Vince loaded their backpacks into the front seat, and they climbed into the back.

The radio was turned to NPR and the older cabbie seemed intent on listening to a debate on LBGT rights.

Janie shifted and snuggled against Vince's left side, which was deliberate. Her sprained wrist lay on the seat next to her, but her right hand rested on Vince's thigh.

The lights faded as the taxi driver drove out of town and onto the pitch-black highway. She hoped the driver was paying attention to the road and not only to the radio. They didn't need to hit a deer; she'd been through enough for one day.

Janie brushed her hand over Vince's fly. Oh, he was hard. Getting her off in the bar must have excited him. Well, one thing for sure, their sex life wouldn't be lacking; she was just worried about all the other parts.

Determined not to let that upset her, she brushed her fingers over his shorts again.

Vince surged under her hand and she smiled. She would see how he liked being played with at an inappropriate time.

He shook his head and placed a hand over hers. Did he think that would stop her? He got her off in a bar. Okay, they'd been in a dark corner, but now they were in a dark taxi. Same difference.

Janie twisted slightly so she was sitting sideways. She hadn't put her seatbelt on because she'd planned this, and she fervently hoped they wouldn't get into an accident.

She undid the button of his hiking shorts and slid the zipper down. She cast a quick glance at the driver, but he was watching the road and mumbling about family bathrooms. He seemed occupied enough.

When Janie encircled Vince's cock with her hand, she realized her mistake. She should have sat on his other side. Being on his left and gripping him with her right hand was awkward. Well, when was the last time she'd gotten off a guy in a car?

When was the last time she'd gotten a guy off, period?

This called for Plan B.

She hoped he was so hot for her it wouldn't take much to get him off because she wasn't an expert at giving blowjobs either.

"Janie," he hissed, and he tried to pull her hand out of his shorts.

Nuh-uh. He didn't let her have a choice in the bar, and she felt like she sold her soul to the devil. It was time for a little reciprocation.

She ran her hand up and down his silky skin. His shaft was rock hard and the tip was wet. Janie ran her finger around the tip, wetting her finger. Keeping eye contact with Vince she brought her finger to her mouth, the glow of the dashboard gauges illuminating his face.

Abruptly, he pulled her finger from her mouth and kissed her, his tongue snaking between her lips with lightning speed.

Janie leaned into the kiss, resting her sprained wrist on his thigh.

She was twisted fully in her seat, but the driver didn't care.

Janie pulled her mouth from his, panting. Her panties

were soaked, and she was more than just a little aroused. She wanted to fuck him, but now wasn't the place. They could go at it when they were back at their cabin. Not much longer, judging by how fast the taxing was moving.

She lowered her head and pulled Vince fully free of his shorts and briefs.

Little Plainee Janie giving a guy a blowjob in the back of a taxi. If only her high school classmates could see her now.

On second thought . . .

"No," Vince muttered and tried to shove her away. But the minute her tongue touched the tip, the pressure changed, keeping her in place rather than pushing her away.

She took as much of him in as she could, knowing it wasn't much, but it must not have mattered because she didn't hear him groan, she felt it.

Saliva filled her mouth, and she bathed his cock. She sucked and moved her head up and down, Vince's hand thrust firmly into her hair.

This wasn't bad. She didn't know why women bitched about giving them.

Then Vince thrust his hips up, forcing more of his cock into her mouth, the tip hitting the back of her throat. Oh. Maybe putting up with that would be a little unpleasant.

She wanted to tease him the way he had tortured her in the bar. She pulled back, his cock almost completely out of her mouth then swirled the engorged tip with her tongue.

"Janie," Vince warned in a threatening whisper.

She continued to play, pulling completely away and shoving her hand down his briefs to cup his balls. The angle of her hand was awkward, but Vince gritted his teeth. "What are you doing?"

"Revenge," she sweetly replied.

Vince groaned into her hair and pulled her into another ferocious kiss. "Jesus Christ, I love you so much."

She pressed a kiss to his lips, and he put an arm around

her. She'd been blackmailed into this relationship (with an orgasm!), but she felt the love in his touch and she vowed to try her best to see the relationship through.

Janie took him back into her mouth, tenderly, and she knew the second he was ready. As she prepared to swallow, hot gobs filled her mouth. She gulped, not wanting to make a mess in the taxi. She *had* started this, after all.

When he was done spurting, she took a moment to swallow and suppress her gag reflex. It'd been a long time since her last blowjob, he hadn't been as big as Vince, and she hadn't swallowed.

Janie licked the sensitive tip before tucking his cock back into his briefs and zipping his shorts. "You'll have to button up," she whispered in his ear, nipping his lobe. "I can't one-handed."

"You are fucking amazing," Vince murmured, quickly buttoning his shorts and pulling her toward him.

Janie became lost in his kiss, and a little voice asked if this indeed could work.

"I love you," Vince whispered, his arm tight around her.

Janie knew it would be a while before she would say it back. If she ever could. She huddled in his embrace for the rest of the ride.

If the driver knew what she had done, there was no indication he did. His attention hadn't been swayed from the radio or the road.

After driving down the two-mile driveway, the taxi driver pulled up to the dark resort office. She forgot they would have to walk over a mile to reach the lake cabins they'd rented, because the store was located between their cabins and other campsites. The driver probably wanted to get back into town for other fares, and Janie would feel bad asking for him to go that extra mile.

Vince unloaded their bags while the driver swiped her

debit card, and she was filled with guilt Vince had to carry both of them to their cabin.

"Will you be okay walking back?" he asked as the tail-lights faded into the distance. He pulled her to him and she rested her scraped cheek gently against his shirt. The scratch was safe under the coating of liquid skin, but her cheek still hurt.

"Yeah. I'm sorry you have to carry both bags."

"Not a problem," he said sincerely. "I just want to get you back and into bed."

Janie opened her mouth to tease him, but he stopped her. "To *sleep*. It's been a helluva day."

They found the path from the resort office to their cabins and started their walk, her feet squishing in her wet hiking boots.

"I hope Chuck and Kara make it back okay without us." Janie chewed on her lip, concerned.

Vince hefted one bag onto his shoulders. "I think the alone time will do them good. They need to talk about a few things."

Janie thought about the secret Kara told her earlier. It felt like days ago. "I hope you're right."

Vince pulled her close for a moment without breaking their stride. "I guess we'll find out."

A bonfire, even this late at night, shone brightly, cutting through a night lit by stars and the moon.

The glow bolstered her spirits and she caught Vince's hand.

Time would tell, but she was excited to see where this relationship would lead.

When Vince squeezed her hand, Janie knew he was too.

KARA AND CHUCK

Kara watched Vince lead her best friend down the path with the cheerful campsite office worker following them to the parking lot.

Shit.

She'd been hoping Vince and Janie would be a buffer between her and Chuck on the hike back to the resort. Kara wasn't looking forward to telling Chuck what her father wanted her to do. She would ruin their vacation. Oh, who was she kidding? Not only their vacation. Her family rubbed Chuck the wrong way, and now her father's request, no *demand*, could very easily tear them apart.

The problem was, she just wasn't sure if it was worth the fight.

Kara trudged back to their tent where Chuck threw a stick for Casey. At least they had the dog to distract them.

Chuck met her eyes. "Is Janie okay?"

"Yeah," she answered, sitting at the picnic table, the bag of Doritos still laying open, flies buzzing around their empty pop cans.

She fanned them away. Kara wasn't even sure why she went on these trips; they weren't her style. Trips to Vegas for the shows and the spas, trips to Cali to get away from the snow and shop Rodeo Drive. Martha's Vineyard. Hyannis Port to mingle with the Kennedys. She loved having coffee with Caroline.

This camping, though. She went because her friends went. And this year, she went because Chuck wanted her to go.

She would have preferred two weeks at the beach on the Florida Keys. Maybe one day she'd tell Chuck. If her news didn't destroy them first.

Casey ran up to her and poked his nose into her crotch. She liked Casey, but Kara preferred little dogs.

Chuck called Miss Fiona a tiny ankle muncher. She called Miss Fiona her little love baby and boarded her at a luxe doggie kennel in the city while she was gone because she couldn't use Janie's. Miss Fiona wouldn't like a trip like this. Not one bit. The deerflies were as big as she was, and Miss Fiona didn't like water.

"Her wrist looked sprained, and she was pretty banged up. It's crazy about her and Vince, huh? I can't picture them sleeping together."

Chuck palmed his wallet from the table. "I think he's been lonely. She might be good for him."

Kara snorted and nibbled another chip. She didn't want to get fat. The hike was good exercise and complemented her daily gym sessions, one of the few positive things she could say about this trip. "She might be good for him, but I don't know if he'll be good for her. He's hated her for so long. I felt terrible they had to share a cabin. If you wouldn't have been so stubborn, Janie and I could have bunked together."

Chuck straddled the picnic table bench and nipped the remaining cheese Dorito out of her hand. "And deprive your friend the best fuck of her life? Did you hear the moaning coming from their tent?"

Kara laughed and shoved his arm. "That was the wind, dork."

Chuck's brown eyes were sparkling with mischief. He grabbed her arm and started to run kisses from her wrist to the crook of her elbow. "Maybe that was you," he teased, scooting closer to her.

His kisses made her shiver. She sat in the V of Chuck's thighs and she let him kiss her, hoping no one was watching. She loved him, but she was wise enough to know love wasn't always enough. Her mother told her so on many occasions. Her brothers all married well and her parents expected her to do the same.

Kara's cell phone chimed.

Chuck withdrew and scowled. "I'm going to grab the steaks. You still want?" he asked, standing.

Kara nodded and slid her hand into the pocket of her shorts. She hated missing phone calls. Her father gave her so much shit.

And if it was Kent . . .

"Answer it, answer it," Chuck grumbled, walking away.

Guiltily, she pulled her bright pink phone out of her pocket and pressed accept. She watched Chuck walk away while one of her clients bellowed in her ear.

Chuck browsed the little convenience store stocked almost daily by a grocer in Poplar Point. The campers shopped there to prepare for their hikes through the park and their road trips. It also carried fresh meat for grilling and delicious produce from a farmers' market down the road. There was nothing like a freshly picked tomato. None of this garbage shipped from Mexico.

He bought a few things that would see him and Kara through until morning, and he selected the food they would need during their time on the trail. He was looking forward to being alone with Kara. Time alone with her was like finding a precious gem. He wanted to treasure it because once they were back in the city, their time together would consist of rushed lunches and watching movies at her place where she would fall asleep by 7:30. He wanted it, though. Watching her throw sticks to Casey, resuming his game, made him want her more, and it seemed like any time he took a moment to look at her, really look at her, his need for her increased. He could never live without her.

Her hair had dried, and it shone in the setting sun.

"Hey, beautiful."

Her pinched face ate him. Her parents were hard on her, and her career was stressful. He hated she so willingly put up with it.

Chuck wanted to take her into their tent and make love to her, but the steaks couldn't be left out, and he was starving. You couldn't live off sex, though he was sure many tried.

"Did you find what you wanted?" Kara asked.

Chuck didn't think he would ever entirely get what he wanted from her. "Yep," he replied cheerfully, lifting the two bags. "And we're set for the hike back. This is some vacation, huh?" he asked, referring to the other couples who joined them every year.

Kara nodded, understanding, as Chuck knew she would. They were in sync with everything but what mattered most. "Our group is imploding."

Chuck lit the charcoal to cook the steaks and grill the corn on the cob. It was a small meal, lacking in the choices Kara preferred, but the steaks were huge and he bought fixings for s'mores.

He sat at the picnic table waiting for the coals to burn hot enough. "Come here," he said, opening his arms and she leaned in, pressing her cheek to his shoulder. "I don't know if Alycia and Bryce will make it. What he did was really shitty. But I can promise that I'll always love you, Kara. I have for a long time." He rubbed his hand up and down her arm. She was wearing shorts and a t-shirt, but the t-shirt was silk and her shorts Donna Karan.

Even in the middle of nowhere, she dressed as if she could bump into anybody.

Kara lifted her face to smile at him and he kissed her, his lips gently touching hers. He ran a thumb over her cheek, his other hand splayed across her back, keeping her in place. His cock hardened and he slipped his tongue into her mouth.

Kara let out a low trill from the back of her throat, her hand clutching his thigh.

"You are so beautiful," he whispered against her lips. "How did I get so lucky?"

"Because I love you back," Kara murmured, kissing him again.

Chuck surrendered to the kiss, but he didn't miss the shadows that flashed across her face.

He grilled the steaks and they ate, the sounds of the other campers drifting around them. Chuck was glad they chose a site farther away. There were people milling about and children played and screamed on the playground equipment, but he was alone with Kara, as long as her phone remained silent.

It was still early when they turned in, but they would start back to the resort with the sunrise.

"Do you think Janie will want to go home?" Chuck asked Kara as she slid on her skimpy shorts and tank to sleep in. It wasn't hot, but the tent was stuffy, the ground lumpy. He always amazed Kara went on these trips when she had her choice of going anywhere in the world. He was incredibly lucky she wanted to spend time with him. Of course, he would follow her anywhere, but he was grateful he didn't have to.

"Vince wouldn't be happy," Kara commented, lying down with Casey beside her, the dog's muzzle resting on his paws.

"I don't know what the hell that's all about. How all of a sudden he's in love," he admitted, remembering his talk with Vince on the dock.

Hate was the opposite of love. Had Vince really loved Janie all these years and made her pay the price?

Kara rolled to her side to face him. It wasn't dark outside, and he could clearly see her: her pale, luminous complexion, the smattering of freckles the sun brought out across her nose. Her pure green eyes framed by thick lush lashes, and her pink lips were shiny from being licked.

"I love you, Kara. Come here and let me show you."

Having sex with Chuck was one of the best things about their relationship, and Kara wasn't ashamed to admit it. The pretty boys her parents always threw at her would rather count their money and sit for a manicure than give her a good screw.

A woman had needs. Chanel couldn't do it all.

Kara eagerly scooted closer and pressed her lips to his. He'd changed into cotton shorts to sleep in.

Casey whined like he didn't want to witness what they were about to do. But the dog didn't have virgin eyes, not with Janie and Vince around. She and Chuck were used to being watched; Miss Fiona always kept guard.

Kara reached for him and he pushed a hand up the leg of her shorts to knead her ass. She didn't know where the man learned to screw but she was grateful for his expertise. Never in their relationship had she not come.

"Wet already?" Chuck murmured.

"Why don't you find out?" she invited, throwing a leg over his hip.

"Mmmmm," he hummed, his finger finding her slick core quickly, easily. She wasn't wearing panties under her pajama shorts.

"Chuck," she pleaded as she gripped his hard-on. He wasn't the biggest man she'd ever had, but he knew how to use it better than the rest.

He twisted his fingers inside her and her hips pressed toward him wanting more.

"God, I love you so much."

That was another thing about Chuck. Sometimes he screwed her, but most of the time he made love to her. How did she discern the difference? Chuck sounded like a fucking Hallmark card factory when he made love.

She adored it.

"Take your clothes off," he demanded, pulling his fingers away.

She eagerly pulled her tank over her head and pushed her shorts over her hips. Kara lay back down on her sleeping bag.

This was her favorite part.

And he knew it.

Chuck started from her chin, running his fingertips along her jaw, down her throat. "You are so beautiful."

She swallowed.

His fingers continued their journey, outlining her collarbone. She wanted to pull her legs up and show him her desire. She was so wet. But he wouldn't let her rush him. Once she tried to force him to touch her and he'd cut her off for the rest of the night. Sex regularly started like this. Slow. Him treating her like gold, porcelain, blown glass. Kara learned quickly he wanted to worship her and she gladly let him.

His fingers feathered over the tops of her breasts, her nipples hardening in response.

Chuck flicked a thumb over one, and Kara's muscles clenched. She could explode any moment.

His hand traced her other nipple. "Like that?" he asked.

She didn't have to answer; he knew she did.

He could probably smell how much she did.

Kara treated herself to her own show and stared at Chuck's cock pressed against his tight stomach. She wanted him inside her so badly she could cry. She was so needy, but then, she always was around Chuck. As he reached her belly button, her stomach quivered, knowing, anticipating, what was next.

Her mound was smooth—she'd gotten a wax right before the trip. She knew how much he loved her that way.

"Open up for me, baby," he finally said.

Slowly, slowly, she drew up her long legs toned by years of ballet and Pilates, so her knees were bent.

Chuck gently pushed them apart. He ran his palms along the insides of her thighs and stopped at her bikini line.

She had no idea how he possessed so much control because she was going out of her mind with wanting him.

Sometimes he moved so slowly she thought he was punishing her.

Impatiently, she lifted her hips.

His thumbs brushed her lips at the V of her thighs, and he gently smoothed the folds apart. Chuck loved looking at her. She loved to watch him look at her. It turned her on in a way nothing else did.

She wondered if he could see her juice run out of her as he opened her.

"Jesus Christ," he muttered.

Kara smiled. She caught his eye and didn't look away as he pushed a finger into her.

"Chuck," she pleaded.

He took position on his stomach and kissed the inside of her thigh.

This was her second favorite part. She absolutely loved being eaten out.

Her hips bucked when his tongue touched her. He shifted his position so he could push down on her hips; he didn't want her to move.

The first time he'd done that it had made her nervous and weirded her out. She wasn't into being tied up. But when she came that time, she'd never come so hard and she'd let him hold her down ever since.

The man knew what he was doing.

With his forearm across her pelvis holding her down, he pushed two fingers into her core. Chuck teased her with the tip of his tongue and kept his fingers buried deep inside her.

She bore down as much as she could, needing his fingers deeper and deeper.

In a rush of pleasure, she exploded and tried to push into Chuck's face to prolong the orgasm.

He nibbled her pulsating clit with his teeth, causing after-shocks to tremor through her body, then he rose on his knees to cover her.

Kara knew this was his favorite part: taking her while she was so slick and pliant, he slid into her in one smooth thrust. She pulled his head down to capture his mouth in a ferocious kiss. Chuck shoved his tongue into her mouth, and she greedily devoured him. She loved tasting herself on his lips. It made her feel sexy and dirty and naughty.

She loved oral sex.

What would her mother say?

Chuck pulled all the way out and forcefully pushed back into her. As he came, she lifted her hips wanting to be as close as possible. After he collapsed on top of her, he nibbled her neck.

She giggled, sensitive after her orgasm.

"You're such a good lay," Chuck teased, rubbing his whiskers against her skin, making her squirm away.

"Crass," she accused playfully. She loved it. None of her previous lovers had ever called her a good screw. Chuck's compliment meant more to her than all other compliments from anyone combined.

Chuck pulled out of her and flopped onto his back, spread eagle.

Kara rolled onto her side and cuddled him. He smelled like sex, sweat, and smoke from the barbecue.

It had taken him a long time to admit how he felt about her, and there were days she wondered if she would have preferred him to remain quiet.

He turned his head to kiss her.

"I love you, Chuck," she whispered, her emotions bouncing off the fabric of the tent.

"I know you do," he said, cradling her jaw with his hand and giving her one more kiss.

Kara fell asleep, content.

༄

Chuck had to admit Kara was a good camper. She didn't complain they were awake and on the trail by six.

Casey, excited to be on their way, barked, running ahead.

"Do you think Janie will be there when we get back?"

Kara shrugged. "You could call Vince and find out. Our phones have a signal."

He knew they did. Kara's phone hadn't stopped ringing.

"Not a big deal, I guess. He wouldn't be awake now anyway." That was the absolute truth. His friend rarely woke before noon. Running his own business was the smartest thing for him to do. He worked from noon until whenever he decided to go home and those hours fit his clientele perfectly. "Did you know Vince's business was in trouble?" He'd been aggravated to be the last to know, though it was Vince's nature to keep things to himself.

"No," Kara responded, surprised. "Janie never said anything, if she knew at all."

"She knew. She helped him with a solution."

They didn't talk much after that, which suited Chuck just fine. He liked the quiet after being in the city—people yammering at him all the time and the crazy amount of traffic he had to deal with daily.

He enjoyed the peacefulness with Kara.

They hiked in companionable silence, and he wished the quiet and the time they spent together would do for her what it did for him. But she always answered her phone when it rang and she spent hours responding to email in the evenings.

How would spending the rest of his life with her would feel? Would he always be second to her career?

Yeah. He knew he was second. Maybe even third. Career, family, him.

He didn't know if he could live like that.

He didn't want to know if she loved him enough to change.

Deep down, he was afraid of the answer.

⚶

Kara picked up on his mood: pensive, reflective.

She was appreciating the peace, taking in deep breaths of clean air and trying to let go of the stress. Oddly, her phone was quiet, yet she checked it frequently. Her battery was almost dead. She'd forgotten her charger, a move that was unlike her. Kara hoped the charge would hold out until they reached the resort and she vowed to only answer the important calls.

She scowled. They were all important. At least, her family

thought so.

Her mother was all but planning her wedding to Kent. All her father talked about was when she'd leave for Chicago. Kent was willing to move with her and already he had his real estate agent searching for property.

What was her hold up?

Her hold up walked slightly in front of her, hefting his backpack as if it were filled with pillows rather than provisions that would last for days.

She wanted to make him happy for as long as she was able.

And if her father had his way, it wouldn't be much longer.

She shook her shoulders as best she could under the weight of her pack, and she willed herself to stop thinking about her family. Kara would never find a kinder, more loving man than Chuck, and it would break her heart and her spirit, to let him go. "Break?" she asked, her voice wavering. She didn't want to cry. Not now. She didn't want to have to explain anything. The longer she could keep it all a secret, the better.

"Sure," Chuck agreed, surprised.

It was good timing. She chose a spot with a clear view of the lake, and she sighed, inhaling the cool air. The sun was shining and the puddles from the other night's storm were gone.

Chuck took off his pack and leaned against a poplar tree, sliding down to sit at its base. After pulling the backpack from her shoulders, Kara sat next to him on the grass. She leaned to kiss him and grabbed his hand, placing it on her chest.

She nudged his tongue with her own and moaned when he kneaded her breast. "Chuck," she whispered. "Please."

"Now?" he asked, frowning, confusion flooding his features.

"Yes." She didn't understand what she was feeling—this

urgency, this sense of emergency. "Don't ever leave me," she cried and buried her face in his neck.

She was being ridiculous, but she couldn't help it. If anyone left, it would be her. Chuck loved her, and she knew he was in it for the long haul. She was the one who didn't know what she was doing, who hadn't committed to the relationship. Wasn't she cheating on Chuck every time she spoke with her mother about the wedding? Because after all, it would take time to book the venue, have the dress made (her mother had already been in contact with Ralph Lauren's people), create the guest list. Kent Hellson came from a distinguished family, (of course he did) and he would have his own guests to invite. Her mother was beside herself to begin. Just one phone call to Kent's mother would start the avalanche.

Tears ran down her face saturating the neck of Chuck's t-shirt.

"What's wrong, baby?" Chuck asked, holding her close. He'd stopped fondling her breast the moment she started crying and now just rubbed her back, doing his best to soothe her.

It wasn't good enough.

"Of course I'll never leave," Chuck said when she didn't respond.

His scent was comforting. Sweat and a hint of smoke from the barbecue last night. Bug spray. Coffee from breakfast. He smelled delicious and he was strong, so strong.

No, he would never leave her. She believed that with all her heart.

Feeling silly, she pulled out of his embrace and wiped her cheeks.

Chuck's eyes blazed with concern. "Kara, honey, are you okay?"

Kara nodded. She didn't want to get into this now. She needed to speak with Janie. This wasn't something she could talk to Chuck about, but if she didn't say something to someone, she would burst. "I'm sorry. I guess I didn't sleep well last night."

"Of course you didn't," Chuck chuckled. "You're insatiable."

Kara gave her cheeks another rub and giggled. "It's because you're so good."

Her head fell back against the tree when Chuck nibbled her jaw. "Flattery will get you everywhere, except back to the resort. Come on, we better move."

Chuck tried to keep the mood light. Kara had never cried before, at least, not around him, and he worried about her. He'd seen her frustrated, angry, fed up with her job, with her family, but he'd never seen her cry.

Their timing was perfect, and they were able to make camp in the same place they'd stopped before with Vince and Janie.

Chuck made a small fire and he lay on the ground, his hands folded beneath his head, Kara's head resting on his stomach.

The day had gone by quickly, and he was grateful. When they returned to the resort, he needed to call his bank. The transfer wasn't something he could do on his phone. Signal came and went, and the text urgently came through this afternoon.

Kara perked up along the way, and she didn't seem particularly upset when her phone's battery died. Tomorrow would be amazing without Kara checking her phone every five seconds, without the pinging notifications of new emails she would need to respond to immediately.

"Feeling better, sweetheart?" he asked, stroking her hair.

"Hmmm," she replied.

She sounded relaxed, happy, and content.

He skimmed the skin over her jaw with his fingertips, and she purred. She was insatiable, but so was he.

Kara sat up, and he did, too. He couldn't picture a more beautiful spot to make love. The fire was snapping at the branches he'd found earlier, the stars were shining, and thankfully, there were few bugs. Chuck pulled Kara to him, and he kissed her, framing her face with his fingers. The tips of her hair brushed the backs of his hands.

"Take your clothes off," he demanded softly, then pressed his lips against hers.

He was ready to go, already anticipating being buried inside her warmth.

Not waiting for her, he pulled her t-shirt over her head and revealed her lacy pink bra. Eagerly, he flicked the clasp. Chuck loved her bras that clasped in the front, finding it so erotic to watch her breasts spill out of them, her bra hanging open, framing them, as it did now, her nipples hardening in the breeze.

He lifted one of her breasts and brought his mouth to the pebbled, sensitive skin.

Kara gasped and ran her fingers through his hair, pushing him into her. He suckled and squeezed her other nipple between his thumb and finger.

"Your shorts," he rasped, and she eagerly pulled away to push them from her legs. He was fully clothed, but she was naked and he drank her in, the bonfire's light flickering over her skin.

Chuck drew Kara onto her knees and he nudged her thighs, asking her to spread her legs, because he wanted to play. Luckily, they were settled on soft grass and the ground didn't bother her. He trailed his fingers down her flat belly and dipped his fingers into her heat.

Kara braced her hands on his shoulders and her head fell back in pleasure.

Moisture pooled in his palm as he pushed three fingers

inside her as far as they would go. With his thumb, he found her clit.

"Chuck," Kara moaned.

Again, his mouth went to her breast, her skin tinged in gold from the fire, pulling her nipple into his mouth and biting at the exact moment she came. His thumb slid over her sensitive spot, carrying her orgasm to the end, her pussy moving against his hand.

"Turn around," he ordered, and he freed his cock from his shorts.

He took a moment to admire her from behind, her ass in the air waiting for him, the insides of her thighs shining from the come that ran out of her during her climax.

Chuck stroked himself just once then pushed into her. He almost lost it, but he gritted his teeth and remained perfectly still, gaining control.

He gripped her hips and slammed into her viciously, coming after only five deep thrusts. "You're mine," he growled.

She whimpered in response.

Chuck withdrew and kissed her ass cheeks up to her lower back. "Mine," he repeated. "Kara."

She turned around tears brimming in her eyes. "I want to be," she whispered, and she kissed him, her arms clinging around his neck.

Chuck didn't know where all her need was coming from. She was so independent, confident. But in the light of the dying fire, she looked like a sad little girl who needed reassurances she would always be loved. "You're tired. You should go to sleep. We're halfway back, and we can slow down a little now. It will be okay."

On her knees, she begged, "Tell me you love me."

He caught her chin in his hand and stared into her eyes. "I do love you, Kara."

But.

There was always a but.

But would it be enough to overcome her career? Her parents?

But would it be enough to overcome her doubts and fears?

※

Kara felt foolish. She'd been overtired from not getting any sleep the night before, then hiking all the next day on top of it. She'd been emotional making love, making demands she hadn't felt she needed to in the past.

The second night on the trail was uneventful. They hiked past the wildflower field they'd stopped at with Vince and Janie on the way to the campsite and were able to find a small clearing off to the side of the path.

They hadn't met anyone on the way to the campsite or on the return trip to the resort, and Kara was relieved. There were times she liked not being around people. Her job as a probate and estate lawyer didn't give her any peace. The minute someone signed on the dotted line, their problems became her problems—and they expected them to be solved as quickly as possible. Her clients felt they were entitled to calls in the middle of the night, answers to their emails at 5 am, and to interrupt Sunday brunch.

And with what her firm charged, they'd be correct.

But it didn't make her feel any better.

Chuck was noticeably happier when she told him her phone died, and they'd a nice evening talking in the clearing. It would be another year before they would have this much time to themselves again.

The thought caused a little tug to her heart. Especially when he was so sweet and only cuddled with her that night, insisting she was tired and she needed the rest.

She was thankful when they neared the resort.

Casey ran ahead, scenting his mistress.

It was full dark by the time they reached the cabins. The time with Chuck had been wonderful, but by the end of the hike she was feigning a lightness she didn't feel. She was emotionally exhausted from the banter she forced herself to make with him, and thoughts of her parents and Kent kept creeping into the forefront of her mind.

Kara dropped her pack on the cabin's little porch.

"I'm going in, babe," Chuck said, pressing a kiss on the top of her head and going inside.

Kara rubbed her eyes and decided to go down to the water; she was too antsy to turn in for the night. She was being dumb. She should go inside and get some sleep, maybe take a bath, or sit in the hot tub.

Only . . . she knew the real reason she was avoiding going inside. She didn't want to plug in her phone. She didn't want to see how many phone calls she missed or how many voicemails she needed to listen to. She didn't want to read the irate texts from her parents, the accusations she was avoiding them.

Kara wondered if her phone would literally burst into flames when she plugged it in.

So she went down to the beach instead and listened to the crickets and the water brush against the dock, the boats bumping against the wood.

"You have no right to say that to me!"

Kara whipped around as the voice slashed through the night and watched Alycia Fischer slam the door of their cabin and stomp her way down the beach, huffing and swearing under her breath.

Kara inwardly grimaced. She'd been avoiding the other couples like the plague for this very reason.

Anger simmered in the redhead's brown eyes along with a sheen of tears, if Kara wasn't mistaken.

"Are you all right?" Kara reluctantly asked.

Alycia snorted. "Nope. What's up with you? When did you get back?"

Kara sat in the sand and untied the laces of her boots to pull them off. After rolling down her sweaty socks she buried her toes in the sand. It felt cool and smooth between her toes.

Alycia sat next to her.

"Just now. How are Janie and Vince? Were they able to come back here all right? How's Janie's wrist?"

Alycia grabbed a handful of sand and let it sprinkle from her fingers. "They're okay. Her wrist is sprained, but she said she didn't want to go home. They've been staying in their cabin, mostly. Are they a couple now?"

Kara shrugged. She didn't know, and she doubted Janie did either. "Maybe. Janie said it was too much to process."

Alycia huffed. "I can't say I blame her. You think you know someone then they go and do a 180 on you. I can't believe what Bryce did to me."

"Are you talking through it?" Kara asked, but her mind was elsewhere. Alycia's and Bryce's problems seemed petty compared to her own fucked up life. They had their chance at happiness; it was nobody's fault but their own if they wasted it.

"Ha! What's there to talk through? He did what he did. We've been together for so many years. I'm scared to be without him—I've had that security for as long as I can remember, yet the thought of being on my own is kind of thrilling."

Kara could understand that. She loved her parents, depended on them, and in some ways, was scared to be without them, but the thought of living out of their shadow was exhilarating. "I suppose I should go in," Kara sighed, gathering her socks and boots. "We'll go for a walk or something," she assured her, patting Alycia's shoulder.

The redheaded woman put her hand over Kara's. "I'm

happy for you and Chuck. And I hope Janie and Vince make it. I'll miss you guys."

"Oh, but—" Kara started.

"No," Alycia interrupted. "I know we've always been a group, but the guys have been better friends than we have. You've always had Janie, and Crystal and Bailey were tighter in high school. If things don't work between Bryce and me, I'm not going to pretend there would be room for me."

Kara didn't want to go into that now. "That's not true," she denied, but there wasn't much conviction in her words. "We'll talk tomorrow. I'm not sure what will happen to our group if Vince and Janie don't make it; things would be very uncomfortable. Maybe this will be our last summer vacation together anyway."

Alycia tried to laugh and teased, "When you and Chuck get married, you could choose a destination wedding and that could be next year's trip."

Not likely. Kara walked over the sand and small patch of grass to the cabin she shared with Chuck. The picnic tables were empty, the bonfire pit cold, and Janie and Vince's cabin dark. They were keeping to themselves, were they? Probably fucking like bunnies. She dropped her boots beside her backpack. Chuck hadn't brought it in, and she left it there.

The cabin door opened with a loud creak and the sound echoed over the water. Briefly, the crickets stopped singing, frightened by the noise.

"It's okay, Dad. You don't have to thank me." Chuck spoke into his cell phone, and his face reddened when he saw her.

What could they be talking about that would cause him to be embarrassed? She hadn't met his parents; Chuck always claimed they were busy. He hadn't come from the best neighborhood, she knew that, and he'd driven half an hour in the mornings to attend their high school for the better programs.

He'd been teased there because of his clothes, but his hard work paid off, as he was the first in his family to go to college.

She kissed him on the cheek and walked down the hall to their room to give him privacy. Kara didn't need to know what Chuck was talking with his father about. There were days she could barely keep track of herself, much less want to do it for someone else. She debated taking a shower or just falling into bed, and she opted for the latter, crawling into her pajamas and tumbling into an exhausted sleep.

Chuck flipped his phone onto the couch cushion and leaned his head back against the soft fuzzy material of the worn piece of furniture. How many people sat here, year after year? The resort was open all year round for people who loved to brave the cold ice fishing or snowmobiling. The park maintained the trail for winter camping and cross-country skiing.

How many people sat here and contemplated life and how fucked up it was?

God, he was so ashamed Kara heard him on the phone. It took him a couple tries to reach his dad, and he was shaking with frustration by the time his dad answered. He was at the theater with Chuck's mother, and he berated Chuck for making him miss the ending of an exciting movie.

Chuck groaned. What the hell did that matter when he was calling to tell his dad he transferred the money for him to fix the car and for his parents to pay the mortgage?

Now his little sister was talking about trying cosmetology school and asking him to foot the bill.

He quietly made his way into the dark bedroom. He was hurt Kara hadn't said goodnight but she was only giving him space, and he appreciated the courtesy.

Vowing to keep his family troubles away from her, he took

off his clothes and slid into bed. No one wanted an albatross around their neck.

No one.

❧

The next morning, Chuck woke spooned against Kara's back, his cock wedged into the crevice of her cheeks. Mmmmm. There was nothing he liked better than morning sex. It released the pressure in his dick like nothing else. He slipped a hand down her pajama shorts and into her panties. She wasn't wet, but he pushed a finger in and slowly pulled it out, hoping to arouse her.

Kara pushed into him and spread her legs to give his hand room to move. "Good morning," she murmured sleepily.

"Good morning, beautiful," he whispered in her ear.

She shivered and her pussy flooded in response.

Gently, he pushed his fingers into her and pulled them out, her hips moving in time to his fingers.

"Oh, Chuck," Kara gasped, and she rolled onto her back to look into his eyes.

His breath caught in his throat. She was so sexy first thing in the morning, with her green eyes hazy with sleep, her eyelids half-mast. Pushing his mouth onto her velvety lips, he eagerly slipped his tongue into her mouth.

On her back, Kara gave Chuck more room between her legs and he added a finger, pressing on her clit with the heel of his hand. "Come on, baby," he encouraged in a whisper against her mouth.

Kara pulled up her tank top to expose her breasts, and he accepted the invitation, sucking on a nipple. She whimpered and as she came, her hips lifting fully off the mattress, her heels digging into the bed.

He gave her a moment to catch her breath then pulled her

panties and shorts down over her legs and threw them onto the floor.

Seconds later he was sheathed inside her, loving the way she wrapped her legs around his waist, pulling him closer. He thought she exuded a hint of the desperation she'd exhibited on their hike back to the resort.

Chuck wanted to reassure her, tell her things would be perfect, their future bright, that he wanted to marry her, but he didn't know about any of those things. The conversation with his father was a reminder he was nothing. Not anything good for Kara, anyway. He was better suited for the Janies of the world, who knew little of the social circles Kara was expected to dance in, who didn't know the difference between a salad fork and dinner fork at the country club events and didn't expect him to know either.

And so he took all he could from her, now, on this vacation, because nothing would ever be different between them. He was who he was, and she was who she was, and dammit, there was no changing that.

Kara sat at the kitchen table staring at her dead phone. Chuck had showered and went out after their morning sex romp. It was just as well; she didn't want him to see the mess that was going to appear the second she attached the charger cord to her phone.

She took a fortifying sip of coffee and connected the cord to her cell. It took a moment for the phone to light up and a few more before her wallpaper and apps appeared. With the sound muted, the notifications of texts, phone calls, and voice mails flooded the screen as her phone caught signal and updated.

Her phone had been dead for over twenty-four hours.

Kara opened her messages app. Her parents texted her over fifty times.

A piece.

She began with the earliest from her father asking, no pressuring her, to decide about Chicago. They escalated into downright threatening messages, demanding if she didn't respond, he would go to the resort and hunt her down.

Cringing at his words of choice, she took another sip of coffee. She did indeed feel like a deer sighted in a hunter's stare, rifle at the ready.

Desperately, she switched to her mother's messages, but they weren't any better. Dresses, dresses, dresses. She wanted to plan a tea with Kent's mother. She wanted to talk to Kara about the venue. Dresses. Her mother didn't threaten her as her father did, but there was no concern for her, not a text asking if she was having a good time. Her mother knew she was with Chuck, and to put it bluntly, her mother didn't give a shit. She viewed Chuck as an interference in her plans to marry her daughter to the highest bidder.

He didn't stand a chance.

Would she still be so reluctant to go along with her parents' plans if she hadn't fallen for Chuck? Probably not. She'd do as she was told like a good little girl, keeping her wants, needs, and opinions to herself.

Swallowing a lump in her throat, she pushed her phone away in disgust. She would enjoy the rest of her vacation. Her parents couldn't stop her from doing that, though they'd try.

Kara brought her coffee onto the little porch of their cabin. It was almost noon. She'd fallen back to sleep after Chuck woke her and had his way with her. He'd kissed her and told her he'd see her later. She enjoyed their relationship, the trust. Kara wasn't worried he'd cheat on her. He'd wanted her for far too long to do that. She would never tell him, but Kara had reciprocated; she'd wanted him for a long time too but had been too scared to do anything about it. She sat on the bench swing, toeing the floor to slowly move back and forth.

She'd never told him because of her family. Kara had no right to give in to her feelings, to tell Chuck she felt the same. She should never have let this start.

Now she was stuck with a mess she was not prepared to clean up.

Chuck waved at her from the water. He'd apparently lured Vince from his cabin, and the two were on Jet Skis, criss-crossing the lake.

Realizing Janie would be alone, Kara carried her coffee to Janie's cabin and pounded on the wooden door. Casey barked and Kara heard Janie soothe him.

She opened the door and Kara flinched as she took in Janie's injuries. Her cheek was scratched and purple, her wrist was wrapped in a splint, and her thigh was scraped and covered with what looked like road rash. But there was a happy glint in Janie's eyes, and her friend shook her head at Kara's whimper of concern.

"It's not that bad," Janie said, opening the door to allow Kara to step inside the cabin. "Do you want more?" she asked, nodding toward Kara's mug.

"Sure," Kara replied, sitting down at the small kitchen table, noting the cabin smelled like French toast. It made her stomach rumble; she'd been too upset checking her phone to eat breakfast. "How are you feeling?"

"Oh, fine." Janie waved her hand in the air. "Vince is always on me to go into town and fill my prescription for pain meds, but really, I'm fine without them." Janie filled Kara's cup with coffee from a clear carafe and filled a mug for herself.

"He's taking good care of you? Alycia asked me last night if you two were a couple." Kara raised her eyebrows and took a sip of the fresh steaming coffee.

Janie rubbed her fingers against her forehead. "I . . . don't know what we're doing. I promised to give him a chance. He's been so sweet, waiting on me hand and foot, and the sex . . . Spectacular."

"But it's not enough?" Kara guessed.

Janie bit her lip. "It's going to take time. I'm getting to know the man he is when he's not hating me." She offered a wobbly smile. "I don't know if I can trust that he loves me."

"He'll give you the space you need if he really does," Kara said.

"Yeah. He's said that. We'll just take it one day at a time, I guess. How about you? How was the hike back alone? I feel so terrible we couldn't hike back with you."

"My phone died," Kara said cheerfully. "It made for a quiet hike back to the cabin. Janie." Misery crept into her voice then, the implications of her father's texts finally sinking in. "My parents won't let me marry Chuck."

Janie squealed. "He asked you? Oh, Kara!"

"No, no. Nothing like that." Kara gripped Janie's good hand. "My parents have picked a man they want me to marry. He's set to move Chicago with me to help set up the firm. He's already secured a real estate agent to look for office space and a condo for us."

Janie sat back, her mouth hanging open.

Kara couldn't blame her. Spoken aloud, the news was ludicrous. "When I get back to the city, my mother is putting together a tea with my future mother-in-law."

"My God," Janie breathed. "That's insane. No one does that anymore. What are you going to do?"

Tears welled in Kara's eyes. Now that she had said the words, admitted them to herself, the news was preposterous and downright scary. She wiped at her eyes before the tears could spill down her cheeks. "I . . . don't know."

"You haven't talked to Chuck at all about this?" Disapproval laced Janie's voice.

Kara laughed. "What would I say? Chuck already disapproves of my social status, my career, my family." She said the words that weighed the heaviest on her heart. "We don't belong together."

Kara waited for Janie's adamant denial, but none came. She was afraid Janie saw the truth in her words. She looked out the kitchen window and onto the beach, tears running down her pale cheeks.

꙳

Chuck was debating a nap when Bryce met him on the dock. After skiing, Vince went inside to plan dinner with Janie and Kara. Now that Chuck and Kara were back from the hike, Vince suggested they eat dinner together. Chuck thought Vince's relationship with Janie lightened the man considerably; he'd never seen Vince so happy. He'd always had his rough edges, but Janie, even in the few days they'd been together, was smoothing them out. He wished Bryce would have sought out Vince to talk with instead of him, but Chuck was killing time and probably looked like an easy target. He didn't want to know what Kara had come back to when she'd plugged in her phone. That, he conceded, might have been better than this.

"God damn women," Bryce groused, stomping along the sun-bleached wood.

Chuck shook his head and looked at his friend with an equal measure of sympathy and disdain. "What?"

"Alycia just won't give me a fucking break." Bryce forked his blond hair with a hand and sat, his arms resting on bent knees.

Wet from the Jet Ski, still wearing his swim trunks, Chuck was sunbathing. It felt good to be outdoors. He played golf frequently while in the city, glad-handing important executives who requested a partner during their business trips. But this was different. There wasn't any faux friendliness, no one to hide from.

One sunny afternoon he'd pretended he needed to take a dump to avoid Kara's father. They'd had the same tee time and Chuck gladly hid in the can rather than make small talk with the man who made his girlfriend's life a living hell. "Why did you two even come?"

Bryce scowled. "I thought getting out of the city would be good for us. I thought, maybe, the women would talk some sense into her."

Chuck didn't know what Kara's stance was on the whole Alycia and Bryce thing. Did she side with Alycia as a woman scorned, or did she side with Bryce, a man who made a mistake? "Women stick together," Chuck finally said, believing that was true.

"Yeah," Bryce agreed glumly.

Chuck pulled his feet out of the water and lay down on the dock's rough planks. The sun shone on his face and he shut his eyes, the warmth seeping into his bones. "Do you want another chance? Or would you rather move on?"

It was a hell of a long time to be together. Only kissing one person your whole adult life, only fucking one person your whole adult life. Chuck didn't have many conquests under his belt—he'd been far too busy studying and pulling As to play in college. He'd also worked through school; his scholarships hadn't paid his entire tuition. But he'd had his fun, and he didn't deny if he settled down now, he'd have no regrets—not as Bryce appeared to have.

When Bryce's dull blue eyes filled with tears, Chuck looked away in embarrassment and to give Bryce privacy to pull himself together. He was no good with emotions.

"I look at her," Bryce began, his voice raspy, "and I see this red-headed, smart-mouthed girl standing on her chair in the front row of Mr. Miller's class." He let out a little laugh. "Bossing some kid around the classroom like she was the queen of sixth grade. Braces and glasses, and just an outline of tits. I remember standing in the doorway of that classroom, Ms. Sheridan, you remember the office lady, standing behind me. She had to show me the way to class because I got lost. I stood there, and there she was. The first day of school. I haven't been without her since."

Chuck wiped at the sweat trickling down his temple, remembering that day with perfect clarity. Bryce standing in the doorway staring, Alycia standing on her chair pointing a yardstick she'd stolen off the teacher's desk. Chuck was the kid she'd been bossing around. That was before the school boundaries had changed, and he'd gone to school with everyone else. "So, what then?" Chuck asked, cracking his eyes open. It took a moment for his vision to clear. Goddamn, it was bright outside. He wished he had his sunglasses with him.

"I wish I knew." Bryce wiped his eyes. "But you have a good thing with Kara. We're happy for you."

It took a lot for Bryce to offer that since the two were so miserable in their own relationship. "Thanks," Chuck muttered. He never thought he had a chance with Kara; he'd always felt so out of her league. Felt it? Fuck that. He *was*. She wasn't rushing him home to meet her father, and the one time he met her mother he'd needed to go to Urgent Care and be seen for frostbite.

With a sinking feeling in his gut, he realized he should cut her loose, find someone on more even footing. He sat up and leaned back on his hands.

At the sound of a cabin door slamming, his gaze shot past Bryce and his unhappy expression to Kara, Janie, and Vince. The sight of Kara in a denim skirt and lacy white tank top turned his heart. He'd never be able to let her go. He'd loved her too long, wanted her too long, to give her up without a fight. Even from the dock's end, he could see the drawn expression on her face, and he guessed the reunion with her cell phone hadn't gone well. He wished he could help her, but their families were topics that were off-limits. Until she opened up, and vice versa, there would be a wall between them. The wall was clear—they could see each other, but they couldn't touch one another and it hurt him. It hurt him she wouldn't, couldn't fix it.

The street certainly went both ways, though he'd never admit to her he'd been supporting his family for almost ten years because his father couldn't do better than a minimum wage job between bouts of unemployment and disability payments.

As Kara walked toward him, he hoped like hell they could work something out because he loved her too much to lose her now.

§

Dinner was a somber affair and Chuck sat near Vince while Bryce sucked up to Alycia, Alycia ignoring him in return. Like he could judge. The lines of communication between him and Kara weren't any clearer.

"This vacation turned around for you," Chuck offered to Vince, drawing from his sweaty bottle of beer.

A smirk crossed Vince's face. "I don't know what happened. I'm just damned glad it did." Vince took a pull from his own beer.

They sat near the bonfire, Nate and Cam on the other side. The women were sitting together, still eating dessert and drinking Irish coffee.

It was a cool night and Chuck had thrown on a hoodie over his T-shirt. "Has your realtor found you a new space yet?"

"Yeah," Vince said, his voice tinged in surprise. "I have an appointment to look at it when we get back. It's in the northern part of town near the industrial park. Greta said it's near a mechanic's shop and the guy rebuilds old cars. She was thinking we could feed business to each other." He looked pleased.

Chuck was relieved for him and asked, impressed, "How'd your agent come up with that?" In his experience, women didn't usually know about that type of thing.

"Her father is a trucker who runs collector cars across the country for people buying and selling them online. She knows a little bit about the industry."

"You lucked out." Chuck drained his bottle and stared into the bonfire. The warmth felt good against his bare legs.

"There's my girl," Vince said, glancing over the fire.

Chuck looked from the flames at Janie walking toward them. She wore grey sweatpants with the word PINK running down the side in hot pink letters, and a hoodie, the hood pulled over her head. It wasn't cold enough for that, but maybe it was her way of drowning out Crystal, Bailey, and Alycia.

Janie sat between Vince's legs and rested her head against his chest. She gave Chuck an angelic smile and snuggled deeper into Vince's embrace.

Vince didn't even notice Chuck's grabbing his beer bottle from him, so immersed was he with Janie, his lips pressed against the top of her head, his eyes closed in utter contentment. He'd been sure he and Kara would be next to marry, but now he was second-guessing himself, seeing how happy Vince and Janie were.

Throwing the beer bottles in the trash, he looked for Kara. He didn't see her talking with Crystal or Bailey anymore, and Alycia was still ignoring Bryce. He decided to look for Kara inside, and when he stepped onto their porch, he heard her whimpering.

As Kara listened to Bailey and Crystal talk babies, or lack thereof, she thought maybe babies weren't worth the effort. Except she was certain whomever she ended up marrying would want one or two or three to run around and carry on his last name.

Kara Matthews. It didn't sound terrible. Her parents would never allow it, but it sounded a lot better than Kara Hellson, and if that wasn't a sign, she didn't know what was. "I'm done in," she said, standing from the picnic table bench and stretching. She was glad she had the foresight to pack her Juicy Couture track suit. Kara didn't want to go inside, but she was tired of visiting. She would've asked Chuck to go for a walk with her but he seemed content to sit and BS with Vince.

"Kara!" Alycia pulled away from Bryce's desperate grasp and scurried across the grass. "Can the four of us, me and Bryce, you and Chuck, go on the pontoon tomorrow?"

Kara rolled the idea around and couldn't come up with a good reason to decline. Alycia's words came back to her from last night on the beach. She didn't want the other woman to feel like Kara wasn't her friend. If Alycia and Bryce didn't make it, it wouldn't affect Kara's friendship with her, despite what Alycia thought. She was friends with everyone as much as she could be with what little free time she had.

She pulled Alycia into a hug. "Of course. It will be nice to spend some time with you. Janie will be locked away in her cabin with Vince anyway." Kara snapped her mouth shut. That hadn't come out right. Alycia didn't look offended though, she just gave Kara a tight hug in return.

"Thank you. I think if I spend any more time with Crystal and Bailey, I'm going to scream." Alycia blushed. "But I mean that in the nicest way possible."

Kara laughed softly. "I know you what you mean."

She tried to catch Chuck's eye before she went inside, but he was talking too intently with Vince to notice. Kara went inside their cabin and shut the door behind her with a sigh of relief. How many more days of this? She counted on her fingers and grimaced. Yeah, she definitely would be having more fun in Cancun, but more than likely Chuck wouldn't be with her, so she had to take the good with the bad.

The glow of her cell phone as it rang lit up the dark cabin, and her grimace turned into a scowl when the display flashed her father's number. She hadn't exactly gotten around to returning her parents' phone calls or texts. She certainly hadn't gotten around to returning Kent's. What was in it for him if he married her? What had her family promised him to take her, and so amicably? Her brothers were vying for Congress. Had they promised to take Kent with them? Maybe even all the way to the White House? Her father hadn't quite made it, but he expected one of his sons to take a seat behind the desk in the Oval Office, and with her brothers' track records and popularity, one of them would.

Before her father's call went to voicemail, she answered, pressing a shaking finger to her phone's screen. "Hi, Daddy," she greeted him, hating the wobble in her voice.

"Kara Millicent St. John!"

Kara cringed.

Remington St. John's voice bellowed through the phone, piercing Kara's eardrum. "How dare you ignore your mother and me!"

Pacing back and forth in the little kitchen, she defended herself. "My phone died." It sounded lame, even to her.

With her phone wedged between her chin and shoulder, she pulled a bottle of red out of the fridge and poured herself a large plastic cup.

Her father's words faded into a buzz as Kara chugged the wine and the alcohol hit her bloodstream.

Kara never drank to get drunk. She drank socially, had been from the age of sixteen. Her mother thought it imperative her daughter learn which wine should accompany which meal.

And not just any wine—hence numerous wine-tasting classes. By the time she was eighteen she could name the top wines in every color from every country. Her parents would be appalled at the Reunite she bought at the liquor store in Poplar Point for $8.99. Hey, it didn't come in a box; that was something.

Tossing back the wine like she was dying of thirst, Kara didn't care her father was saying she was no good and wishing she'd been born a boy.

It was the nastiest he'd been with her.

"Daddy, please," she begged, the second cup of wine sloshing around in her stomach.

"Don't pull that shit with me, Kara," Remington hollered, and Kara pulled the phone away from her ear. "When you come back to the city, I expect you in my office on Monday morning at eight sharp. You will then tell me you will relocate to Chicago and that your mother can begin planning your wedding to Kent Hellson. There will be no more cajoling. I am at the end of my patience. Do you understand me?"

Tearfully, Kara assured him she did and disconnected the call.

Slobbering and dizzy, she sat at the table and tried to stop crying. She couldn't let Chuck see her this way. She was a strong woman, confident, brave. She made a six-figure salary and chaired million-dollar fundraising committees. She was not a blathering drunk, sick from cheap wine.

Get it together.

Kara's tenuous resolve broke when Chuck came into the cabin, looking adorable in his Minnesota Vikings hoodie. "Chuck," she gasped and launched herself into his arms.

"Oh, baby," Chuck murmured.

Kara's vision was a sliding mass of color, twirling and twisting. Beyond drunk, the alcoholic warmth spread through her body, and all the feelings of love she had for him pulsated and slithered around her heart threatening to shoot from her tingling fingertips. Leaning into him, she breathed in the smell of beer and fire and outdoors. She loved him so much; she was afraid he'd never truly understand how much. Kara peered at him, joy and sorrow dueling in her heart. His brown eyes were full of concern and love, his mouth tilting downwards in a troubled frown.

"You're drunk."

It wasn't an accusation, only a statement of fact. Kara leaned against his hands laced behind her back, trusting him not to let her crash onto the floor. She'd always trusted him with everything. Until now. "Yes," she agreed, giggling, her emotions turning on a dime.

It was hot in the cabin, despite the cool temperature outside, and the heat flushed her cheeks. "Make love to me, Chuck," she breathed.

His face swam and suddenly the kitchen light was too bright, the glare hurting her eyes. She needed the darkness of the bedroom. Kara pulled from his embrace and shut off the kitchen light. The cabin was doused in blackness, only the shadows from the hot flame of the bonfire danced along the walls. In the dimness, Kara banged her hip on the edge of the kitchen table. She swiped at her cup and drained it. The cups were huge—she drank half the bottle. *Oh well*, she thought, grabbing the wine bottle, *let's not waste the rest*.

"Whoa, I think you're done. Let's get you to bed." Chuck pulled the bottle from her hand, twisted the cap back on, and placed it in the fridge.

A cap! Kara covered her mouth, but it didn't stop the hysterical giggle that bubbled from her throat. Never in a million years would her mother allow her to drink a wine that needed a twist-on cap!

"Bed," she echoed, her mind sliding from one topic to the next. She felt better with the lights off. Kara unzipped her salmon pink hoodie and dropped it to the floor. She forgot she'd asked Chuck to make love to her. Good thing he brought it up again. It was a fabulous idea!

"Yes, to bed." Chuck nodded, pulling her upper arm. "Why'd you go so crazy, Kara? You rarely get like this."

That was true! Kara bobbed her head vigorously in response. The last time she got this drunk was at a fundraising dinner for the Children's Miracle Network. Chuck hadn't been invited and later that night her father told her why. That was the night he'd introduced her to Kent and told her of his plans for the two of them.

"Bad news," she said gravely, sitting on the edge of the bed.

Chuck knelt and pulled her sandals off her feet. "Lift up," he asked, and Kara stood so he could pull her track pants down her legs and over her feet, throwing them aside.

"What kind of bad news?" His voice was taut, like a rubber band stretched to the max.

"Things," Kara replied and laughed. She couldn't tell Chuck! What would he do? She pulled the tank top she was wearing under her hoodie over her head so she was clad only in panties and matching bra.

Chuck stood, and Kara ran a finger along the elastic waistband of his shorts. "Make love to me, Chuck," she pleaded. "Help me." If only there was help. She was afraid nothing could help her now. Kara was in too deep—and no one told her father no.

"Kara, you're drunk. You need sleep, not sex."

Kara grabbed Chuck's groin and smiled when she found him hard. "I want to." She lost her balance and fell backward onto the bed. Her mind was fuzzy, and it took her a moment to realize she was staring at the ceiling. A breeze from the open window blew into the room, and she heard her friends talking over the crackling fire. It was cooler than in the kitchen, but she couldn't move her limbs to crawl under the covers. "I'm cold," she whispered instead, hoping Chuck would warm her.

She watched as he shed his clothes and pulled the blankets back. Kara scrambled under them, grateful to be warm, and molded her body to Chuck's, relishing the feel of his hot body against her. She desperately wanted him inside her, so she kissed him, but she had to pull away to slide her panties off, pushing them to the end of the bed with her foot. She kissed him again.

"Kara, are you sure?" he asked as she rubbed against him, his breath feathering against her cheek.

"Yes." She pushed her breasts against his chest. Kara wanted to take her bra off but she didn't want to waste the energy. She wasn't sure if she could undo the hooks anyway. Instead, she grasped his hand and shoved it under the blanket. Hips tilted upward, she spread her legs. "See?" she murmured, and his hand tight in hers, she guided his fingers to the apex of her legs. "Please Chuck, make it go away."

Make the emptiness go away.

He slid one or two or three fingers inside her. She didn't know for sure, she only groaned, grinding her hips against his hand to increase the pleasure.

Kara kissed him, pouring all her fear into the motion. She needed rescue. Chuck's love for her was her only possession, and she wouldn't have it much longer. Alcohol mixed with her desperation and she slid her tongue into his mouth, wrapping her arms around his shoulders, her head coming off the pillow.

Chuck shifted their positions so he leaned over her.

"Yes," Kara cried, widening her legs. "Yes."

"Shh, shh," Chuck whispered. "The window's open." He covered her mouth with his and swallowed her cry as she came.

"Inside, inside," Kara whispered, clutching at his shoulders, "I need you inside of me." She calmed when Chuck rolled on top of her. His arms encircled her and he pulled her close as he thrust in and out of her.

"Kara," he panted in her ear. "It's all right."

He came, and through her drunkenness, she wished she wasn't on the pill. She wished his seed would take root, but she buried her face in his neck as he rode out his orgasm and knew that would never be.

Nothing would ever be all right again, but she had this vacation and she had Chuck.

For a little while.

Cradled in his arms, she was safe, but she knew it wouldn't last.

Chuck knew Kara was awake by the way she burrowed her face into his neck. He lay awake until late, worrying about her. Her problems with her family were none of his business. There was something big going down, but until she confided in him, there was nothing he could do. The bad news she mentioned last night bothered him. She must have been on the phone with her either her mother or her father, but never had they driven her to drink—that he knew of. She kept him out of her family life and usually he appreciated that. Now he was anxious, and he wanted her to share what was going on. He wasn't naïve enough to think he could help, but things with her seemed to be getting worse and worse.

"What's on the agenda today?" he asked, nuzzling the top of her head with his nose.

They smelled like sex and sweat. He wanted a shower and coffee, though he couldn't decide which first.

"Pontoon with Bryce and Alycia," Kara mumbled.

"Are you serious?" Chuck groused.

Kara laughed against his shoulder. "She ambushed me last

night. She said she wouldn't feel like part of the group if she and Bryce divorced. I feel bad for her."

"I feel bad for me," Chuck lamented, running his fingers lightly over Kara's back. She wore a powder blue bra and nothing else. It was fucking sexier than hell. "How are you feeling?" The sex had been as good as always, but he'd felt wrong, somehow, making love to her, even though she wanted it. It would have taken a miracle to stop after she forced his hand to her pussy. She'd been sloppy wet, just the way he loved her.

Her desire for him was off the charts, and he worshiped her for it.

"I have a headache," she admitted, propping herself onto an elbow so she could look into his face.

Chuck caressed her cheek with his palm, cupping her jaw. "You can talk to me. You know that, don't you, Kara? I love you so much. I'd do anything I could for you."

Rolling on top of him she said, "I know. I know, Chuck. Let's not talk now."

He brushed her hair out of her face as she pushed herself onto him, and he tried to forget about the worry he knew was there, even after she closed her eyes.

This wasn't so bad. Truthfully, Chuck preferred to spend time with Vince and Janie, but this had always been a group vacation, so he needed to spread the love. Besides, now that Vince and Janie were together, it was difficult to persuade them to leave their cabin.

He used to really like Bryce, once upon a time. He still did, well, kind of, but Chuck rarely saw Bryce anymore. His hotel job took most of his time, and the rest he gave to Kara.

She lay at the front of the pontoon, clad in a little baby pink bikini. Alycia was with her, in a suit that covered her more extensively. She'd always been too bossy for his taste, but Bryce needed the direction, and as far as Chuck knew, never minded Alycia wore the pants in their relationship.

"Making any progress?" Chuck murmured.

They were fishing off the end of the pontoon, and Chuck pitched his voice low so the ladies couldn't hear. Alycia brought along an ancient cassette player and a warbling-sounding mixtape was playing old Bon Jovi and Firehouse. The songs reminded him of high school, and his mother and father telling him if he wanted to go to college he would need to work hard and earn good grades to win scholarships because they couldn't afford to help.

"Nah," Bryce said, scratching a mosquito away from his cheek. "I should have known two weeks away from the city wouldn't do anything. She's talking counseling, whatever."

"You don't want?"

Bryce shrugged. "You know how you're so deep that no matter what you do, nothing will help?"

Chuck *did* know. He felt like that with his family. No matter how many bills he paid, there would always be more.

"I'm at the point where I can do whatever she wants, but it will never be enough."

Yep. Chuck nodded, thinking about the mortgage payment he'd transferred to his parents, even though his father promised he'd be able to pay it himself this month.

It'd never be enough.

§

Kara dove into the cool water of Lake Harriet. She opened her eyes under the water, the sunlight penetrating the surface making it look a murky green. How would it feel to stay down there forever, to suck the water into her lungs, to let the water fill her body, her mind, her heart? She felt so helpless, as if she had no control over her own life. Kara was a puppet, her father holding the strings. Only they weren't strings, they were wires, and Chuck held only a pair of dull kiddie scissors. No one could free her.

The natural buoyancy of her body popped her head above the water. Alycia, Bryce, and Chuck were treading water near her and Chuck splashed Alycia playfully. Kara swam to him and looped her arms around his neck. She hung on to him and allowed him to keep her afloat with his powerful arms and legs cutting through the water.

The lake chopped with waves, and if Kara dipped too far near the surface, the water splashed into her mouth and eyes.

It felt good after lying in the sun with Alycia.

They hadn't spoken much. Kara didn't want to talk about her job or how things were going with Chuck. Alycia spoke little of her job as the accessories department manager at Macy's, and of course she didn't talk about Bryce, not when Chuck and Bryce were in earshot. Mostly they lay in silence and listened to the music Alycia brought along, and the water slapping the side of the pontoon.

Distracted with her own, she didn't think much about Alycia and Bryce's problems. Not that they were such problems. You played, you paid.

Chuck never asked her what she thought about any of their friends. Thinking about them made Kara feel almost better about her own life. Almost.

"You okay, baby?" Chuck murmured in her ear.

The lake water was chilly and even with the sun beating down on her, goosebumps dotted her skin, and she started to shiver. Kara wiped water out of her eyes and tried not to think of the fish swimming under her.

St. Barth's this was not.

Water clung to Chuck's eyelashes and spiked his hair. His skin was turning a delicious golden brown. God, he was handsome. "Yeah." She offered him a smile and kissed him.

Kara laughed when they started sinking because Chuck wrapped his arms around her and stopped kicking.

"Get a room!" Bryce hollered, joking.

Kara stuck her tongue out at him, then deflated when she saw Alycia's frown and the hurt in her eyes.

"Good idea," Chuck agreed. "Let's go back to the cabins."

They climbed the little ladder at the back of the pontoon and Kara dried off, slipping a white terrycloth cover-up over her bikini and binding her hair with a scarf.

Chuck hadn't motored them far from the cabins, and the ride was short. He probably didn't want to be trapped away from the resort for long if Alycia and Bryce didn't behave themselves, and Kara didn't blame him. There was an odd current running between the couple. Or was that her and Chuck? Kara couldn't deny that things were far from copacetic with them, too.

"Thanks," Alycia murmured as they neared the dock. "This took up a nice part of the day. I'm going to eat some lunch and then take a nap."

"It was no big deal," Kara replied. "I wish we could have talked more."

Alycia pulled her into a quick hug. "I'm tired of talking. The peace and quiet were good for me." She stepped from the pontoon and without a backward glance, trotted down the dock, her red curls bouncing behind her.

While Kara helped Chuck secure the pontoon to the dock, the *blip blip* of a cop car's siren startled her, and she almost slipped into the water. The sound was out of place in the quiet of the lake's shore.

"What's going on?" Bryce asked, jumping from the pontoon.

"No clue," Chuck said, giving the rope a final tug.

Janie and Vince hurried out of their cabin.

Alycia stood on the grass and Bryce ran to her, hovering protectively.

Kara swallowed a lump in her throat. Had her father sent someone to fetch her? She could picture it now—being taken away in a cop car because she wouldn't answer his texts. It was juvenile and manipulative, and just like her father to humiliate her that way to keep control.

Bailey and Cam met them outside as the police officer opened the door of his cruiser. The only couple missing was Crystal and Nate.

"Where's Nate and Crystal?" Kara asked as Chuck put an arm around her.

Before Bailey could answer, the officer stepped from the car and slammed the door of the cruiser that indicated he was with the Popular Point police force. He was dressed in a navy blue uniform, and even though it was short-sleeved, Kara winced in sympathy. The poor man must be baking in this heat.

"Can we help you?" Vince asked, standing close to Janie.

Kara's mouth twitched in a smile. *That* relationship she hadn't been sure about, but Vince treating Janie with such loving concern was changing her mind. Janie wasn't the only one used to Vince behaving so callously toward her all these years. But contrary to what Janie said, a little bit of fucking apparently did Vince a whole lot of good.

"I just came from the resort's office and convenience store," the officer began, an 8 by 10 picture in his hand. "We received a 911 call this morning. The clerk at the store was assaulted during a robbery—"

Alycia gasped.

Kara clutched Chuck's arm. Things like that didn't happen in a small town like Poplar Point. Not like the city where last year someone was shot and killed by a druggie on a lethal high three blocks from her father's firm.

"We believe the man to be a transient who has been in and out of our jail and mental health clinic in Poplar Point numerous times. Unfortunately, he disappeared from the clinic during a staff change. Without his medication, he's prone to violence. We want to be cautious, and we're warning everyone in the area to be careful. Try not to go anywhere alone until he's apprehended. He's on foot, so we believe it shouldn't take long. Is anyone here armed?" The officer scanned their faces.

Kara shook her head though the officer wasn't looking at her. No one was armed here. She had taken a self-defense class five years ago. That was it.

"No," Vince answered, stepping closer and reaching for the photo. "We're on vacation from the city."

Vince studied the picture, and Kara peered over his shoulder at the mug shot of an older gentleman, his hair white, a grey beard covering his jaw.

"He's done this before?" Kara asked.

The officer cleared his throat. "He has. Unfortunately, the environment of our jail is not conducive to the state of his mental health. The hospital's mental health clinic can only do so much. We're a small town with little funding for that kind of thing, and staffing for that floor is thin. I know those aren't valid reasons for why this gentleman is out on the streets, but Poplar Point is not the only town dealing with issues like these." He gave the group a feeble smile. "Keep in mind, we think he's gone. He's been known to surface in other towns near here. He was able to make off with quite a bit of cash from the convenience store register, and we're hoping it will tide him over until he can be apprehended. But please keep your eyes open for anything suspicious and call 911 right away. Do not try to contain him on your own. His family lives in the city, and they've been alerted. They've had trouble keeping him under control and don't know what to do. It's a bad situation all around."

Chuck took the picture, glanced at it briefly and handed it to Bryce and Cam. When everyone had taken a look, the officer thanked them, returned to the patrol car, and slowly turned it around.

Kara watched as he drove back down the gravel driveway toward the office.

"Well, that's just great," Chuck muttered. "I vote we get a refund from the resort and get the hell out of here."

"No!" Kara burst out. God, no. If she went back to the city now, before she could decide what to do about her father, mother, and Kent, she would be trapped forever. She needed to talk to Janie . . . and to Chuck. She had to tell him; there was no excuse.

Letting him go would be the hardest thing she would ever do.

"No?" Chuck growled. "Are you crazy? There's a mentally unstable and dangerous man wandering around, and you want to stay here?"

"The cop said he's gone."

"Vince?" Chuck spat.

Vince tensed his shoulders, Janie in his arms, his chin resting on the top of her head. "We should probably go," he said, though it was evident cutting the vacation short was the last thing he wanted to do.

Chuck nodded. "Good man. Bryce? Cam?"

Kara held her breath.

Bryce looked relieved, and he was nodding before Chuck even finished saying his name.

Cam shrugged.

"Wait a minute!" Kara cried. "What about the women? Don't we get a vote? And Crystal and Nate aren't even here. Where are they anyway?" She clutched her swimsuit cover-up around her. She was perspiring, but not from the heat. Fear caused the icy trickle of sweat to slide along her back. She'd been counting on having another week with Chuck before having to face her parents.

"They went hiking," Vince supplied tersely. "They won't be back until tomorrow."

Kara blew out a sigh of relief. "We can't up and leave them. What would we do? Nail a note to their door?"

"Okay." Chuck rubbed his hand up and down her back. "I don't like it, but fine. We'll talk to Crystal and Nate when they get back, then we'll decide as a group, okay?"

Shaking, Kara pressed her head into his shoulder. She needed this last week. She'd never see Chuck again after this vacation. She'd move to Chicago, marry Kent, be the good wife and daughter her parents expected her to be.

"I'm going to grab some food. You want?" Chuck asked.

Kara's stomach rolled with nerves, and she shook her head. The thought of food made her gag. "Janie, can I talk to you?"

"Yeah, sure." Janie tipped her head for a kiss and Vince fluttered kisses over her cheeks.

"Don't go far," Chuck warned her, glaring.

"I won't," Kara promised.

Chuck and Vince disappeared into Vince and Janie's cabin, and Kara watched them go.

Bryce stood uncertainly, running his fingers through his hair before he went inside his own cabin.

Kara looked at Alycia. She seemed uncomfortable standing in her swimsuit with the built-in skirt, like she didn't know what to do. Bryce had gone into their cabin, and if she didn't want to be with him, she didn't have anywhere else to go. Kara wanted Alycia to go inside so she could talk to Janie alone, though it would be rude to ask for privacy. They were all friends.

Bailey and Cam, who had been quiet during the officer's briefing, walked to the beach.

Kara led Janie and Alycia onto the pontoon because she wanted somewhere quiet to sit, and there weren't many places where they could talk without interruption. Her stomach pitched with the waves.

"What's wrong, Kara?"

Kara sat on a bench that ran along the side of the pontoon's front and stared out over the lake. It was so peaceful on the water.

"Is it about the homeless guy?" Janie tried again.

Alycia and Janie were flanking her on the bench, but Janie didn't see them; her watery eyes only following the swooping of a seagull in the sky.

"Chuck and I are over."

Alycia hummed in sympathy, and Janie squawked her denial.

Kara sounded dramatic but she didn't care.

"But you looked . . ." Janie faded, tucking a piece of hair behind her ear.

Fine. We looked fine, just five minutes ago, Kara said to herself. "We're okay," she whispered, still looking into the shimmery horizon. "My parents are making me marry someone else." Kara shot from the bench to the end of the pontoon, knelt, and threw up. The bile burned her throat. She hadn't eaten breakfast, and her stomach churned with the bottle of wine from last night.

Alycia handed her a tissue.

Kara took it gratefully and wiped her mouth. "Sorry."

Janie and Alycia sat near her, and their presence was both soothing and grating. She needed the support of her friends, but she also wanted to be left alone. It was probably better if she wasn't alone because she was at the end of her rope. The noose tightened around her neck, her feet scrambled for purchase, but there was nothing she could grab onto for help.

"Surely they can't force you," Alycia said.

"You don't know my father," Kara replied bitterly. It wasn't the entire truth. They all had been friends long enough they met each other's parents at some point in time; only Kara knew them best.

"You haven't told Chuck," Janie guessed.

Kara shook her head in misery. "No. I'll have the rest of this vacation, and that'll be it. I'll have to tell him this isn't going to work out. There's nothing I can do." Kara rested her head against the ladder's handrail and cried.

❦

Chuck worried about Kara. She'd come inside after talking to Janie and Alycia looking drawn and pale. Just for a second, he hoped she was pregnant, but he knew she wouldn't allow an accident like that to happen. Not with her career. Not with the way her parents rode herd on her. No, something else was going down, but like hell if she would tell him.

Vince made lunch—thick ham sandwiches with a bag of chips and a couple bottles of beer. Chuck wanted to suggest to Kara that she eat, but she didn't look like she could keep anything down.

He convinced her to go back to the cabin, raising his eyebrows at Vince and Janie before following her out the door.

She went directly to the bed and sat at the end. "Do you love me, Chuck?" she asked hollowly, her eyes not seeing him standing in the doorway. She was still wearing her suit and cover-up, her sunglasses resting on the top of her head, her short hair covered by a lime green scarf.

Chuck still wore his swim trunks, and his skin crackled with sun and lake water. "Of course I do. Kara, what's going on? You have to talk to me, love. You haven't been yourself this whole trip. You can talk to me." Chuck knelt by her feet and gathered her hands in his. She had such small hands. Smooth, soft, turning a pretty shade of tan from spending time in the sun. He despised the thought of her going back to the city, of returning to eighty-hour weeks to make her family happy. Her pale skin, her skeleton-like frame from not taking the time to eat. Chuck tried to take care of her the best he could, but it wasn't enough.

She took his face in her hands, leaving his palms resting on her thighs.

Kara's eyes cleared, and for a moment he saw the woman he fell in love with—her expression brimming with love, with happiness, for them.

"I will always love you, Chuck," she whispered. "No matter what. Please remember that. Whatever happens, I love you."

That sound like a goodbye if Chuck ever heard one, but he tried not to think that way. It was just a reassurance—one he needed desperately because while he could accuse her of keeping secrets, he was guilty of doing the same.

"I know," Chuck said. "We have a long road ahead of us." He blew out a frustrated breath. "Kara, I have things I need to—"

"No. Not now."

Chuck nodded, understanding. It wouldn't do to tell her now, to tell her he'd never be truly free of his family. Love only went so far, and he didn't want another week of vacation to endure after she realized his baggage was too heavy to help him carry.

"Will you make love to me, Chuck?" she murmured.

He didn't answer, instead pressing a kiss to her knee, and trailing his lips up her leg. He pushed the hem of her short cover-up higher and continued to kiss the inside of her thigh.

"Chuck, I need more."

"Lift up, then," he requested, and Kara lifted off the bed so Chuck could pull the bikini bottoms from her legs and toss them aside.

"Like this?" he asked, and she nodded, spreading her legs. She lay back onto the mattress, near the edge of the bed.

Chuck loved looking at her. Loved spreading her open, watching her juice trickle out of her, coating the crack of her ass, loved seeing her swollen, ready for him. He took pride in the fact she loved him, wanted him so much she quivered with it. Slowly slipping a finger into her, he savored her heat, growing hard watching his finger move in and out of her, breathing in her musk. "Put your feet up."

Yeah, that was it.

Kara was spread wide, her skin smooth and pink.

Chuck lowered his head and sampled her, relishing the clenching of her muscles around his fingers as he touched the tip of his tongue to her delicate skin.

Slowly, in a steady rhythm, he licked, pulling his fingers out, then pushing them into her.

"Chuck, I'm going to come," Kara gasped, readjusting her feet on the mattress, spreading her legs as far as she could.

"You like that, baby?" he murmured.

"Yeah," she whimpered.

Chuck pulled his fingers out and positioned her feet so they rested on his shoulders. Draping an arm over her pelvis, he pushed down so she couldn't move her hips.

Kara moaned.

Gently, Chuck slid three fingers into her, and once again nuzzled her with his tongue.

As she came, he pushed his fingers into her as far as he could, smoothing his tongue against her clit.

Kara cried out, a mewling noise that contained more pain than pleasure.

Chuck's cock throbbed. He wiped his mouth with the back of his hand and leaned over to kiss her, but she was crying. He couldn't ask for more now. Instead, he kissed the tears from her cheeks. "Kara, love, look at me."

She turned her head away.

"Kara, look at me," he requested firmly.

She finally looked at him, her green eyes swamped with tears.

"Why don't you shower? I'll make you something to eat. Then we need to talk. I mean it." It didn't matter how much of their vacation they had left. They couldn't go on this way.

"I don't deserve you, Chuck," Kara whispered, sitting up and smoothing the tears from her face.

"That's bullshit. Go take a shower, rinse that lake off you. Though it did taste good," he teased, smacking his lips, hoping to make her smile.

She laughed. "Gross." Kara slid off the bed and went into the bathroom, quietly shutting the door behind her.

Chuck was tempted to follow, but his arousal deflated at the sight of her tears and only the need to comfort consumed him.

In the kitchen, Chuck assembled ingredients for omelets and toast while he sipped a beer.

Faintly, Kara's ringtone sounded. Chuck knew it was Kara's father by the Imperial March Kara had attached to the number.

After a quick look at the browning omelet, he grabbed her cell phone before the call could go to voicemail.

"Mr. St. John, sir," Chuck answered. Normally he didn't touch Kara's phone, or she, his. But he didn't think Kara could handle speaking with her father now and letting it go to voicemail would make the next time she spoke with him even worse. So he answered, thinking he would take a message.

"Who the fuck is this?" Remington St. John roared into the phone.

"This is Chuck Matthews, sir." He hated how timid and weak he sounded when he was trying for polite and cool.

"Where the hell is my daughter?" Remington's voice shook with rage.

It was a wonder the man hadn't had a heart attack or stroke. His blood pressure must have been off the charts.

"She's in the shower, sir. Can I take a message?"

There was silence and Chuck wondered if the man hung up on him, but then Remington's voice came softly over the line. "You may tell my daughter that her mother arranged the tea with her future mother-in-law to discuss preliminary wedding details."

Dumbfounded, Chuck gulped. Vivian called Chuck's mother and arranged a tea? With a ball of fire in his stomach that threatened to burn him from the inside out, Chuck realized that wasn't what Remington meant at all.

"A wedding, sir?" Chuck choked. He felt like he had a spoonful of peanut butter lodged in his throat threatening to suffocate him.

"Yes. To Kent Hellson. She must have told you?"

Remington paused, waiting for a response.

Kara was engaged and she hadn't told him. It explained the tears. Why she got drunk last night.

When Chuck didn't answer, Remington continued, "Surely you didn't think you were good enough for her? Did you, Charles?"

Chuck grimaced. He hated his given name.

"You may be the manager of that hotel and I admit, I am rather impressed with how far you've come despite your family, but you are still nowhere near good enough for my daughter. Kara has so much to look forward to. The Governor's Mansion . . . maybe even the White House, if Kent plays his cards right, and I'll be sure to see that he does." Remington's tone hardened. "We were overjoyed when Kent proposed and Kara accepted. She asked for time to tell you. Time she apparently used unwisely. Charles, you may take a message for my daughter. You tell her time has run out."

Kara's phone beeped, signaling Remington hung up, and Kara's fairy wallpaper and app icons popped onto the phone's screen. Only the smoke from the burning eggs in the frying pan jerked Chuck from his shock.

He was scraping burnt egg into the garbage when Kara came into the kitchen dressed in khaki cotton shorts and a butter yellow top.

Brushing her hair, she wrinkled her nose. "That smells horrible. What happened?"

Chuck couldn't meet her eyes. He worked on the charred egg with the spatula. "Your father called."

"Oh." Kara's brush clattered to the linoleum floor. "You didn't talk to him, did you?" Her voice shook.

"I did." Chuck calmly finished scraping the pan. To make another omelet he would need to wipe the bottom with a paper towel.

"Oh."

Finally, Chuck met her eyes. Kara's pallor pissed him off. He wouldn't let her play the victim. This was his fucking heart they were talking about. Slamming the pan on the stovetop, he glared at her. "He asked me to pass along a message."

"Oh."

"Is that all you have to say? 'Oh?' Don't you want to know what he told me to tell you? Or maybe you already know?"

"W-what did he tell you?"

"*Oh*," Chuck said, feigning nonchalance. He picked up an egg out of the carton sitting on the counter near the stove. Casually, he dropped it from one hand to the other. "He said to let you know your mother set up a tea with your future mother-in-law."

Kara covered her mouth with her hand, but a whimper still escaped, filling the entire kitchen with just that small sound.

"Now, I'm a naïve, trusting son of a bitch, and I thought, just for a second, that you got up the guts to tell your father that you wanted to marry me and that the tea was with my mother." He continued to toss the egg, back and forth, one hand, then the other. It was the only thing keeping his hands off her. "But then, well, I remembered we've never talked about getting married. I've never asked, mainly because I never thought I had a chance in hell, and you've never said either way, so I realized pretty fast your father wasn't talking about Vivian and my mom. You're engaged, huh? When were you going to tell me, Kara? In the middle of fucking me?"

She flinched. "It's not what you think."

"It seems pretty cut and dried to me," Chuck disagreed. He almost felt sorry for her. Almost. Her face was paper white, tears leaking from her bottle-glass green eyes. Black circles rested beneath them and her lips trembled.

Her hands shook as she took a step forward, but the dangerous glint in his eyes must have warned her off. Kara stopped and instead reached out to him pleadingly. "My father, he's making me—"

Chuck laughed. "*Making* you? Kara, you're thirty-one years old. No one can make you do anything. And your fiancé? He's on board with this? Or is your father black-mailing him? Bribing him? Promised him a seat in Congress or some fucking shit?"

Who would turn Kara down? A gorgeous, intelligent blonde who was a fucking dream in bed . . . "Have you been fucking him too, Kara? Have you been spreading your legs for him? Letting him bury his face in your pussy? Making you come? Do you cry out his name while he's deep inside you?"

"No!" Kara burst out and Chuck was pleased to see some flash in her eyes. *That's right, baby. Fight. Fight for us.*

"There's only been you since we got together. Only you."

Chuck believed her. He took up any free time she had. Unless she was fucking the guy on the couch in her office, Kara didn't have time to screw another man. It didn't mean he had to let her think she was getting off easy. "Yeah, well. I don't know what you want me to say. I don't fuck with engaged women, so I guess this means we're done. Pack your bags and go back to the city. Go to tea. I'll catch a ride with Vince. Don't worry about me.

"But then . . ." Chuck narrowed his eyes at her, ". . . you never have, have you?"

Kara ran out of the cabin, barefoot, the screen door slamming behind her.

Unleashing his anger, Chuck threw the egg against the door, taking not one ounce of satisfaction as it exploded against the wood, yolk and shell flying everywhere.

Kara could barely see and she clipped her leg against the rough wood of a picnic table bench. She skirted the bonfire pit, ran past Vince, and headed toward the trail. Kara needed to get away and she ran as fast as she could, though her pace wasn't fast enough to run from Chuck's anger. She couldn't run barefoot—she wasn't like Janie, barefoot the entire time they were here.

Vince hollered something at her, but she ran on, gasping, pain from her feet competing with the pain in her heart.

Chuck knew.

She lost him.

A shriek of agony tore from her throat.

Kara ran on past the little overlook with the useless fence. She slowed and looked over her shoulder, making sure no one was following her. Vince could have sent Janie to see what was wrong, but Kara wanted to be alone. When she went back, she'd need to pack, go back to the city.

Chuck had thrown her out.

He had every right.

Secure in the fact she was alone, she let the sobs come. She stumbled along the hiking trail, veering off the path at the last second onto a barely-there-trail that led who the hell knew where.

It suited Kara. The farther she ran from the cabin, from Chuck, the better off she'd be.

She lurched through the bracken, the sticks poking at the delicate soles of her feet, plants brushing creepily at her legs. Bugs buzzed around her head. The heat of the day hadn't abated and sweat ran down her neck, down her back.

Kara didn't care about any of that.

The pain and betrayal on Chuck's face ripped at her heart.

Hadn't she known this was going to happen? Hadn't she *known*?! She had, and she'd ignored it all this time. Had thought maybe things would work out and bet Chuck's heart on her father.

She lost.

And Chuck paid.

Not only Chuck. This pain, this pain threatening to cut off her air supply, was real. Her love for him was real.

Kara slowed and picked her way along the forest floor. Was she walking a path? She didn't know. She didn't care.

She wiped sweat from her forehead before it ran into her eyes. Not that that mattered, either. There were so many tears, she wouldn't be able to discern tears from sweat. Kara couldn't see, though there was nothing *to* see but trees and green plants. Besides the buzz and droning of the bugs, there wasn't any sound. It was so different from the city— ringing phones, people chatting, always, always, the sound of traffic.

Her only sanctuary in the city was Chuck. Snuggling on the couch with him and Miss Fiona, making love under the covers in a dark, quiet bedroom. He was her oasis, her sanc- tuary in the dry desert wasteland that was her life. How would she survive without him?

A deerfly bit her shoulder, and she smacked it away. How could something so little cause so much pain?

Sinking to her knees, she fell on her hands, then onto her stomach, resting her head on her arms.

Home.

Such a foreign-sounding place. Where was that? Her condo? Her lonely condo with a small TV she didn't have time to watch and only Miss Fiona for company. It always felt like home when Chuck was there.

Chuck hated her condo. He said it felt sterile, isolated. Her condo was different from the townhome Chuck rented. He liked having a yard—a place to grill, to sit outside to soak up the sun after a day of sitting in front of a computer. He liked mowing grass, planting flowers.

He was ultimate husband material.

Kara would never be his wife.

Did she want to be?

That was a dumb question, of course she did.

But what else did she want?

She'd given so little thought to it.

She fell into an exhausted sleep, *what did she want, what did she want, what did she want,* looping around her mind.

Chuck was readying the small aluminum fishing boat when Vince and Janie found him. He'd cleaned up the egg, turned off the stove, and packed a sleeping bag and small backpack of things he'd need to spend a night on one of the islands.

He didn't want to be around when Kara came back for her bags.

He couldn't.

Chuck watched his future run out the door in a flood of tears, and he couldn't do that again.

"Did you and Kara fight?" Vince asked, looking down on Chuck who was in the boat, checking the motor.

"Yes." Chuck didn't want to talk about it. Not that there

was anything to talk about, really. She'd chosen her path, and it was not his.

"About what?"

Normally Vince wasn't so chatty, and Chuck scowled. He liked his friend when he was being more silent, but whatever. "Kara's engaged."

Chuck snorted when Vince could only stare.

"And not to you?"

"And not to me," Chuck nodded. "I'm sure he's some Harvard boy her daddy picked out." His gaze slid to Janie who stood behind Vince chewing a fingernail. "You knew about this?"

She looked like a student who didn't have the answer when the teacher called on her. Her brown eyes widened and she bit her lip, probably weighing how much to say. It wouldn't matter. He was done with Kara; what Janie said would matter not at all.

Janie sighed. "She told me at the campground. Not about . . ." She trailed off. "Not about her engagement, but about . . ."

Chuck should have figured there was more. Dealing with Kara's family, there was always more, and he should be thanking his lucky ass he didn't have to fucking deal with it anymore. His own family was enough, but instead, all he felt was filleted, like the walleye they caught and sliced and diced for frying. Rolling his eyes he said, "You don't have to break some sisterhood pact, Janie."

"Well, you know about what's-his-name so . . ." Janie sighed. "Her father wants her to move to Chicago to open a new branch of their firm."

"Well," Chuck snapped. "She's free to go. In fact, I'm going to an island to wait her out. When she comes back to the cabin with her tail between her legs, tell her I'm gone and I'll catch a ride back to the city with you, or Bryce and Alycia. It doesn't matter." He ran a hand over his face. It was almost dinner and his stomach rumbled. He hadn't made an omelet, too upset with Kara to eat. Now his stomach turned with hunger and nausea. The sloshing of the water against the side of the boat didn't help.

Vince shook his head and hunkered down on his haunches to look Chuck in the eye. Janie sat next to him, cross-legged.

"Let me get this straight," Vince started through clenched teeth. "Kara's *engaged*, and she's moving to *Chicago* to work because her family is making her?"

Chuck barked a bitter laugh. "What makes you think her family is making her? She could want this, man." He snapped his mouth shut. It was something he didn't consider. Kara could want to move, to marry that schmuck, be the hotshot lawyer, play the political wife. Her tears could have stemmed from the fact Chuck had found out, and in the worst possible way . . .

. . . Or the best possible way.

Let her father break the news to him so she wouldn't have to.

He was letting his mind run wild. He didn't have to answer Kara's phone. That had been his mistake.

"That's not true, Chuck," Janie retorted. "She's so broken up about this. Why would she want to marry some guy she barely knows? She doesn't want to move. Kara loves you."

Janie was only trying to help, but it didn't work. "Not enough," Chuck said softly, untying the boat from the dock.

"Do you want me to go with you?" Vince offered, resting a hand on Janie's leg.

Shaking his head, Chuck threw the rope into the bottom of the boat. "No. I need time alone. It would just be great if you could make sure she makes it back to the city all right. It makes me nervous when she drives while she's upset." Which was a lot of the time.

"Yeah, sure," Vince agreed and gave the boat a nudge with his hand.

Chuck grabbed a paddle and pushed away from the dock, waving half-heartedly at Janie and Vince in goodbye.

Kara was the love of his life, but they had never been single at the same time—for years. Poor timing. He would be dating someone, or she would. Usually some preppy guy her parents shoved at her. When she broke up with the last guy and he had just disentangled himself from a current girl-friend, he'd pounced. And she hadn't run.

He cranked the motor and made way for the island farthest from the cabins. He packed the recent Stephen King and he was looking forward to plowing through all one thousand pages.

He'd build a fire, read through the night, and maybe, just maybe, forget Kara ruined his life.

Kara's ribs and boobs hurt from falling asleep on her stomach. A wind had picked up and dark clouds loomed in the sky. She sat and looked around, seeing nothing but trees, trees, and more trees.

She rubbed her hands over her tear-crusted face and studied the bottoms of her feet—they were sore but not bleeding. That would have made walking back to the cabins difficult. Kara stepped away from the so-called trail and relieved herself. It was disgusting she didn't have toilet paper, but she didn't know poison ivy from a rosebush so she only pulled up her panties with a grimace, grossed out she couldn't wipe. Even with a leaf.

Kara backed away from the place where she peed so she wouldn't step in it. Maybe next year she could convince Chuck—

She pressed her lips together. She and Chuck wouldn't be doing anything together ever again. More than likely next summer would be full of plans for her wedding to Kent and then the obligatory honeymoon. She wouldn't know where until next year; her mother would choose the hottest place—and she wasn't talking about the temperature.

Kara took a tentative step forward. Where was the trail? She tried not to panic and rested her back against a tree. If she chose the right direction, she was near her and Chuck's cabin and could make it back with little fanfare. All she needed was to find the hiking trail she ran on before veering off in a panic. If she chose incorrectly, she could wander the woods for days.

Shit.

Kara slid to the base of the tree. It would be best to wait. But how many hours would she be lost before Janie told Casey to look for her? Because let's face it, Janie would be the only one to think to look for her. Crystal and Nate were returning to the cabins from hiking, but it would be a miracle if she heard them and they found her. Bailey and Cam were keeping to themselves. Alycia might think to ask where she was, but if Vince told her she ran off, Alycia wouldn't think much more than that.

Kara sat for a few minutes enjoying the cool breeze. She shredded a leaf. She shredded another leaf. Her stomach growled. She batted at a fly, killed a mosquito, inspected her feet again in the waning light. She chewed on her lip.

That was it. She couldn't take it anymore.

Kara stood, stepping gingerly. She had to move. It might not be very smart, but she hadn't exactly been exhibiting any degree of intelligence this whole time, had she?

She wanted to blame her father. Goddamn it. She bet old Remington had been shaking with glee when he had Chuck on the phone, and he was able to tell him to fuck off and leave his daughter alone. It was just like her father to take joy in making other people's lives miserable.

Kara paused. Was this the right way?

Well, fuck it. She'd go where she wanted. If it fucked her over, it would serve her right. She should have been honest with Chuck. Correction. She should never have gotten involved with him to begin with. She knew all along their relationship would end this way.

Not this way, particularly. With her father involved, it could have ended a lot worse.

Chuck lay next to a dying fire, gazing up at the stars. Was Kara gone? Packed her suitcase full of designer clothes and driven off without a backward glance? Maybe she'd cry a little. He was sure she regretted how things ended. Kara may be blind where her parents were concerned, but she wouldn't be deliberately cruel. She loved him, but she couldn't tell her family to back off. Who was he kidding, anyway? It's not like he'd done such a stellar job of that—paying his parents' bills. Some would call him an enabler. Wasn't Kara doing the same thing? She allowed her father to boss her around just as he allowed his father to use him for money.

Chuck tried telling himself it was different, but how different was it? He'd never done the math, had never wanted to. How much was he left with at the end of the month when all was said and done? He lived okay, but if he wasn't funneling half his paycheck to his parents every month, he could afford to take Kara somewhere besides Poplar Point. He couldn't afford two weeks in Paris, but he'd be able to do something better than this.

Good luck with that! Chuck couldn't even imagine the names his father would call him. If he told his sister he wouldn't fund her schooling, she'd never speak to him again. He would hate that; thinking of his parents and sister cutting him out of their lives sliced him to the quick.

Kara probably felt the same. He couldn't ask her to exclude her family from her life, even if they deserved it. He didn't know much about them—just that her father worked her to death, was too hard on her, and now sold her to the highest bidder.

Chuck shifted on the hard ground. He was getting too old for this. After his heart healed he needed to find a woman who was emotionally available and looking to start a family. Maybe his next vacation would be to Disneyland, and they could sleep on beds.

Rolling onto his side, he reached for his phone. Of course, no signal, but it would have been nice to know Kara made it back to the city. She would go back, wouldn't she? Janie could have convinced her to stay in Janie and Vince's cabin, but surely Vince would see how stupid that was.

Maybe Kara would stay and try to work it out.

But there was nothing to work out unless she wanted to go against her father. And he couldn't blame her if she didn't. Didn't he hide from Remington himself?

Chuck rested his head on his arm and stared across the water. There was a red light blinking in the distance. Focused on that, with the embers of the fire warming his face, he willed sleep to come.

❧

This was getting ridiculous, and Kara was starting to get scared. It was dark now and she put the time at past ten o'clock.

Of course she didn't have her cell on her. She'd left it in the kitchen when she ran out.

What the fuck was Chuck doing answering her phone anyway? He'd never done that before.

Stomping through the woods, Kara thought maybe she'd picked up the little trail she'd been on before she had to pee. She hoped she had because this was stupid. Being lost in the woods. And what would she do if she couldn't make it back? Stumble around all night?

For God's sake.

What was Chuck doing? Was he worried about her? He probably didn't care. No, he cared. He wanted her gone. He was probably pissed she hadn't left for the city so he could enjoy the rest of his vacation without her.

It was all so fucked up.

Her father was an asshole.

And her mother was a bitch.

She'd love to see their faces if she told them to leave her alone.

Kara stumbled on a broken branch, scraping her foot. She couldn't see clearly in the hazy dark, and her foot felt like it was bleeding.

Great.

Kara sucked in a breath. Could she tell her father to leave her alone? What had Chuck said to her when they were fighting? No one was making her marry Kent and move to Chicago.

Her father was making her.

Yet . . . she was 31 years old.

Who made her do anything anymore?

The laws made her wear a seatbelt and buy car insurance. The IRS made her pay taxes. Her condo association made her pay fees.

These were all entities bigger than her father. Okay, probably not the condo association, but Kara got the idea. Her father was only one old man.

Kara scratched her leg and kept moving.

Fuck, she felt dumb.

Where in the hell was she? No, not literally. She hoped she was walking in the direction of either the cabins or the resort office.

No, where was she in her thoughts?

Her father was just one old man. What would the repercussions be if she told her father she didn't want to marry Kent or move to Chicago?

Well, the worst thing he'd do is fire her from the firm, probably cut her off. Maybe write her out of his will, if he'd even included her in the goddamn thing. He'd always treated her second rate because she was a girl.

She'd been working for his approval all her life, which had gotten her jack shit.

So if her life sucked with her father in it, her life could only improve with her father out of it, right?

Didn't need a law degree to make that correct assumption.

Her mother might be sad for a bit, but she loved her daughters-in-law. They too, had been born and bred for the lives they were living. The only difference was, they acted like they enjoyed it.

She and Chuck could elope, run off to New England somewhere, stay at a bed and breakfast, eat pancakes with real maple syrup.

Unfortunately, Chuck wasn't speaking to her right now. Might never speak to her again.

No. He wasn't like that. If she explained, if she told him she decided to tell her father that she wasn't going to marry Kent, that she wasn't going to move to Chicago, he'd talk to her. Maybe he wouldn't take her back, but he'd let her explain.

Kara could tell Chuck her plans, and if he didn't take her back, she could go through with what her parents wanted. That way she wouldn't be left high and dry.

It was also a coward's way out.

She'd talk to her father first, tell him to go to hell, then she'd see if Chuck still wanted her.

If he didn't? What would she do if he didn't?

She wouldn't have a job, she'd have parents who despised her. Okay . . . she could live with that.

She didn't like her shitty job anyway. Kara had only gone

to law school because her father strong-armed her. She could go back to school. What classes would she take? Kara wasn't worried about money. She was good at squirreling it away, and she could live comfortably off her savings for a couple of years. She could take some business classes. Kara was interested in non-profit sector work. She could offer her services pro bono on the side. Maybe consult.

The ideas excited her. Without her father's collar around her neck, and her mother jerking the leash, Kara could be free, a mutt running through a park, unhindered, the world under her paws. Er, feet.

Chuck loved her.

He'd take her back when she could prove to him she was serious about making changes. The changes she'd need to make so they could be together.

Determined, Kara marched on.

She didn't know where she was, but she knew where she was going.

And didn't that sound like an eighties song?

❧

With a heavy heart, Chuck motored back to the resort a couple hours after sunrise. He needed a shower. Breakfast. He thought about the egg he threw at the door yesterday when Kara ran away from him.

Maybe not eggs.

His phone pinged with texts and phone calls he'd missed while he was gone as it caught the Wi-Fi signal from the cabins.

Kara, maybe.

His parents, definitely. There was always a need for more money. Disability didn't stretch far.

He left the phone in the pocket of his shorts, too tired of it all to check his messages.

Vince was pacing the dock when Chuck approached the cabins, and he stared as Chuck cut the engine and cruised through the calm, shallow water toward the dock. He threw the rope and Vince tied the boat to the dock.

Vince didn't say anything to him until Chuck's feet were planted firmly on land.

"Kara didn't come back last night."

"Of course she didn't come back," Chuck bit out. "She went back to the city. I told you to make sure she made it home okay."

Vince grabbed Chuck's arm. "No. She ran off after your fight and didn't come back. Her SUV is still here. Janie checked your guys' cabin—her things are still here."

Chuck's heart turned into a block of ice. He swallowed thickly and fought a sudden burn beneath his eyelids. "Did you call the cops?"

"Yeah. With that homeless man out there, we didn't take any chances, but . . ."

"But what?" Chuck called Kara's phone. She might be ignoring everyone, but she'd answer his call, even if he had to call every ten seconds all goddamn day. He would find her.

Chuck stomped up the porch stairs to his cabin. He'd join in the search as soon as he changed his clothes and brushed his teeth. There was no point in going out half-cocked. He'd talk to the cop, find out where—

Kara's ringtone jarred him from his thoughts.

Shit.

When Kara took off she hadn't taken her phone with her.

Fuck.

". . . But we didn't call them until just a couple hours ago," Vince finished, catching up with him.

Chuck glared. "A couple hours ago?"

"She's a grown woman, Chuck. If she needed space, we wanted to give her space. Besides, the cops never do anything right away."

"They might have with that psycho on the loose," Chuck exploded, disconnecting the call to Kara's phone and throwing his onto the kitchen table. "Where is everyone?"

"Janie's out with Casey, letting him sniff around, some of the others are in Poplar Point looking for Kara. If she got turned around, she may have made it to the highway and hitched into town."

Chuck snorted.

Kara would never hitch.

"We have to cover all the bases. The cops are at the convenience store. There's talk the DNR will cruise the shoreline. She might have fallen and . . ."

Drown. That's the word Vince didn't say. There was a chance in the dark Kara lost her way and accidentally fell into the lake.

"She wouldn't *do* that."

Vince followed him into the bedroom where Chuck stripped and changed into clean clothes. Tiredly, he washed his face in the bathroom with cold water, hoping the chill would clear his head.

"That's why they call stuff like that accidents, Chuck."

"She wouldn't do that," Chuck repeated in a whisper, staring at his blood-shot eyes in the mirror.

"Look, I know how bad this is. When I watched Janie fall on those rocks . . . she was lucky all she did was sprain her wrist and get scratched up."

"It's not the same," Chuck disagreed through clenched teeth. "Kara is fucking missing."

"Then let's go look for her. I was only here to wait for you to come back. I didn't know how long you would stay out there."

Chuck trotted down the gravel path that led from the cabins to the convenience store. They could have driven the mile, but he wouldn't have been able to sit in Vince's truck for even five seconds. He needed to move.

The officer who told them about the homeless man and the assault stood by his squad car, speaking into a mouthpiece clipped to his shoulder.

"Did you find her?" Chuck burst out, out of breath.

Vince came up behind him and placed a hand on his shoulder.

"No. We're going to bring in the search and rescue dogs from the city. A little boy wandered off last summer and the dogs took less than two hours to find him . . ."

A rustling from the trees beyond the store's parking lot jerked Chuck's eyes from the police officer.

He was already running toward her when Kara emerged from the tree line.

❧

Kara had never been so happy to see Chuck in all her life. The argument, her family, Kent and her engagement, they all faded away as she ran to him.

The rocks cut her feet and her skin burned from bug bites. She was tired, having stumbled like an idiot through the woods most of the night. And, oh my God, was she hungry and thirsty.

But even all that disappeared when she all but fell into Chuck's open arms, and he held her close.

"Kara," he moaned into her neck. "I was so fucking worried."

Kara soaked in his love and concern. "I'm okay. I was scared, but I was on some kind of little trail. I got turned around, I think, and I needed to rest, but I've never been so glad to see this store." She opened her eyes, and over Chuck's shoulder the police officer she recognized from the other day was talking to someone on a walkie-talkie clipped to his uniform. Vince, looking like he hadn't slept all night, was on his cell phone, punching buttons.

Had everyone been up all night looking for her? That made her cry and Chuck soothed her, running his hands up and down her back and murmuring, "It's okay, it's okay," into her ear.

Chuck pulled away so he could look into her eyes, his hands cradling the sides of her face. He pressed a kiss to her forehead. "She needs medical attention," he told the officer.

The officer nodded and spoke once more into his walkie-talkie. He requested an ambulance to the Poplar Point Resort convenience store. It was the second time this week it was needed there.

After giving Kara a kiss on the cheek, Vince trotted back to the cabin to wait for Janie.

Kara hadn't been sure about Vince and Janie, but Vince was a good man, and she hoped they would make it.

She and Chuck, on the other hand, she wasn't so sure about. She sat with him on a bench in front of the store. It wasn't open yet, and besides the officer's squad car, the parking lot was deserted. Chuck held her close with his arm around her shoulders, and her hand in is. His thumb ran comfortingly along her knuckles. He wasn't talking to her, and she didn't want to say anything to him. She wouldn't tell him the conclusion she'd come to until she spoke with her father. Chuck would never believe she had the guts to tell her father no.

She was reclaiming her life, and she could only hope that after her life was completely hers, Chuck would want to share it with her.

In the back of the ambulance, Chuck sat near her on a narrow bench barely big enough for his ass.

The emergency technician gave her a Gatorade to sip to treat her dehydration and cleaned the bottoms of her feet and the bites all over her body. Kara leaned back against a small pillow on the gurney and dozed, too tired to even let the sting of antiseptic keep her awake.

She didn't know how long she slept. When she blinked her eyes open, Chuck was sitting next to her, holding her hand, staring at her worriedly. "Sally said you're good to go," he said. "You need to schedule a check-up when you get back home."

Chuck's expression shuttered, and Kara turned her head away. For Chuck, nothing had changed. She was still engaged, she would be returning to the city alone to have tea with her mother and Kent's.

Kara would speak to her father. Then, and only then, would she approach Chuck and ask him to give her another chance.

Slowly, she sat up. Her muscles ached and her skin blazed from bug bites and sun exposure. In her worry, she hadn't noticed the bugs biting her, at least not to that extent, but apparently the mosquitoes and deerflies had decided to use her body for a tasty buffet. "What time is it?" she asked groggily.

"Almost dinner time. Kara, you've slept most of the day. You're lucky another emergency didn't happen or they would've had to kick you out." Chuck offered her a small, teasing smile. He hopped out of the back and assisted her onto the ground and into flip flops Kara guessed he'd asked someone to bring her from their cabin. Her feet hurt, and she leaned into him for support.

Kara blew a sigh of relief when Vince pulled his truck into the parking lot, its tires crunching the loose rock. There was no way she could have walked back to the cabin. "Thank God," she murmured into Chuck's shoulder.

"I didn't think you'd want to walk anymore today," Chuck said, opening the truck's door.

Kara was grateful to disappear inside. Now the store's parking lot was scattered with people staring at her and the ambulance.

Sandwiched between Vince and Chuck on the short ride to

the cabin, Kara relaxed, her head resting on Chuck's shoulder. She didn't care if he was tense. She didn't care if he was pissed at her. He still loved her. You couldn't turn something like that on and off. And despite his anger, he kept his arm wrapped around her and helped her from the cab of the truck.

"Kara!"

Kara smiled at Janie, at the relief and joy in her voice, and Casey's happy bark.

Janie ran across the grass and Kara leaned into her embrace.

Crystal and Nate both gave her a hug, Crystal laughing and crying. "We are so sorry we didn't see you! If we would have known you were out there—"

"Don't be silly," Kara objected. "How were you to know? You couldn't have known where to look."

"You look exhausted," Crystal said, hugging her again. "Get some rest." She gave Kara a quick kiss on the cheek.

"I plan on it." Kara let Chuck help her up the porch stairs, Casey following her into their cabin. "Where are the others?"

"They stayed in town to eat dinner. Kara, can I make you something to eat? You must be starving."

"No, I'm okay." She hobbled straight into their bedroom. At first Kara had been embarrassed the technician looked her over for ticks and other bugs, but she was happy now. She vaguely remembered the tech checking her, even her pubic area, though that must have been quick being she was bare down there, in case she needed to be tested for Lyme disease. Knowing she was bug-free made her feel better, and she quickly pulled off her soiled tank and grimy shorts and slid into bed. If Chuck didn't want to sleep with her, he could sleep in the other room.

Her eyes closed in fatigue, Chuck's voice, urging her to eat, sounded far away. She was afraid of what she'd see if she looked at him now.

It was better not to look.

Kara woke up at six the next morning. The sun was rising, casting the sky in a glorious orange hue. Birds were singing, and through the open window, Kara heard the crickets and the water making the fishing boat and pontoon bump against the dock.

Rubbing her eyes, Kara rolled onto her side. Chuck slept next to her, his face pinched, even in sleep. The whole thing was such a mess, but she would fix it.

Today.

She took a hot shower, the water stinging her bites. The bottoms of her feet were tender, and her legs were covered with little scratches. It felt good to wash her hair and shave her legs. Kara dressed in a pink sundress and made coffee. She popped some ibuprofen with her first cup then checked her phone, which was still on the kitchen table right where Chuck had left it. Her mother and father had both been texting her, her father about Chicago, her mother about the tea with Kent's mother.

The texts and voicemails didn't bother like they would have. She'd hardened her heart in preparation for what she knew she had to do. Not only for Chuck—but for herself.

The missed calls and texts from her friends made her smile, and tears filled her eyes.

Chuck had called her too.

She knew he still loved her.

It was time to prove she loved him back.

Kara made toast and nibbled as she went through her email. None of it mattered anymore. She skimmed her work emails, guessed what cases would be assigned to whom. She drafted her notice in her head. Remington St. John wouldn't accept a two-week notice. When she told him she was done, someone would clean out her desk and leave the box at reception. Knowing she'd never set foot inside her father's firm ever again lightened her spirit. She should have done this years ago.

"Good morning," Chuck said, walking into the kitchen, his hair in spikes, rubbing the sleep from his eyes.

Her eyes went straight to his morning boner, prominently showing through his boxer briefs.

Sleeping with him right now wouldn't be a good idea, even if Chuck gave her the best morning sex she'd ever had. If she played her cards right, she'd be able to have morning sex with him for the rest of her life.

"We need to talk."

His tone sent her heart plummeting.

Be strong.

Casually, she licked butter from her fingers. She wouldn't talk to Chuck until she spoke with her father. It wasn't too early to call him, but she needed to wait until he was alone in his office. He had an hour to himself every day from eight to nine when he would drink his coffee and go through his email.

She would call him then. Kara checked the time on her phone. She had half an hour to kill. "No."

Pushing her paper plate away, she stood. Without meeting his eyes, she left the cabin and quickly walked the fifty feet to Janie's cabin, hoping against hope her friend was awake.

Janie was in the kitchen pouring dog food for Casey, and she motioned for Kara to come in. Kara let herself into the cabin, and she sat at the table and allowed Janie to pour her a cup of coffee.

"You're lucky I had to pee," Janie teased, sitting next to her at the table.

They both knew Janie's penchant for sleeping in, especially now that Janie stayed up with Vince, doing deliciously naughty things.

"What happened yesterday? Vince said he saw you run off. You and Chuck had a fight?"

"Yeah." Kara took a sip of coffee. "My father called while I was in the shower and Chuck answered my phone. My father told him about Kent."

Janie shot her a look full of guilt.

"What?" Kara asked. "Whatever it is, it can't be as bad as my father telling Chuck I'm engaged."

Grabbing Kara 's hand, Janie sighed. "After you ran off, Chuck went to one of the islands to wait while you packed and went back to the city."

"And?" Kara prompted. That wasn't the news she expected to hear.

"And I told him about Chicago."

Kara shrugged. "That's nothing compared to what my father told him. It's okay, Janie."

"I stood up for you, I really did."

Kara checked her phone. Ten to eight. Close enough. "It's time I stood up for myself. Thank you for being my friend, Janie, but it's my job to fix this."

As she listened to her father's cell phone ring, Kara walked onto the dock and stared into the misty horizon.

&.

Chuck held his head in his hands as he sat at the kitchen table. The slamming door of the cabin beside theirs snagged his attention and through the storm door's screen, he watched Kara walk across the grass, her phone to her ear.

Probably calling dear old dad to tell him she would be home today, put the engagement announcement in the paper.

He couldn't let her marry someone else. He loved her; she was his. Chuck claimed her every time he made love to her. There would be no one for him but her.

He would talk to her one last time. He would try one last time.

❧

Kara felt like throwing up.

"Kara!" her father bellowed when he answered her call. "I had an enlightening conversation with Chuck yesterday."

She wanted to punch his face through the phone, his voice was so smug. If only he knew what he'd done actually caused her epiphany. Ashamed, Kara admitted she had come very close to doing what her father wanted. That time was gone.

"When will you finally return to the city? Your clients are not very happy with you, Kara, and your mother is beside herself. She wants to start designing your dress for the wedding."

"I'm not going to marry Kent, Daddy. I'm marrying Chuck."

If he'll still have me.

"Over my dead body." Remington's voice dropped to an icy whisper. "You will do as you're told and get your ass back to the city, marry Kent, and relocate to Chicago. I need you there. Your brothers are too busy to do what needs to be done."

Kara turned around when she heard footsteps on the wooden dock.

Chuck stood there, warily watching her. Dressed in black cotton shorts and a black and beige striped t-shirt, his brown eyes followed her every movement. He'd taken a shower; his hair was still wet.

There was a hopeful expression on his face, and it spurred her on.

"Daddy," Kara started, her eyes never leaving Chuck's face, "I've done what you've told me to do all my life. Which schools to go to, which jobs. How to dress, who to date, thinking maybe, maybe somehow I would earn your approval. But I never did. Not in the way my brothers have."

"Now you just wait—"

"N-no, Daddy," Kara interrupted her father for the first time in her life. "No. I *have* been waiting for you and mother to love me. You talking to Chuck yesterday made me see that you never will. I'll always just be someone to boss around. I want my life back. I'll work where I want, marry who I want, live where I want. I officially quit. Goodbye, Daddy." Kara disconnected the call and ignored it when it promptly played the ringtone assigned to her father.

"Chuck?" she asked tearfully.

"Did you mean it, Kara?"

Kara lifted her chin. "I meant it. Last night when I was lost, I wasn't just lost in the woods. I was lost in my heart, in my soul. Without you, I'll never know the way. Please give me another chance."

Tentatively, Chuck moved closer. "You want to get married, baby?"

She wanted him to hold her, to kiss her. But he'd been hurt terribly and she didn't blame him for not trusting her.

"If you still want me."

Chuck sighed. "I'd never want to be with anyone else."

Kara rushed into his arms, her phone clattering onto the dock. She pressed her lips to his, and she reveled in the feeling of his arms wrapped around her.

Her cell phone rang again and Kara reluctantly broke the kiss. She picked up the phone; it was her father calling. She was tired of him thinking she was at his beck and call, but isn't that what she'd been all these years? She'd done every little thing he'd asked, no commanded, she do, and nothing changed. It was time to take her own life back, it was more than time to unlock the handcuffs that bound her wrists.

Stepping to the end of the dock, and putting as much power into her swing as she possibly could, she threw her phone into the water. It broke the surface of the lake with a satisfying splash.

Chuck stared at her with wide-eyed disbelief.

"I told you, I'm done. My family will have to change if they want me back because now I belong to you." She searched Chuck's eyes, the dark brown that turned to coffee and cream when he was aroused. His eyes looked like that now. "Will you love me forever?"

"There's never been any doubt, Kara."

"Then, it's still early. Let's go back to bed."

❦

When Chuck followed her onto the dock, when he heard Kara talking to her father, he thought it was over. He thought she was telling him she'd be on the road and back to the city by lunchtime. What he'd heard her say filled him with joy—and with dread. She'd told her father to fuck off, just as he always hoped she would. But he hadn't told her about his family. He hadn't told her about the money, the albatross around his neck.

Mist rose from the water, and she stood there in the sunrise, her blonde hair shining, her green eyes full of hope and promise. How could he tell her the future might not be what she wanted it to be? She'd done her part, but now he had to do his.

"Yes, let's."

He took Kara's hand and together they walked toward their cabin. Janie, still dressed in her pajamas, stood on her porch, a cup of coffee in her hand. She rose the mug to them in toast, and his elation got the better of him. "We're getting married!" he called to her, but Kara tugged on his hand, urging him forward. There was no time for Janie to offer her congratulations.

In the bedroom, Chuck pulled his t-shirt over his head. He

stopped Kara from taking off her dress to give her a kiss. She wrapped her arms around his neck, pushing her body into his. "I'll try to make you happy, Kara," he promised, rubbing the ends of her hair between his fingers.

"I've never been so unhappy, so scared. The look in your eyes when you asked me about Kent. I swear to you, Chuck, I never slept him. Since we've been together, there's only been you."

"I believe you, sweetheart. I never thought you would. It was just something I said because I wanted to hurt you as much as I was hurting." Chuck unbuttoned his shorts and pulled them off with his briefs so he stood naked in front of her. "Take your clothes off."

He crawled into the bed and pulled the blankets over him. Chuck watched her tug her dress over her head and smooth her aqua panties over her hips. Kara undid her bra and let it fall to the floor. She was so beautiful naked: the graceful line of her neck, her breasts the perfect size, her flat stomach, her long, smooth legs. She was stunning, and she was his.

Kara joined him in bed and smiled. "Does this mean we're engaged? Did you ask me to marry you on the dock? Did I say yes?"

Chuck rolled onto his side and propped his head onto his hand. With his other hand, he ran his fingers over her stomach, along her hip, skimming her smooth skin. She widened her legs. The urge to tell her now hit him, but he fought it back. Instead, he slipped two fingers inside her, leaned over and kissed her, tasting the flavor of coffee in her mouth. "Will you marry me Kara, no matter what?" It was a stupid thing to say. Making her promise something like that wouldn't help him, not if she hated what he had to tell her.

"Yes," she breathed against his mouth.

Love swamped him and he rolled on top of her, positioned himself between her legs and slowly filled her. He didn't want this to be fast; he wanted to go slowly, tenderly, and he slid his hands under her pillow and kissed her as he started to move.

Being inside her when he thought he'd lost her made his desire for her spike, and he came after only a few deep thrusts. Gasping for breath, he buried his head against the warm curve of her neck, kissing her shoulder, nibbling her collarbone and then side of one breast. He took her nipple between his lips.

Kara arched her back.

Chuck knew she didn't come, so he pulled out of her and rolled to her side, finding her clit with his fingers. He leaned over to kiss her again, and she spread her legs, moving her hips. He took her other nipple into his mouth and bit the sensitive skin between his teeth. She mewed, running her fingers through his hair.

He knew the moment she was about to come, and he increased the tempo and pressure making Kara come with a whimper, crushing the side of her face into her pillow, her eyes squeezed shut.

He tucked her into his side, exhausted from spending the night on the rocks, from being stressed out while she was missing, from being heartsick he'd lost her forever. Kara wiggled beside him, and with his cheek pressed against her hair, he worried.

Now it was his turn to do the hard part.

Kara's growling stomach woke him, and he looked at his watch. It was almost noon. Kara was awake next to him, staring at the ceiling.

"Regrets?" he asked.

"About us making love?"

Chuck enjoyed the sparkle in her eyes, the tension erased from her face. She wasn't reaching for her phone, a pinched look marring her beautiful features. Kara was light and free. He'd always wanted to see her this way. "No. Telling your father off."

Rubbing her eyes, Kara looked back up the ceiling. The afternoon light crept through the closed blinds, making the white walls of the cabin glimmer.

"No. No." She licked her lips and reached out to touch his arm. "I should have told him a long time ago, I just didn't have anything at stake. Until I almost lost you. What you said to me made sense. He wasn't making me do anything. I was following along."

"I'll always take care of you, Kara, you don't have to worry about that."

Kara huffed out a little laugh. "I don't need you to take care of me. I just want to share my life with you."

"Well," Chuck said, leaning over to kiss her, "how about I take care of you a little bit and make you some breakfast. You need to eat, and I'll make fresh coffee."

Chuck fried bacon and breakfast potatoes and started another pot of coffee. He scrambled eggs and had everything set out on the small kitchen table when Kara walked in. "Did you fall asleep again?"

"I dozed," she admitted. "I feel . . . weird, not having my phone."

Chuck pulled out a chair for her and she sat. Putting a plate full of food in front of her, he said, "Eat." He sat next to her with his own plate and cup of coffee. "But a good weird?"

Kara sampled her eggs and picked up a piece of bacon. "Yeah . . ." she mused, crunching. "Yeah."

Chuck loved her smile. He hoped what he told her wouldn't make it disappear. He cleared his throat. "Kara, I accused you of not being honest, but I'm to blame for that as well. There are things I haven't told you about my family, things that you have a right to know if we get married."

Chuck looked down at his plate . . .

❧

. . . and Kara's stomach dropped. Hadn't they been through enough? She bit her lip. "It can't be any worse than my father arranging a man for me to marry, choosing my career path, accounting for every second of my every day. It can't be any worse than what he did to you, and I let it happen. You'll never know how sorry I am I let it get to that point." She took his hand and brought it to her lips.

"Kara, we've both been guilty of letting our parents get the best of us. You know my parents have never been financially secure. They loved us, but once you start sinking . . . my father never tried to keep his head above water and, he's been using me to make ends meet since I graduated from college. I pay their mortgage, pay to have their cars fixed, pay for repairs to their house. Now my sister wants me to pay her tuition so that she can go to school."

Kara winced. She didn't know how much Chuck made. It hadn't made a difference to her. It still didn't; she could pay her own way.

"What do you want to do?" she asked. This was his choice. It was his family.

His eyes pleaded with her. "I can't leave them hanging."

"No, and I wouldn't ask you to. I can sell my condo, we can live in your townhouse, or we can buy something else. We won't be hurting for money," Kara teased, her tongue in her cheek.

"I don't want you to be responsible for my parents."

Kara laughed. "Really? I would rather stare down your parents' mortgage payment than see my father ever again. The more I think about it, the more I think I'm getting the better end of the deal."

If money was all that was worrying Chuck, they would be all right. It seemed silly, now, they almost let their families tear them apart.

"We're going to make it, aren't we?"

Kara stood and straddled Chuck's lap. She wrapped her arms around his shoulders and rested her forehead against his. "We'll make it."

Through the open windows shouting floated to them, carried on the summer breeze blowing through the poplar trees.

Kara opened her mouth to speak, but Chuck interrupted her.

"We'll never end up like that. I promise."

Alycia moved into Kara's line of vision through the screen door. She stood on the beach, hunched over, her shoulders shaking.

Kara knew nothing in life was a guarantee. Both hers and Chuck's families could make more problems for them than they could ever anticipate.

All they could do was promise each other they'd do their very best.

And staring into Chuck's glowing eyes, Kara knew that was a promise worth keeping.

ALYCIA AND BRYCE

Four months ago . . .

Music thumped, an electro dance clubhouse mix, strains of Madonna's "Erotica" woven into the beat. The room was tinged in a light rose, misting a pink-lemonade glow over the crowd and the women on the mini-stages that dotted the expanse of the floor. Bryce Fischer followed his friends, weaving around occupied high-top tables to one with a white 'reserved' placard sitting in the middle near a burning candle.

The table was located directly in front of a stage, a stripper just finishing her dance, and Bryce caught a glimpse of blonde hair, white milky skin, and ass cheeks dusted in what looked like glitter, just before she disappeared behind a curtain.

A cocktail waitress holding a small, round black tray approached as Bryce and his friends each claimed a seat. The slim woman was elegantly dressed, her brown hair pulled into an sophisticated French twist, her blue eyes done perfectly in grey eyeshadow and black eyeliner. Blood red lipstick coated her lips, and a diamond necklace sparkled at her throat. Her black dress was long, and strapless, showing off her ample cleavage. A crystal belt accentuated her tiny waist, and a slit ran from not quite her hip down to the floor. Her platform heels gave her at least an extra four inches of height.

Bryce was surprised his friend had chosen such a classy place. When Rick suggested a strip club, Bryce imagined some seedy joint downtown with strippers getting high in the back, shooting up between dances. Here there wasn't any hooting or hollering, there weren't any drunk men trying to pull the strippers down from their stages to give them kisses or feel them up. The men wore suits or dress shirts, their ties undone, enjoying the end of the workweek. There were even a few women in the audience, and they were dressed much like the cocktail waitress, for a night on the town.

"I'll have a G and T," Rick told the waitress to get them started.

Bryce's blood was already humming from the bars they'd visited and he wanted to keep the feeling going. He wanted to relax, have fun. "Scotch, neat, and make it a double," he said, and the waitress nodded and smiled, writing his order down in a large loopy scrawl. He drummed his fingers on the table and looked around to the other stages in the club while the rest of his friends gave their drink orders to the waitress. One stripper was slowly pulling off white gloves as she danced, her silver dress sparkling as she flirted with the pole —and the audience. Another stripper across the club was already down to her bra and panties and she slithered on the stage floor in some kind of dance routine.

The music changed to something Bryce didn't recognize and a woman stepped onto the stage in front of their table. His friends cat-called to her and the immaturity of it sounded out of place, but a smile played on her lips.

She was one of the most beautiful women Bryce had ever seen. Her hair was the color of a freshly minted copper penny, strands of gold weaving throughout her tresses. He couldn't see the color of her eyes from where he sat, but her luscious lips sparkled and the stripper's peaches and cream complexion shimmered with a gold dusting across her décolletage. A rust colored dress accentuated her hourglass figure.

The stripper started moving, swinging her hips in time with the music.

Returning with their drinks, the cocktail waitress placed them on the table. She leaned into Bryce and whispered in his ear. "Mandi will treat you well."

Her name was Mandi. It could have been a stage name, but Bryce thought it fit her. She didn't seem to be the stripper type, but she was too gorgeous to be sitting behind a desk typing and filing all day. Maybe she was trying to break into modeling, and this was a way to earn a paycheck until she made the big-time.

He took a sip of his Scotch and enjoyed the alcohol fizzing in his blood, the pounding of the music in his head. Bryce watched Mandi, and his heart stuttered when her eyes met his.

Rick nudged him and yelled over the music, "She likes you!"

The idea pleased him. He'd been with the same woman so long, he often wondered if he'd "lost it." But when Mandi winked at him as she played with the strap of her dress, teasing them, teasing *him*, his back straightened with pride. Bryce worked out and ran several miles a week; he didn't want to become complacent. Alycia had slowly been putting on pounds all these years. Not that she was getting fat . . .

Mandi saucily knelt and undid the small buckles of her silver stilettos. She pranced around in a small circle before smiling at Bryce and kicking a stiletto off her foot toward him.

He watched her kick off the other, and it landed neatly next to the first. She must have done that a million times, and an inexplicable feeling of jealousy swept through him. He didn't want her kicking off her shoes for other men. He didn't want her dancing for other men, period.

Bryce tried to taper down the feelings that swirled in his Scotch-addled brain. He didn't know this woman; for all he knew her husband was sitting in the audience watching the show. She could have children waiting at home for her.

And he certainly wasn't the jealous type. Men looked at Alycia from time to time. In high school she'd been popular, a cheerleader, and as the smallest, she was always being thrown into the air and caught by the male members of the squad. There had been boys, and as they grew older, men, who asked her out, who looked her up and down, never hiding the admiration in their eyes. It hadn't made him jealous; it made him proud. Proud he was the one she chose to be with.

Mandi shimmied out of her dress and let it pool on the floor. Underneath, she wore a black corset and matching panties. She turned around and wiggled her ass at them; the corset was tied with a black satin ribbon and the bow sat at the small of her back. Bryce wondered if she had a tramp stamp.

A pair of pink lips decorated one ass cheek of her panties.

Bryce wanted to put his lips there.

He chugged his Scotch and tried like hell to get that visual out of his mind.

The waitress placed another glass in front of him before he

could even look around for her, and he took out his wallet and tipped her a twenty for such attentive service.

She gave him a naughty smile and licked her lips. "Thank you."

Mandi sashayed around the stage swinging on the pole and hanging upside down, her hair swishing back and forth along the shiny black floor.

His friends started to get antsy, but they refrained from yelling at her, thank God. If they wanted to act like that, they should have chosen a less classy place to party.

Bryce was glad Rick decided on The Candied Apple. Mandi was a dream in her corset, her ass curved perfectly beneath her black silk and lace panties, and her legs, even without her stilettos, seemed to be miles long.

Mandi pranced on her tiptoes, playfully seduced the pole. She turned and pulled the ribbon at the small of her back to loosen the corset. It slid over her hips and down to the floor. Covering her breasts with her arms, she looked over her shoulder, winking at their table. Her hair fell down her back in thick copper and blonde waves.

Lacing her fingers in her hair, she twirled around, displaying her magnificent breasts dusted with a gold powder that sparkled in the spotlight trained on her.

They watched her dance for a few more minutes, and after the music stopped, Mandi blew them a kiss before picking up her discarded clothing and disappearing behind the heavy black velvet curtain.

"She was fucking hot!" Rick exclaimed, downing his gin and tonic.

Bryce silently agreed, running his finger between the collar of his shirt and his neck.

After a brief break, another stripper took Mandi's place, but in Bryce's opinion, she wasn't nearly as pretty. She had a hot body too, well, she would or she wouldn't have been a stripper, but her black hair was short and spiky and her eyes and lips were too small for her face.

Bryce's friends didn't seem to mind, enraptured by the woman slowly rolling fishnet stockings down her legs.

Their waitress brought them new drinks and offered them cigars. Bryce took one and brought it to his nose. It was a prime brand and he appreciated the quality, even if he wouldn't smoke it.

Bryce's vision blurred and his stomach churned with the steak dinner they'd eaten at the gentlemen's club Rick belonged to. The steak had been prime too, his plate putting him out fifty bucks.

Rick loved living the high life; Bryce was just along for the ride.

Another girl took the place of the last and Bryce started to get bored. He looked around the club, hoping to catch Mandi on another stage, but he didn't see her.

It was near closing when Rick stretched, his eyes hooded by alcohol and exhaustion. "This has been fun, boys, but Melissa will kick my ass if I'm out any later. See you all at the church. We start dressing at nine sharp. Pictures at eleven."

Bryce was amazed Rick was able to hold all those details in his booze-soaked brain.

Sliding from his tall stool, he too, was ready to leave and he stumbled over Mandi's silver stilettos. "I better return these," he muttered, picking them up. He lost his balance and clumsily leaned against his chair, and it screeched across the floor as it broke his fall.

"Give them to our waitress and let's go," Rick said, pulling on his arm.

"Nuh-uh." Bryce shook his head and tightened his grip on the shoes. He could see Mandi one more time. Through all the alcohol, his brain declared that a perfect idea.

"Your call," Rick allowed, slapping him on the back. "See you in the morning."

Bryce didn't wait for his friends to leave before searching the walls, looking for a way to get backstage. Even drunk, Bryce didn't think it would be easy to see Mandi. This place was a class act, and he was sure the girls were kept safe from creeps who thought they could get a little extra for the exorbitant cover charge.

He spotted a darkened hallway and lurched toward it, the club slowly emptying as the lights brightened, encouraging the last of the club's patrons to leave. He passed other girls still scantily clad, or dressed in robes. One was fully dressed in jeans, t-shirt, and leather jacket with a duffle bag hanging from her shoulder.

"Help you?" she clipped, then blew a bright pink bubble.

"I'm looking for Mandi. She kicked her shoes off the stage."

The woman raised an eyebrow but jerked a thumb. "Back that way. The door is cracked open."

"Thanks," Bryce mumbled, turning around and going back the other way.

He found the black door that was slightly ajar and pushed it open.

Mandi was sitting at a vanity taking off her makeup. Her copper hair was pinned on the top of her head, and she wore a cream satin robe. Her eyes met his, startled, and nervously she ran the tip of her tongue over her lip.

Bryce thought she looked incredible, her light brown eyes sparkling.

"Can I help you?" Mandi clutched the lapels of her robe together so they wouldn't gape.

Bryce stepped inside the changing room, the shoes dangling from his fingers. "You left them by our table."

Relief flooded her features. "Oh! Thank you, but the staff would have brought them back. They aren't mine. They belong to costumes." Mandi tilted her head toward the racks of colorful dresses and several cubbies for shoes in the corner of the room.

Mandi took the stilettos from him and placed them in an empty shoe cubby. "Do you want to sit and have a drink?" she asked, her apprehension at his intrusion disappearing.

Bryce took a seat on a pale blue leather couch.

She grabbed a bottle of, he wasn't sure, he couldn't read the label from where he was sitting, but he took the crystal-cut lowball glass she handed him and took a tentative sip.

Mandi knocked hers back then poured another. She sat near him on the sofa, tucking one leg under her ass.

Before, Bryce thought she was pretty, but this close she was fucking gorgeous. Her eyes were a light amber, almost gold. Freckles dotted her nose, and her lips were a light soft pink.

A tendril of hair slithered down her neck and Bryce reached out to touch it.

Mandi didn't pull away, instead leaning in and tilting her head. "What brings you back

here . . .?"

"Bryce, Bryce Fischer," he filled in, running a finger down the soft skin of her neck. Her skin still sparkled with the gold glitter she wore onstage. "Why do you dance here?"

Booming music shook Mandi's changing room, and she laughed when he jumped. "The cleaning crew started cleaning. They blast music every night." Mandi bit her lip. "I have to pay the bills like everyone else. I'm taking college classes during the day. I know, so cliché." She blushed and looked down into her drink.

"No," Bryce murmured, impressed, lifting her chin with a finger so she would look at him. "I think that's great."

"I should get dressed and go."

Bryce's heart sped up. He didn't want to leave yet. It was strangely comforting to be sitting in Mandi's dressing room, the music filtering through the walls. Bryce could just make out Bruce Springsteen. "No, wait. Tell me what you're going to school for."

Mandi smiled at him and leaned against the back of the couch clasping the glass to her chest. "You know, no one has ever asked me that before. The girls here don't care, and well . . ." Her face fell for a moment, then brightened. "I'm going for graphic design. I love playing around with pictures."

Bryce was drawn into the pride and obvious pleasure in her voice. He set his glass on the black tiled floor and then took her hand. "That's incredible. You should be proud of yourself."

"I am," she whispered. "I want to do better for . . ." She stopped and averted her eyes. Then she put a hand to his cheek. "I just want to do better."

Bryce understood what it was to want to do better, want more, and in that second he wanted Mandi more than he had ever wanted anything in his life. He didn't just want her body, but that was true, his cock straining the fly of his tan dress pants. No, he wanted her body, but he also wanted her spirit. He wanted to capture the pleasure and pride in her eyes. He hadn't felt like that in such a long time. He'd been going through life in a haze, and Mandi's bright eyes were a beacon in the fog.

Swept up by her verve, he cupped her jaw in his hand, and captured her mouth with his, even though alarms that sounded louder than the city's tornado warnings shrilled in his head.

Mandi surprised him by returning the kiss, and The Boss's "Secret Garden" permeated the walls, weaving love and lust around the room.

Bryce's hand trailed down the elegant line of her shoulder and into her robe; his fingertips skimmed her breast, his thumb grazing her nipple.

Mandi gasped and tore her lips away. "Bryce," Mandi started, but hearing his name on her lips sparked a passion

Bryce had never felt before, and he ravaged her mouth, pulling the robe from her shoulder.

She dropped her empty glass onto the floor, the thud lost in the music still pounding in the main room of the club. Mandi wrapped her arms around his neck, giving in to Bryce's kisses.

His tongue slipped inside her mouth, and he lay her back against the couch cushions.

"Bryce, I don't do this. Just because I take my clothes off for money doesn't mean I'm a hooker. I'm not a prostitute."

"I'm not using you," Bryce said, pulling his tie loose and unbuttoning his shirt.

It was imperative he take his clothes off so they were skin to skin. He wanted to touch all of her at once. "I'm loving you."

He stood to take his pants off and unbuckled his belt. Mandi lay on the couch, her robe open, her skin glittering gold. She was a goddess, and she was his.

Naked, Bryce kneeled on the couch, gently he lifted one of her legs, and guided it to the sofa's back. Mandi's other foot touched the floor. He was grateful Mandi was naked under her robe and her trimmed coppery pubic hair intimately framed the apex of her legs.

Bryce chuckled—the carpet matched the curtains.

Overcome with the urge to taste her, Bryce slid his hands under her ass and lifted her hips. He was scrunched at the foot of the couch, but he didn't mind. He wasn't thinking about anything but sampling her.

He didn't care this was wrong. He didn't care his wife was at home sleeping in their bed. He didn't care that he would probably hurt her beyond repair. All he could think about was the newness of Mandi's body, the way she made him feel. The way his cock surged at the thought of shoving it inside her. This wasn't the same old kind of sex.

Mandi would only be the second person he'd ever slept with, and he wanted her so badly he could taste it.

So he did, and he lowered his mouth to her, gently licking and suckling as if she were a ripe peach, her juice coating his chin.

She murmured encouragement and thrust her fingers in his hair, pushing his face forcefully between her legs. Her clit bulged under the tip of his tongue, and he teased her, playing with the nub. He ran his tongue from the crack of her ass to her clit and back again, over and over. He pressed two fingers inside her just in time to feel her come.

Bryce suckled her, torturing her, until she pulled away. "Turn over," he commanded, wiping his mouth with the back of his hand.

Mandi scrambled to flip over, her ass high in the air, her arms braced on the armrest of the couch.

Bryce grabbed her hips, his dick rock solid. He hadn't had sex this good in years. Mandi was different, exciting. And she wanted him.

He watched as his shaft moved in and out of her, slamming into her again and again. He came, the pleasure crashing into him from the top of his head all the way down to the tips of his toes.

That he was buzzed helped. The alcohol allowed the guilt to be buried by the bliss of screwing someone new. Mandi was a bright shiny copper penny; she was lucky, and he found her, heads up right under his nose.

Mandi still wore her robe, the creamy satin framing her perfect ass. She curled on her side and he spooned her, the couch barely wide enough for them both.

He tucked his arm under her head and wrapped his other arm around her stomach.

The music was still blasting and Bryce recognized Carrie Underwood's "Before He Cheats."

Too late, Bryce thought groggily before sleep pulled him under. *I already did.*

§⁰

Present day . . . Poplar Point

Alycia needed something good to happen to her. Janie found a man, Kara got engaged. It was Alycia's turn, though she couldn't see what good exactly could happen to her in Poplar Point on vacation with her cheating-ass husband. She sat at the end of the dock seeking peace and solace.

It was difficult to come by.

Even with the hour-long Skype therapy session she just completed.

What it boiled down to, what it always came down to, was could she forgive Bryce and move on?

"Hey, you."

Alycia looked over her shoulder when Bailey Scott greeted her.

Bailey was a little thing, five foot nothing, slender with huge blue eyes and long, black wavy hair. Thin, she was all elbows and knees, and reminded Alycia of a gamine Audrey Hepburn. Alycia felt like a whale beside her, though in comparison, she wasn't that much heavier and not any taller. Bryce insinuated she'd put on weight over the years. It wasn't so much that she'd put on weight, but that she didn't want to show him she *hadn't*. Of course, she was paying for that now.

Hadn't her mother always said if he wasn't getting it at home, he'd go somewhere else?

"Hey. I thought you were hanging out with Crystal."

Bailey shrugged. "Crystal and Nate went into town. What are you doing?"

Alycia held up her iPad. "I just finished a Skype chat with my therapist."

"Ah."

"What's that?"

"I know how that goes, but I have to find a new one. Mine keeps telling me things happen for a reason. If that's really true, what's my reason?" Bailey sank to the wood. Her denim capris and white blouse made her look crisp and cool in the oppressing heat.

Alycia didn't want to admit her therapist uttered the same bullshit time after time. If things really did happen for a reason, if it was fate, or destiny, or some such nonsense, what was *her* reason. What was Bryce's reason?

Oh, she knew Bryce's "reason." He'd been drunk. But you couldn't convince Alycia that under the alcohol Bryce hadn't known what he was doing.

Alycia's therapist continually told her to look inside herself. All she saw when she did that was a mass of confusion, hurt, and betrayal bound together like a ball of rubber bands.

"Mine does the same," she tried to joke. "I think that's their Plan B when they don't have anything else to say."

Bailey laughed.

Alycia was glad she could make Bailey smile; she'd smiled so little herself, lately.

"I've been seeing mine for so long, it's probably truer than you know. Maybe a new therapist could offer some different insights."

"Yeah," Alycia agreed. She hadn't been seeing her therapist long enough to bore the poor woman, and she was trying to convince Bryce to go with her. That would certainly spice up her already tense and tearful sessions.

Bailey sobered. "But your situation is pretty black and white, isn't it? Either move on or *move on*."

Alycia knew what Bailey was saying. It was the same

thing she told herself. It would be so much easier if Bryce left her.

But he didn't seem inclined to do that.

Alycia didn't know if she was grateful for that or not. She closed her iPad's case. "Come on, let's go swimming. We don't have many days left here. Might as well enjoy it."

Looking around at the cabins, lake, and beach, she tried to appreciate the nice day. She wasn't sure what would happen once she and Bryce were back in the city.

She wasn't too eager to find out, either.

Bryce and Cam paddled the canoe along the shore. Loons and mallard ducks bobbed in the water, soaking up the heat.

Cam wasn't saying much to him, but that was fine by Bryce. He knew he was a laughingstock among his friends. He'd screwed a stripper at a bachelor party. How clichéd could he get? It made him an asshole, and he knew he deserved it. Vince barely spoke to him, well to be fair, Vince didn't speak to anyone since he started banging Janie, but Chuck couldn't hide the disgust in his eyes whenever Bryce tried to talk to him. His work buddies weren't as bad. They'd seen Mandi and weren't as close with Alycia as his school friends were.

Chuck was right—probably hadn't been the brightest idea to go along on their annual summer vacation. But he had a lot to think about too, and selfishly, it helped to be around people who had problems just as bad, or worse, than his own.

Kara's having gone missing had shaken him, and when he was in Poplar Point looking for her with the others, he'd slipped into the men's restroom at the diner and given Mandi a call, worried about her.

"How are you holding up?" Cam asked.

The question made Bryce feel guilty. It should have been

his question to Cam, but he decided to answer truthfully. Maybe it would get him out of the doghouse with his friends. "I've been better. I honestly don't know what I'm going to do."

"What do you want to do?"

Bryce's mouth opened in surprise, then snapped shut. He adjusted his sunglasses that were slipping down his nose and wiped sweat from his forehead before it dripped into his eyes.

The sun beat down on them and there was a hint of a breeze, but it didn't cut through the heat. The rocky shore was beautiful, pine trees and poplars crowding the ground.

A huge bird, perhaps a falcon, made huge swooping glides in the sky.

He considered Cam's question. What did he want to do? Stay with Alycia, try to work it out? Take a chance with Mandi?

Making decisions had never been his strong suit, which was probably why he got along so well with Alycia. With her, there wasn't anything to think about. She took care of it all.

"I don't know," Bryce said, shoving his paddle into the water, propelling them forward. "What would you do?"

Cam laughed. "You're asking me, when you know the bullshit I've been putting up with? If I was in your shoes, I would cut and run so fast. Sometimes I just don't understand why it matters."

Bryce heard that. He was damn lucky he and Alycia didn't have children. People who had kids got divorced all the time, but he was already a creep. Fucking a stripper while his little kids were sleeping at home would have taken it to a whole new level.

"You don't want kids?" Bryce asked.

Cam chuckled, though it was bitter and full of disillusionment. "You must not. You and Alycia have been together long enough you could have a baseball team by now."

It wasn't something Bryce considered. He had a good job

—not as good as something he could have gone to school for, like Chuck, but he made okay money. In the beginning, Alycia needed to work to help pay for household bills and rent for their apartment. She didn't need to work now, but she liked her job and there was no reason for her to stay home. Surprisingly, they never talked about kids, happy to be with each other until recently. "I guess not."

Sitting on the bench ahead of him, Cam shook his head but didn't look Bryce's way, instead speaking to the bow of the canoe. "Don't you two talk? No wonder you don't have any kids. You have to fuck your wife to knock her up."

"You try being with the same woman for twenty years," Bryce grumbled.

Cam snorted. "That's what you sign up for when you get married, dickhead."

Bryce knew he signed his life away scrawling on that dotted line—he just hadn't read the fine print.

Content for the first time in days, Alycia lay in the sun on the soft sand of the beach, Janie near her, Casey sleeping on her other side.

She hadn't seen Kara since Chuck announced they were engaged, but that was okay. She hadn't seen Janie much either, and it was a treat to lay with her and sunbathe. Bailey had declined swimming and took a walk alone. She spent a lot of time by herself, but that wasn't Alycia's business. She wanted to support her friend, but in all reality, she didn't know what to say.

"How's your wrist?" Alycia asked, sitting up to gulp some water. She loved the feeling of the sun baking her skin as if she had to store up the sunshine for the winter months.

"Not bad. I can't take the splint off yet, but the throbbing stopped."

"That must have been scary." She couldn't imagine having an accident and falling into the lake. With her luck, she'd drown, and nobody would care.

When there was talk of searching for Kara's body after she went missing, Alycia freaked out. Bad things came in threes.

"Not as scary as how pissed Vince was. You should have seen him at the clinic." Amusement colored Janie's voice.

Alycia was familiar with the tone. It was the tone of a woman who was loved, and she was secure in the knowledge that she was.

She'd felt like that once.

"He loves you very much." Alycia wasn't jealous; Janie deserved some happiness.

Janie giggled. "Yeah."

Cam and Bryce came into view, paddling from around the dock. They jumped out of the canoe into the waist-high water and pulled it onto the beach.

Alycia stared at her husband. Her life had been so wrapped up in his—from when they were little kids—that continuing on without him seemed unfathomable.

His skin was finally beginning to tan, and the sunburn on his cheeks made his icy blue eyes pop.

Bryce hadn't gone through an awkward puberty phase, but he'd stuck by her when she'd gone through hers.

He flicked her a glance before walking over the sand toward their cabin. Bryce seemed to be in a mood, and Alycia wondered what Cam told him. As far as Alycia knew, Cam idolized Bailey, so Cam probably told him what a dumbass he was. Alycia had suspicions that Bryce's friends weren't too sympathetic. Not that she wanted them to be hard on him, but there was a sense of satisfaction she couldn't deny.

Alycia stood and followed her husband over the grass and into their cabin. Shaded from the sun, the cabin's interior was significantly cooler than outside. The lower temperature was a pleasant break.

"Bryce, did you have fun with Cam?"

Bryce took a bottle of water from their refrigerator and downed it in several long gulps before answering her. "Yeah, it was okay."

His swim trunks were dripping on the kitchen floor.

"Do you want to talk?" Alycia asked. She wanted to share what her therapist told her and wanted to try to convince him, again, to go with her.

"No!" Bryce threw the empty bottle against the kitchen counter where it bounced like a ping pong ball until it landed on the floor. "All we do is fucking talk. It doesn't get us anywhere."

"Then what do you want to do?" Alycia asked mystified. Talking was all they had left.

"I want to fuck my wife. Is that too much to ask, Alycia? Huh? Apparently, it is because we haven't had sex in months. Months! What the fuck is wrong with me that you won't touch me?"

Alycia's cheeks heated with rage. "You're putting this on me?" she shrieked.

She knew their friends on the beach could hear them, but what else was new? They'd been airing out their dirty laundry this whole trip. They didn't have any secrets. "I'm not the one—"

Bryce bore down on her, fire flashing in his eyes.

She took a step back, but that seemed to spur him on.

"Don't even say it. You've been throwing it in my face for weeks. You know what Alycia?" he asked, pulling her into his arms, grasping thick handfuls of her hair in his fists, jerking her head back to make her look at him. "You know fucking what? I didn't have to tell you." His face was millimeters from hers, his breath fluttering over her cheeks. "I didn't even have to tell you." He grabbed Alycia's hand and pushed it against his hardened cock.

Alycia forgot how big he was. How long had it been since

they'd had sex? Staring into Bryce's face, her mind tripped along the months, realizing Bryce had been way off with his estimate. It hadn't been months. It'd been years.

Bryce crushed his mouth onto hers; Alycia didn't bother to struggle. In fact, heat pooled in her belly and her nipples tingled beneath her swimsuit.

She ran her hand up and down his length and he moaned.

Bryce took control in a way he never had. Was this how he'd been with his stripper?

Alycia tried to pull away in disgust at the thought, but Bryce didn't let her, instead tightening his grip and shoving his tongue into her mouth.

She was in equal parts turned on and repulsed. Alycia tried to pull away again, but Bryce wrapped his hand around her upper arm and dragged her into the bedroom. His bedroom. They'd been sleeping in separate beds since the day he told her he cheated. That morning he'd confessed what he'd done when she found him looking like something the cat puked up, and he'd had to drag his ass off the couch to shower and dress for bridal party pictures. Humiliated, she'd skipped that wedding, and they hadn't shared the same bed since.

Now Bryce led her to the bed he'd been sleeping in, the scent of sweat and heat permeating the air.

He'd never been rough with her, in fact, she was used to calling the shots in the bedroom. But now he yanked her swimsuit straps down over her shoulders and her breasts sprang free of the spandex and built-in bra.

Alycia wanted to move, or run, or at the very least, swear at him, but she was rooted to the spot and only stood when Bryce grabbed her breasts and kneaded them painfully, squeezing her nipples.

Aroused by the pain, her muscles clenched in desire. She tipped her head back, asking for more.

Bryce shoved her onto the bed and pulled her one piece suit from her body.

She lay there, naked, feeling decidedly vulnerable. They'd never had sex in the daylight before. She'd always been so prim and proper, lights out, under the covers. She made him do her that way.

He'd always done whatever she said.

Alycia watched him peel his wet swim trunks from his legs, and they landed with a wet splat on the hardwood floor.

Bryce crawled on top of her, and Alycia shivered. His skin was cold and wet from the lake.

Bruising her lips as he kissed her, he pushed his tongue into her mouth, and he rammed his fingers into her.

Alycia cried out. She was tight. She was dripping wet, but she was tight, and Bryce's hands were big.

"Be quiet," Bryce growled as he continued his assault with his fingers. Abruptly, he stopped, completely covered her, and crammed his cock inside her.

Alycia moaned and brought her legs up, hoping it would open her. He was huge, and it had been so long. It helped for a few moments, but he increased his tempo, his hip bones slamming into the insides of her thighs.

She tried to move her head to say something, anything, but Bryce was beyond speaking, and he held her head tightly with his hands fisted in her hair, his mouth on hers, suffocating her.

Finally, he came, pumping fast and furiously.

He pulled out, and thinking he was done, she tried to roll away.

"I don't think so," Bryce murmured, and he lowered his mouth to one of her breasts and took a nipple between his teeth. He was half on her, half on the bed, and he thrust his fingers inside her pussy and found her clit with his thumb. "Come for me," he demanded, rubbing with more pressure than was necessary.

But it felt good. It had been so long since she'd been touched by someone other than herself that even the harsh way Bryce handled her was a release. She came against his hand, her sensitive skin pressed into his palm.

He captured her mouth once more crushing her lips, then pulled away to stare into her eyes. "If I want it, I'll take it."

Alycia lay on the bed as Bryce went into the bathroom and started the shower.

Her lips stung with his kisses, her breasts ached, and her pussy throbbed.

That had been some of the best sex of her life.

Holy shit.

❦

Bryce fumed in the shower, his anger mixing with the steam of the hot water.

He was tired of talking.

They'd been talking for four months, and they never got anywhere. Alycia kept asking him to go to therapy, and what for? So some feminazi therapist could tell him he was an asshole for cheating on his wife with a stripper? It's always "with a stripper." Like she wasn't an actual person.

In the early morning when he woke, he'd been by himself on the couch in Mandi's dressing room. She'd left him her phone number, but that was all. Later she said it was because she'd seen his wedding ring and didn't want to pressure him into calling her.

He had though, anyway, to assure her he didn't think of her as a one-night stand. Bryce might not know her favorite flavor of ice cream, but he cared about her.

He rinsed the shampoo from his hair then leaned against the wall, letting the spray hit him on the side of his face.

To her credit, Mandi didn't make demands. They texted and emailed. He sent her flowers, and he'd taken her to lunch on several occasions. He met her daughter. And whenever they got the chance, they made love.

Alycia didn't know any of that. And he wasn't inclined to tell her. He didn't know what he was doing, how he was feeling, so her hounding him didn't do any good. It only pissed him off because he had nothing to say.

Bryce shut the water off and reached for a towel. All he knew was they couldn't go home and do what they'd been doing for the past four months.

In the bedroom, Alycia perched on the bed, wrapped in a towel, waiting for her turn in the shower.

The creamy skin of her shoulders made him hard, and he wanted to fuck her again. He wanted to take back all the time she'd stolen from him.

But he didn't want her scared of him. Taking what was his this one time was one thing, but ultimately, he didn't want it if she didn't want to give it.

He grabbed underwear from the dresser, and when he turned around she was gone, the bathroom door closed.

Kara was sitting at a picnic table outside when he went to find his friends and figure out dinner. They'd been barbecuing as a group, and that suited him. He wanted to spend as much time with them as he could because after this vacation, there was a very good chance he'd never see them again.

Alycia told him they were the odd couple out in their group, and he believed her now. Of course, that was because they were treating him like the jackass he was. No, he would probably move on, maybe spend more time with his work buddies.

Or fuck everyone and be with Mandi.

"Hey," Bryce greeted Kara, forcing a cheerfulness into his voice he didn't feel. He tried to push back the dark thoughts and remain upbeat.

She wrinkled her nose at him but smiled. "You and Alycia fighting again?"

"You heard or you wouldn't ask."

Kara shrugged.

Bryce sat next to her. "You look weird."

Kara did look off, her eyes slightly glazed as if she were sitting in a fog.

"I'm feeling a bit lost without my phone."

"You told your old man to go to hell, huh? Must have felt pretty good."

Kara opened her mouth to speak then closed it, looking off to the side at the beach, then back at him. "It did, but it made me feel sick, too." She took a swallow of her diet Coke with lime. "We're in the same kind of situation, you know."

Bryce snorted. What would he have in common with a high-class attorney? "You sleep with any strippers lately?"

Kara laughed.

Bryce could see what Chuck loved about her. Kara was tall and rail thin. Her blonde hair was lightening in the sun, and a tan made her look as if she was glowing from the inside out. Delicate, her features were small but fit her face. She could have been a model. But Kara wasn't his type. She was too fussy for him.

"No. I mean, we're both being pulled in two directions. My father was trying to get me to do what he wanted, but I was being pulled in a different direction by Chuck."

Bryce met her eyes and flinched at her serious expression.

"You have to choose which direction you want to be pulled in, or you'll be torn in two. Are you still in touch with," Kara paused, "her?"

Bryce appreciated Kara's respect toward Mandi. Unfairly, Bryce thought Kara would be the last person to give it to her.

"Mandi. Yeah. We talk. I've been seeing her."

Bryce wasn't sure he should be saying all this, but Kara didn't seem like she was asking to be mean or to make fun of him later behind his back. He decided to trust her; he needed to talk with someone. Tired with the whole mess, he rubbed his eyes. "I don't know what's going to happen. I just met her. I enjoy spending time with her—I like her as a person, you know? But then there's Alycia. We've been together forever and thinking about moving on without her gives me the shakes."

Kara tapped her fingernails on the side of her can. "I felt the same about my parents. I wanted them, needed them, was dependent on them. But it wasn't healthy."

"You make it sound like you *want* me to leave Alycia."

"Only if you don't want to be with her. I chose Chuck over my parents. Will there be repercussions? Sure. Would there have been if I had chosen my parents and lost Chuck? Yeah. So I had to think. Which consequences did I want to face less?" She lifted her hands in the air to mimic a scale. "Chuck or my parents?"

What would life be like choosing Alycia over Mandi? Choosing to honor his marriage vows, going to counseling, maybe finally having children?

"When I was lost in the woods, I had a lot of time to think about how life would feel if I didn't have Chuck. It didn't make me feel very good. Thinking about how life would be with my parents made me feel worse. All I'm saying is, you and Alycia, all of us, we're still young. Don't stay with Alycia out of pity or obligation, or because you married her when you were nineteen years old. Stay with her because you want to make it work, because when you look at her, you can't imagine life without her."

"What if it doesn't work between Mandi and me? I'd be alone." Bryce realized that was what was holding him back.

Selfish.

"There's no guarantee," Kara said. "Chuck and I could be done next year, and I'd have flushed what relationship I had with my parents down the toilet. Listen. I gave up a husband, granted, he was a man my parents chose for me, but he was still a nice guy despite that. I also gave up a high-paying job and political aspirations when I told my parents to fuck off. If things don't work out with Chuck, well, I won't have any of that, and I won't have Chuck either. But I'll have my life. Bryce," she said gently, resting a hand on his arm. "Life is short. If you want Mandi and she wants you, go for it. Alycia will be okay. I wanted Chuck, and now he's mine." Kara beamed.

"Thanks, Kara." Bryce kissed her cheek. "I haven't had anyone I could talk to about all this."

"It's okay, and believe me, I know it's a lot easier said than done. Chuck and I will likely have to put up with a lot from my parents. I'd bet a million dollars they'll harass us once we're back in the city. So I'll tell you this: If you stay with Alycia, do it all the way. Don't give her crumbs. And if you realize you regret the choice, get out fast. Straddling the fence doesn't do anyone any favors. I straddled the fence between my parents and Chuck, and all I did was hurt Chuck. And myself."

Bryce nodded and for the first time accepted that he was the only one who could make his own choices.

Alycia was bored. She tried to figure out why this year was different. It wasn't her relationship with Bryce. If she was being honest, her relationship had been on a downward slide for the past few years. She needed to do something or she was going to go crazy.

Maybe she'd run to the convenience store down the drive. She could grab a latte and a new magazine. Maybe some candy. Then she'd start a new series on Netflix. Her Facebook friends were raving about a new show called *Stranger Things*, so maybe she'd give that a shot. She didn't have anything else to do.

Alycia dressed after her shower and brushed her hair.

What had gotten into Bryce? He'd never been so . . . so . . . she was trying to think of derogatory terms to describe what he'd done, only she couldn't.

In shorts and a tee, with her debit card tucked into her back pocket, Alycia let herself out of their cabin.

Bryce was talking to Kara of all people, and she ignored them to walk around the cabin toward the gravel road.

"Alycia, where are you going?" Bryce asked, running behind her.

Alycia huffed with impatience. "I'm going to the convenience store for candy and a new magazine. Why?" She frowned. "Do you want something?" she asked reluctantly.

"You shouldn't be walking alone with that guy out there. I think the police would have told us if he was picked up."

Alycia stared. His eyes were a brilliant blue; so blue, in fact, people asked him all the time if he wore contacts. His jaw was scruffy, and he needed a haircut. He wore a Minnesota Twins t-shirt and basketball shorts, and he was barefoot. It was ludicrous she could look at him and see no one who meant anything to her now.

"Since when do you care?" Alycia sniped. "Did you care when you watched that stripper take her clothes off? Did you care when you were fucking her? Did you even remember my name when you had your face between her skanky legs?"

Bryce paled and his eyes filled, but his remorse didn't soften her.

She lifted her chin. "I didn't think so."

Alycia hurried down the gravel driveway, her heart pounding.

Her therapist told her to stop raking Bryce over the coals like that. But the problem was, she couldn't help it. She knew it wasn't doing their relationship any good and that she was only pushing him away.

Bryce wasn't in their cabin when she came back from the

store. In her room, she hid past midnight with her latte, candy, and her laptop.

He didn't come back.

§⚘

Bryce watched Alycia trot away confused about what she wanted from him. He'd apologized and he'd groveled, the whole time Mandi's face swimming before his eyes as he kneeled at Alycia's feet.

He'd made a mistake, but as the time went on, he wondered how big of a mistake it actually was.

He packed his backpack and took off down the trail. Not the path everyone hiked year after year. No, this one was less traveled, and not far from their cabins. Bryce took his cell phone from his pocket and walked until he started losing bars. He couldn't lose signal completely because he needed the Wi-Fi. Bryce found a fallen tree and leaned against the log, setting his backpack at his feet. Tipping his head back, he listened to the birds, the squirrels rummaging through the leaves. He wondered if this was how Kara felt when she was trying to find her way back to the cabins. So close to people, yet so very alone.

He brought up Mandi's phone number and listened to her line ring. It was perfect timing—she would be getting ready to go to the club.

"Hey, baby." Mandi's voice came through the line, and Bryce slid to the ground, his back against the log, the bark digging into his shoulder blades. Bryce blew out a breath. He'd needed to hear her voice, but he hadn't realized just how much.

"Hey," he choked, and imagining the accusation in Alycia's eyes, he swallowed a lump in his throat.

"Bryce," she whispered. He heard a door shut on her end of the line. "What's wrong?"

"I don't know what to do," he gasped, and he pressed his lips together.

Mandi was silent. "I don't know what to say, baby. You're married, and I'm . . ."

"Don't say it. Don't you dare say it."

"I am what I am, Bryce."

"You're not going to dance forever. I told you—"

"You told me you wanted me to stop stripping. Yes, I know, but it's the easiest way for me to make money. I need to pay my bills, baby," she quietly pleaded. "What do you want me to do?"

"Tell me—"

"No. I'm not going to tell you to leave your wife. If I tell you anything, I'll tell you to work it out with her. Have some kids. I'm not a home wrecker, Bryce. I didn't want any of this to happen. You're just so . . . you're just so sweet and . . . you treat me like a person, not a whore. Do you know how incredible that is to me? That you can look me in the eye, even though you know what I am, and still . . . want to touch me? You didn't even use anything that night."

Bryce could picture her in her snug jeans, a pretty blouse, her amber eyes lined with glittery bronze eyeliner. Her glorious hair pulled back into a high ponytail. It wasn't just her looks, it was all of her, the whole package. Like how she could make banana bread from scratch without a recipe, how she could talk about front page news, or how she could change a tire on her car. He'd wanted her from the moment he saw her, and he wanted her still, with a ferociousness he couldn't describe. But he wasn't free to take her.

"You've been with her for a long time, Bryce. I'm not anyone you should throw that away for. Can't you see? You have so much history with her, so much love. She's been your everything, and you're going to make her walk away."

"Are you saying you don't want me, Mandi?" Bryce rasped.

"I'm saying it's not my place to want you. You're *married*. I should just cut this off right now—"

"No! God, no, Mandi please." A tear leaked down his cheek.

"Then tell me what you want, Bryce! I can't do this for much longer. I'm not going to be your mistress. My daughter deserves a father. Brothers and sisters. I can't find a man to marry and share a future with if I'm fucking you just because you feel like hiding from your wife."

Bryce flinched. Their relationship was more than just sex. They both knew it. "Then, just give me a couple more days. Just two. It's all need. I know this situation sucks, and I'm sorry. I just, I don't know what I would do without you, Mandi. You're really important to me, you know?"

"I know. I do. But your wife, she's important to you too, isn't she? Listen, darling," she whispered into the phone, "if . . . this doesn't work, and trust me, I will completely understand if it doesn't, we'll always be friends, right?"

Bryce swallowed against a bitter taste in his mouth. He wasn't sure if he could be friends with Mandi and not imagine what their life could have been like had he chosen her. "Yeah. Sure. If you say so."

"Bryce," Mandi chided. "We need to act like grownups here. People's hearts are at stake."

He knew it was selfish, but he feared for his heart, too. What he needed to do was talk to Alycia, really talk, no yelling, no screaming, no name-calling. Just talk. Because, honestly, if she couldn't forgive him, there was nothing left to fight for.

If she *could* forgive him, he needed to decide if their relationship was worth keeping.

"I know. I just want to do the right thing." Bryce stood and slung his backpack over his shoulder.

"You will. But don't do it for me, and don't do it for your wife. Do it for you."

"Thanks. Mandi, you have no idea how much it means to me that you're with me."

Her voice lighter she said, "I think I have an idea. Good-night, Bryce."

Bryce shoved his phone into his pocket and backtracked, being careful not to step into sight of the cabins, though he was sure Alycia wasn't looking for him anyway. He found the main trail and stopped at the overlook. He spread out his sleeping bag, intending to sleep under the stars.

He planned what he wanted to say to Alycia and prayed she would listen.

༄

Bryce let himself into their cabin before the sun rose. He was tired and felt stupid sleeping on the ground when he wasn't even half a mile from the cabin and his bed. Things needed to change, quickly, because this was ridiculous, and Mandi was right. They were all grownups, and it was time they started acting like it. Kara was right too; he needed to stop straddling the fence. But he was a coward, he fully admitted that, and he wanted to talk to Alycia before he made any hasty decisions.

She was sleeping when he let himself inside. Her laptop sat on her bed, and she was still dressed in her clothes. It looked like she was maybe waiting for him to come back, but he knew her better than that. She'd probably just fallen asleep in the middle of watching a show.

Bryce stripped, fell into bed, and was sleeping in two seconds flat.

He woke around noon stiff and sore, and he took a hot shower. With a bagel in his hand, he headed outside to see if he could find Alycia. There was no point in putting this off.

"Bryce!" Kara called.

Chuck and Kara, Cam and Bailey, and Alycia were sitting at a picnic table, a board game waiting in the center.

"It's great you're awake. We're going to play Trivial Pursuit, and we can team up in couples now." Kara waved him over, and Bryce grimaced. He wasn't in the mood for a group activity; he just wanted to talk to Alycia, figure out his game plan.

Alycia glowered at him and was sitting with a red Solo cup in front of her. She could be drinking anything, and if she decided to get drunk, talking to her would be impossible. Fuck.

He sat down next to her, and she leaned away, putting at least a foot of space between them.

"Where were you?" she hissed. "I was up late waiting for you."

"Sorry. I fell asleep outside. I had no idea you'd be so concerned," Bryce jabbed at her then bit his tongue. Didn't he just *say* they needed to talk without all the recriminations? "Sorry, sorry."

"No. No, you're right. You didn't deserve how I treated you yesterday."

"Hey now," Kara announced, handing out empty pie shapes around the table. "We don't have much more of this vacation left, and we haven't done much as a group, so we need to make the best of it." She pointed at her eyes, then at Bryce and Alycia in the "I'm watching you" motion. "We're all going through stuff, but we need to set it aside at least for the afternoon. Vince and Janie went into town for food. We're going to have a big kick-ass barbecue tonight. Now, how do we figure who goes first?"

"Highest number," Chuck said, and he rolled the die.

"Hey, did you know Michael Stratton died yesterday from cancer?" Cam asked as he rolled the die for himself and Bailey.

"What? No way!" Kara gasped.

"Yeah, I saw it on my Facebook feed this morning. Someone posted his obit."

"Oh my God, he was too young for that," Bailey murmured.

"That's fucked up," Bryce muttered and was surprised to feel Alycia put a hand on his thigh under the table. Bryce handed her the die so she could roll for their place in the game, and she rolled a six.

"Nice," Chuck told her and read them the question after Bryce moved their pie onto the board. "What year was the first Super Bowl played?"

"1967," Bryce crowed, and Chuck gave him a high five.

"When is Michael's funeral? Did the obit say?" Kara asked Cam as she opened a bag of Fritos.

Cam nodded and grabbed a handful. "This Saturday. While we're here. I didn't know him well enough to go, but does anyone want to drive into the city for it?"

"He hung out with Vince the most," Bryce said, then shoved the rest of his bagel in his mouth. He'd have to go into the cabin for something to drink. He wanted to make a pot of coffee. While he'd slept okay in bed after he came back from the overlook, the stress was taking its toll and he felt tired all the time.

"Do you remember when the tenth-grade science teacher, oh, what was his name?" Alycia asked, rolling the die for their next turn.

"Mr. Peterson," Bryce said, picking up the conversation, knowing exactly where Alycia was going. "Yeah, he flunked Michael, and he buttered up Mr. Peterson's car."

The group laughed, but it sounded melancholy.

"He had a wife and a couple of kids, right?" Kara asked, picking up a card. "Who wrote the fairy tale 'The Ugly Duckling?'"

"Hans Christian Andersen," Alycia answered.

"And just like that they have control of the board," Chuck drawled in a sports game announcer's voice.

"Yeah, she's in my book club," Bailey said. "It's so

horrible."

The news unsettled Bryce. Life was too short to be unhappy. "We need to talk," Bryce whispered to Alycia.

"Tonight," Alycia answered with a pleading look on her face. "Okay?"

He took in her expression. "Okay," he agreed, rubbing her back.

They were finishing the game just as Vince and Janie came back with the groceries. While Janie went inside Kara and Chuck's cabin to put the bulk of the food away, the group filled Vince in on his friend's death.

"I should go back," Vince said reluctantly, kicking at the ground. "We've still been in touch, and I should offer my condolences to his wife. He was feeling okay a couple of weeks ago."

Bryce wanted to go too, but not to go to the funeral and offer condolences. He wanted to escape what was going to happen later. But he couldn't do that either; he promised Mandi he would figure this out.

Vince shuffled toward Kara and Chuck's cabin, his head bowed in sadness, his truck keys jiggling in his hand.

"We shouldn't let this get us down," Chuck said, picking up the game pieces. "Let's do something fun."

"Did someone say fun? That's been in short supply around here," Nate said as he and Crystal approached their group.

Bryce agreed with Nate. He couldn't think of a less fun vacation.

"I don't think anyone's been having fun," Alycia grumbled, draining what was in her cup.

Chuck heard her. "So it's time to fix that. Let's go tubing."

Everyone groaned.

"You're the only one who likes to do that," Kara told him, swatting his arm. "No one wants to be whipped around on a hot inner tube at thirty miles an hour."

"Does anyone else have an idea?" Chuck raised an eyebrow.

"I'm in," Alycia said suddenly. "I'll go change."

"See," Chuck teased. "It's a great idea."

Bryce didn't know why Alycia suddenly wanted to go tubing, and he squinted at her as she went into the cabin for her suit. Whatever. There was time enough to talk to her tonight. Maybe he could use Chuck as a sounding board first. He'd actually be able to talk to him with Vince gone.

He changed into swim trunks, and everyone was waiting at the boat when Vince waved goodbye. Janie remained behind to finish her stay at the resort, but she was sitting out tubing because of her wrist.

Kara sat out to keep Janie company on the beach.

Alycia hopped into the speed boat and sat near Bailey and Crystal in the front, and Bryce sat near the motor with the guys. Bryce didn't mind tubing, but he was antsy now that he and Alycia had a plan to talk. He liked being on the water, though, and it was a beautiful day. The sun was blinding as there wasn't a hint of clouds, and he figured this would be a great way to work up an appetite for the barbecue tonight. Chuck seemed determined to keep the group together, but Bryce thought it was bad timing. All he wanted to do was talk to Alycia, but that was damn near impossible while being dragged into these group activities.

Bryce pulled a beer from the cooler and sipped it as Chuck motored them way from shore.

Alycia knew what Bryce wanted to tell her, and she thanked God Chuck wanted to do these group activities. It was a convenient filler, a valid excuse to avoid Bryce. He was going to tell her they were done, that he was moving on with Mandi. She had yet to process how she felt about that.

The roar of the motor and the boat slamming against the choppy waves made talking to Bailey or Crystal impossible, and Alycia was glad. There wasn't anything they could do for her anyway.

Bryce was still in contact with Mandi—she'd checked his phone while he was sleeping. He'd called her yesterday after Alycia bit his head off before going to the store. She wondered what Mandi told him. Did Mandi say that if she was going to treat her husband that way, Alycia would deserve it if he left her? Why hadn't Bryce left her before now? The bachelor party was four months ago.

The wind whipped her hair in her face and she brushed it back to look down the boat's length at her husband.

They'd been together for so long. They'd jumped right into adulthood, skipping college, taking jobs to pay rent and other bills. She'd worked her way up in Macy's from a part-time cashier. Bryce skipped from job to job, always going up, but not as quickly as if he'd gone to school. They didn't have the time away from home, the flings, the keggers—they missed all that. The only thing they did right was to not pop out a couple kids immediately after getting married. At least they'd kept their wits about them on that. Her mother had even taken her to the clinic and said if she was determined to get married, be married first and have kids later. So they worked, had dinner parties with their friends, and fell into an old couple routine by the time they were twenty-three.

Alycia snorted, and Bailey shot her a puzzled frown. She shook her head and turned away to look over the water. It sparkled a royal blue, the rocky tree-filled islands dotting the waterscape. It was beautiful out here, and she envied Janie who would get to finish out the vacation alone. She wanted that, too.

She stumbled to the cooler at the back of the boat and grabbed a drink.

The boat hit a large wave, and she tumbled backward into

Bryce's lap.

"Careful," he warned and wrapped his arms around her.

Relaxed in his embrace, Alycia unscrewed the top of a wine cooler and threw it into the ice box. She wet her mouth with the orange-flavored drink. On top of the wine she drank during Trivial Pursuit, her limbs were loose and a happy static filled her brain.

Chuck slowed the boat to an idle.

After the loud roar of the motor, the quiet echoed in her head.

"I wanna go first, is that okay?" Chuck asked.

No one contested him. Alycia would probably take a turn if Bryce could keep Chuck in hand. She sat next to Bailey and offered Crystal and Bailey a wine cooler. Bailey accepted one, surprising her, taking a long swig from the bottle. Bailey was on ovulation medication, if Alycia wasn't mistaken, and she shouldn't have been drinking. Alycia brought it intending to drink it herself, and she was only being courteous offering it to her friend.

Something must have happened for Bailey to go off her meds.

Alycia glanced at Crystal, but Crystal looked away. It was definitely something they couldn't talk about now.

Chuck attached the inner tube to the back of the boat with thick red straps and threw the huge black tube into the water where it landed with a loud *slap* against the surface. He jumped in and crawled on top of it, shaking the water from his hair like a soaking wet dog. "Come on," he demanded, pounding on the rubber. "Give me your worst." A challenging grin filled his face as the others hooted and cat-called warnings to him.

Cam started off slowly enough and eventually the guys were doing everything they could to make Chuck flip off the tube.

Clinging to the boat to steady herself, Bailey yelled in

Alycia's ear to be heard over the sound of the motor and wind, "If they're going to do that to us, I don't want to ride."

Alycia slid into Bailey as Cam took a tight turn hoping to make Chuck fly off the tube. This went on for a while until Chuck let go purposely, his body skidding over the water, like a rock skipping over the surface.

They circled back for him, and Chuck was laughing when Bryce helped him into the boat.

"Who's next?" Cam called looking around.

"I'll go," Bryce volunteered.

Alycia hoped the guys weren't too hard on him. She knew she and Bryce were fighting a lot, but she didn't *really* want his friends to take out their feelings on him. It didn't seem like it, not with all the fighting in public they were doing, but this really was between Bryce and her, and she hoped he kept his friends after this. She knew she would lose Janie and Kara, and probably Crystal and Bailey too, but maybe that was for the best. She should move on, find new friends, so she wouldn't have to hear all the time about how Bryce was doing.

They gave Bryce an easy time of it, and she was glad. He didn't let go like Chuck did, so when the boat slowed he stood on top of the big tube, wobbled for just a moment then fell backward into the water. After he climbed into the boat, he raised his eyebrows at her. "You said you wanted to do this. Are you ready?"

Alycia threw her empty bottle into the cooler, the glass clinking against the ice. It would feel good to jump into the water after sitting in the sun all afternoon. "Take it easy on me, will you, guys?" she teased and tried not to show any apprehension. The guys were like barracudas and they would prey on her fear.

She jumped in and let out a gasp as the chilly water swallowed her, and she was shivering, her skin broken out into goosebumps, when her head broke the surface. After a bit of difficulty climbing on, they were off, Chuck keeping the speed manageable for her. It was a pleasant ride, the boat cutting loose on the open water. The lake was choppy and Alycia pressed her face into the rubber, hanging on as the inner tube hit wave after wave.

Gradually Chuck went faster and faster, but Alycia was glued to the tube and couldn't motion for him to slow down.

A large wave came out of nowhere, and the tube hit it in the perfect place at the perfect time, bucking high over the water. As it slammed into the lake, Alycia lost her grip, and she too, crashed into the water with a belly flop that would have earned her a gold medal in the Olympics if there were such a sport.

Water pushed up her nose and in her mouth, her skin stung everywhere, and her face felt numb.

Her eyes were shut against the water, she couldn't breathe, yet Alycia wanted to cry out in pain. Disorientated, she struggled to lift her face above the surface to suck in some air, but her hair was wrapped around her neck, and she didn't know which way was up.

She should have worn a life vest, but the thought came too late.

Just when she imagined she would die in the water, strong arms encircled her and pulled her head above water. Alycia coughed and gagged, throwing up water. Her hair was still in her face and she grabbed at it, desperately trying to move it away from her eyes and nose.

"Calm down, calm down, I've got you."

Alycia recognized Bryce's voice through her panic, but she couldn't relax. She still gasped for breath, urgently trying to push her hair from her face.

Finally, she won the war against her hair and she could see. Coughing, her nasal passages stinging from the water, she clung to Bryce, sobbing.

Her skin burned like it was on fire.

Bryce swam them to the boat, and Chuck pulled her out of the water.

Alycia's whole body shook, and she tried to gain enough composure to breathe. Someone wrapped a towel around her and sat her down on a seat. She coughed, gagging up lake water, and her eyes smarted from the water, sun, and tears.

Bryce sat next to her pressing his warm body against her, and he put an arm around her cradling her to his side. "Shh, shh," he whispered near her ear. "It's going to be okay."

Chuck knelt next to her. "I am so sorry, Al. I should never have gone so fast. You were being such a good sport and you were able to hang on . . ." he trailed off helplessly.

Alycia rubbed her eyes. "It's okay—" she started but Chuck tried cut off to protest. "No, really it is." She continued, "The tube hit a wave at just the wrong time . . ." She had to stop in a fit of coughing. Her lungs still hadn't cleared from all the lake water.

"We'll take you back to shore," Nate said.

Bryce guided her to the front of the boat and sat, gripping her tightly the whole way back to the cabins.

She leaned into his embrace knowing this was one of the last times they would be close without any animosity between them.

When Bryce watched Alycia flip from the tube and flail in the water, he'd been scared shitless. He'd been shaking just as badly as she was when they sat in the boat, her trying to get the water from her lungs, him just trying to calm the fuck down after watching his wife almost drown.

He sat with her now, on the couch, both dripping, soaking the fabric. Bryce didn't care. He kept smoothing his hand up and down her arm, his lips pressed to her head. He didn't know how could he leave her alone, defenseless, for another woman. Alycia wouldn't be able to take care of herself without him. He'd stood guard by her side for two-thirds of his life. The realization that he'd lived more of his life with her than without her shook him. It felt as if she'd always been a part of him, and now he was about to walk away.

Lifting her chin so he could peer into her brown eyes, he studied her face. Her skin was pale against the pink splotches on her cheeks from hitting the water and around her eyes where she'd rubbed at them. "You really slammed your face into the water," he said, smoothing his thumb over her cheek.

She shrugged. "It's not a big deal." She bit her lip and met his eyes. "Thanks for jumping in. I was pretty rattled."

"You're my wife, Alycia. I love you."

He hadn't given her any reason to believe him during these four months, but he wasn't lying to her. A marriage didn't have to have passion to succeed. A man could love his wife and not be in love with her.

"Come on, you're still shaking. Why don't you take a nap? There's plenty of time before the barbecue." There *was* plenty of time. In fact, everyone had gone back out tubing when they dropped him and Alycia off. Nate hadn't had his turn, Bailey wanted to try it, and he was sure Chuck would go again. They would be on the water for hours.

Alycia nodded and she followed him into the bedroom.

Gently, he peeled her suit from her, so unlike the other time when she'd made him angry. Her skin was ruddy and raised in the places it had come so forcefully into contact with the water, and it looked tender to the touch. "Does your skin sting?" he asked, running his fingertips along her cleavage, down her breasts, and to the rosy skin on the tops of her thighs.

"A little," she whispered as she dropped the towel to the floor. "Will you make love to me, Bryce?"

The words warmed his heart, yet made him sad. It had been such a long time since she'd shown any interest, and now she was asking after knowing about his affair. It humbled him; she was a million times better person than he was.

"Yeah, baby. I want to."

He started by running kisses over her bruised thighs. Goosebumps chased his lips as they grazed over her skin. "Let's get into bed," he said, "you're cold."

Bryce pulled the comforter from under the pillows and slid in next to her. It was too hot outside for blankets, but he still flipped them over their heads, making her giggle.

He captured her mouth with his and nudged her thighs apart. She hadn't groomed herself, and the down of her soft curls made him hard. With probing fingers, he found her, and slid two into her dampness as he slipped his tongue into her mouth.

Alycia wrapped her arms around his neck and pulled him closer. She rocked her hips under his hand, and he found her clit with his thumb.

He wanted to try something new, and he skimmed his fingers to her ass. She stilled when he nudged her opening with a finger, but he continued with the tip of his slippery finger, pushing inside the tightness.

Alycia moaned, and it spurred him on, wiggling his finger into her a little at a time. This wasn't something he'd ever considered doing with her, but Mandi liked and asked him to do it.

Thinking of Mandi while in bed with his wife made him feel all kinds disgusting, so he focused on giving Alycia as much pleasure as he could. When his finger was buried into her ass to the last knuckle, he pushed a finger into her pussy, too. "Touch yourself," he murmured into her ear. He applied as much pressure as he thought she could stand.

She rubbed her clit with her fingers, and he felt her bearing down.

He pulled both fingers out and pushed them back in, and

Alycia gasped in what could have been pain, pleasure, or both. Bryce took one of her nipples into his mouth and bit, his fingers finding a rhythm to her gyrating hips.

"Bryce," she whimpered, and he knew she was about to come.

He thrust his fingers into her as deeply as he could, and sucked on her nipple as aggressively as he dared.

She came, gushing, her hips full off the bed.

Alycia flipped the covers from over their heads, gasping for fresh air.

Bryce missed the scent of hot sex under the blanket, but he took a deep shuddering breath. His fingers were still inside her and he slowly pulled them out, aware she would be tender after coming. He gave her a long kiss and pushed his cock into her hip. He rolled on top of her as he kissed her, but she pulled away.

"Wait," she whispered. "Let me."

Alycia pushed him against the mattress and stroked him, rubbing his pre-come around the tip. When she leaned over him and took his cock in her mouth, he groaned in pleasure, almost spurting.

It had been many years since Alycia had given him a blowjob.

Mandi liked to give them.

Bryce groaned and guiltily pushed Mandi from his mind, instead focusing on Alycia's mouth and tongue on his skin.

She started fondling his balls; she must have remembered he loved that.

Bryce tried to hold off, but he was swept away in pleasure. He rammed his fingers into her hair and pushed her head down, forcing his dick deeper into her mouth, almost down her throat. He came, huge jerks bucking his body.

Alycia struggled for a moment, then accepted his come and swallowed it as he squirted inside her mouth.

When his grip on her hair loosened, Alycia lifted her head

and glowered, wiping her mouth with the back of her hand. She flicked her hair out of her eyes. "What'd you do that for?"

Bryce grinned. "You never have before. I wanted to see if you would. Now kiss me."

Alycia cuddled next to him, propping up on one elbow. "You didn't give me much choice," she groused playfully, before lowering her lips to his.

They snuggled in bed, the sounds of their friends coming and going in the late afternoon; Kara complaining she was hungry, Casey barking, Janie's laughter.

Relaxed, Bryce thought this was how summer vacation was supposed to be. Yet Mandi's face came into focus behind his closed eyes.

He wondered what he be throwing away, and what would he be gaining, if he chose Mandi.

Choosing what to do shouldn't be a list of pros and cons. His heart was on the line, and Alycia's, too. Mandi never said she loved him, never said she wanted a future with him. She promised she wouldn't crowd him, and she wasn't, but that kept her from telling him how she really felt.

Bryce ran his hand over Alycia's shoulder. She was sleeping, the accident no doubt taking its toll.

He'd lost years off his life watching her struggle in the water. He was her husband—it was his job to look after her. Yet their relationship had fallen into some kind of nothingness. They shared the same space and breathed the same air, but they weren't together and they hadn't been for a long time. They deserved more.

Alycia woke alone. Her body ached, her head pounded, and she was sore between her legs.

Too much activity after going too long without. And the ass thing. God, that'd felt good, but it was the first time he'd ever done that to her. Would he want to be more adventurous in the bedroom from now on? She wasn't sure she would like that. With as aggressive as he'd been lately, she wasn't sure she had a choice. If they stayed together, she would need to be prepared to be married to a different man. The way they'd done things for the past twenty years wouldn't cut it with him anymore.

She went to the bathroom and bit her lip when she saw a faint smear of blood on the toilet paper after wiping. She couldn't say the pain had been a turn-off. In fact, Alycia admitted, she wouldn't mind if he did that to her again.

He'd really gone at her and the thought of his fingers doing those naughty things made her wet.

She went back to bed, not ready to face the group. Alycia threw the covers over her and spread her legs.

Gently, she prodded at her sore ass, but the discomfort made her tingle, and she rubbed her clit, widening her legs. After years of playing with herself as her only source of pleasure, she knew exactly what she liked.

With her fingers enveloped between the slick folds of her pussy, she pinched her nipples with her other hand, the tingling pain making her come. Alycia rubbed furiously, moaning, coaxing every last bit of pleasure from her body.

After taking a moment to slow her pounding heart, she rolled out of bed and started the shower.

She wished there was someone she could call, someone she could talk to, but maybe that wouldn't be much help to her anyway. She knew he was still talking to his stripper, but maybe they were just friends.

Yeah, right.

Alycia showered and dressed for the barbecue and bonfire. Chuck was all but making them attend. She would have loved to stay in the cabin and hide—finish watching *Stranger Things*, but she went outside, trying to be a good sport.

The sun was starting to set, the frogs and crickets doing their thing.

Everyone was outside except Vince, but Janie didn't seem to mind he was gone, talking animatedly with Kara, her hands gesturing in the air in response. Casey's head was in her lap as he napped.

"Hey," Bailey greeted her, the words slurring, as she lifted a plastic cup in her direction. She was dressed in light blue running capris pants and a matching striped Under Armor shirt, a hoodie tied around her waist.

The woman was seriously drunk.

"Hey," Alycia replied, concerned. She sat near Bailey at a picnic table and looked for Cam. He was building up the logs for the bonfire. "What's going on?"

"We're done," Bailey announced.

The words made Alycia's skin break out in goosebumps. "Done doing what, Bailey?" Alycia asked carefully, meeting the woman's blue eyes.

"Trying."

Alycia's heart sank, and she wrapped an arm around her as Bailey sobbed into Alycia's shoulder.

Cam's eyes met hers over the clearing, but he quickly looked away. How much of Bailey and Cam's decision had been Cam's?

Alycia didn't know the intimate details of Cam and Bailey's relationship, and they'd been dealing with their issue a lot longer than she'd been dealing with Bryce's cheating on her.

But apparently Alycia had been blind to a lot of things, including how miserable Bryce was.

She reminded herself too, that Bailey was closer to Crystal, and she shouldn't feel guilty for not being there if she wasn't needed. But she did sit with Bailey most of the night, keeping an eye on Bailey's alcohol consumption.

Alycia plied Bailey with hamburgers and chips hoping the

food would absorb the alcohol in Bailey's system.

It was near dark when Bailey wiped her eyes and licked her fingers of chocolate from the brownies they'd eaten for dessert.

"Thanks, Al," Bailey hiccuped.

"Sure, hon," Alycia said, rubbing her back. "I can't say it will work out, but I sure hope it will."

Bailey smiled for the first time that evening. "Thank you. You have no idea how hard it is to hear 'it's part of God's plan,' or 'things happen the way they're supposed to happen.' How easy it is for them when they're so secure in their own lives."

When Bailey stumbled to her cabin, Alycia snagged a bag of puppy chow and walked to the pontoon, sitting heavily in one of the captain's chairs. She grabbed a handful of the chocolate and powdered sugar Chex mix and dropped the pieces into her mouth one by one.

If, well, when, no if, it came down to divorce . . . Alycia wrinkled her nose. If, when, whatever. If they did, people would look at her much like they looked and gossiped about Bailey. What was so wrong with her she couldn't keep a man, what made her husband look for someone else?

Alycia was under no illusion that society wouldn't pin this on her. It would be her fault he wasn't happy. After all, *she* hadn't thought about straying. She wouldn't even know where to begin looking if she wanted to.

Bryce had at least connected with someone on an emotional level, in addition to a physical one.

Alycia hadn't connected with anybody lately. Especially not Bryce.

She'd been walking through life in a daze—work, home, sleep. She and Bryce hadn't traveled, though they could afford to now. No trips to Mexico, just because. No road trips to Florida. No Grand Canyon, no Yellowstone National Park. No trips to Paris, or trips to see the glorious beaches of

Australia or Greece. They didn't have kids, what was stopping them? They only went on this trip every year.

Kara always said this time could be better spent. In the past, she thought it was the snob in Kara talking, but now she agreed.

Not that it mattered now. This would be their last trip here because even if they stayed together, this vacation was getting old, and she didn't want to do it anymore.

"Hey, want a cup of coffee?"

Only Janie would drink coffee at eleven o'clock at night, but Alycia accepted the steaming mug, anticipating the slightly bitter taste against the chocolate in her mouth.

"Thanks," Alycia said, then bit back a sigh of annoyance when Janie sat in the other chair across from her, tucking one foot under her butt. She wanted to be alone. "I'm sorry about Vince's friend," Alycia said, giving Janie the bag of puppy chow along with her condolences.

"It was a shock, I think, for all of us," Janie replied, munching. "No one likes to be reminded of their mortality."

"It *is* a reminder how short life is. I was just thinking how Bryce and I never do anything, never go anywhere. We don't have kids, not even a dog to look after. Why aren't we out there," she gestured to the water, the moon reflecting off the still surface, "living it up? Brunch, vacations, we don't do any of it."

"Do you think that would have helped?" Janie raised her eyebrows.

Alycia shrugged. "Maybe. It didn't help that we didn't. We sit around the house looking at each other. He lost interest and found someone who didn't bore him."

"So why didn't you do something?"

Janie sounded interested and Alycia thought she might be taking notes and adding to her "what not to do" list for her own relationship.

"It didn't occur to me until it was too late," Alycia

admitted bitterly. "Isn't that how it goes? Don't get your car serviced until it breaks down. Don't pay your credit card until the bill goes into collections. Don't get a check-up until you have a heart attack. I didn't know it was something we should be doing."

"Don't you like spending time with him?" Janie chewed on a fingernail for a second then took a sip coffee.

There wasn't much of a breeze and the mosquitoes buzzed around them. They swarmed near Alycia's ear, and she swatted at them, unnerved.

"Janie, the man has always been around. He's been my shadow since sixth grade. I've loved having him around. But even when you promise to never take someone for granted, doesn't it always happen anyway? You take for granted the garbage will be taken out, that the mortgage will get paid. You take for granted there will always be someone to sleep with. It's not wrong to grow comfortable with someone until it is."

Alycia didn't expect Janie to understand. In fact, she probably wouldn't find someone her age who *would* understand. Maybe someone ten years, or twenty years, older than she and Bryce. They were in an odd situation at thirty-two.

"So what will you do?"

Alycia reached across the narrow aisle of the boat for another handful of puppy chow. "He hasn't decided as far as I know."

"You don't have to wait for him to decide. Why can't you?"

Alycia munched the chocolate mix. "Maybe I don't want to take responsibility for the outcome. What if I ask him to stay and we're miserable? If I tell him to go, and things turn to shit, I'd be to blame."

Janie snorted. "That's kinda dumb. You have to make a choice. I chose to give Vince a chance, not just float along like a gob of pollen in the wind."

Alycia held back a laugh. "A gob of pollen?"

"You know what I mean," Janie said, irritated.

"Yeah, I do. Honestly, deep down, I don't know if Bryce would stay if I asked. Maybe he'd stop seeing the stripper and try to make things work. My tubing thing this afternoon freaked him out a little. But Janie, honestly, I don't know if I want him to. Then on the other hand, what would I do without him? I fart in front of him, he holds my hair when I puke. When I had a stomach bug, I had diarrhea all over our bed. He didn't say one word. He only helped me shower, changed the bed, and took the bedding to the laundry mat while I napped. How would I find another man who will do that for me?"

"You'd find someone, Al. Bryce loved you, loves you. You'll get that back. Don't be scared to try if that's what you want."

"Easy for you to say, miss, 'I just fell in love,'" Alycia grumped, though she wasn't mad.

"It doesn't matter," Janie said firmly, draining her coffee. "I'm never going to fart in front of Vince."

Alycia laughed. "Just wait until the first time he traps you under the blankets after he lets a silent but deadly one go. You won't be able to wait to pay him back."

"Ew," Janie said, laughing with her. "I'm going inside. The bugs are driving me crazy."

"I'm going to stay out here for a little bit longer. Thanks for coming out to talk to me."

Janie kissed her cheek. "You're welcome. Goodnight."

Alycia sipped what was left of her coffee and stared at the stars.

She didn't know what she would do, but anything she chose had to be better than this.

❧

Bryce sat near the bonfire burning marshmallows. No, he didn't like to eat them that way, though he knew some freaks did. He remembered reading somewhere burnt food was a carcinogen, and that stuck with him. He didn't even char his steaks anymore, though he liked them that way best.

Chuck was quiet, probably upset his little bromance with Vince was interrupted by Michael's death. The thought was unkind, but he couldn't help feeling bitter. He was drunk and tired and confused as hell. He wanted to talk to Mandi, but he knew at this time of night she was dancing, and that pissed him off even more. The knowledge she was showing her breasts to other men put him in a rage, and he made her swear she wasn't fucking anyone else.

That was a hell of a joke now.

She promised, saying she'd fallen for him when he asked what subject she was studying in school.

That was him: Mr. Sensitive.

He watched the marshmallow burn on his stick. It tore him to pieces to know she was still dancing, but when she told him how much she made, the figure made his head spin. She could pay all her bills, rent, her daughter's sitter, groceries, car payment, insurance and anything else, and still have money left over.

Mandi could make it without him and the fact rankled.

She wanted him but didn't need him.

Wasn't that better? Bryce tried to convince himself it was.

Alycia didn't seem to need or want him. At least she'd let go of some of her animosity, some of her anger, toward him. The sex earlier had been good, but nothing like what they used to have. He laughed to himself as the burning marshmallow dropped into the fire.

"What?" Nate asked, sipping a beer and eating one of the burgers they'd grilled for dinner.

"Oh, just remembering my first time with Alycia."

Chuck grunted in encouragement for him to continue.

"We were watching a movie in her parents' basement. Lying there on the couch in the dark under a blanket. God, we were barely sixteen. One thing led to another and we were just like, let's do it. Let's get it over with. We didn't even have any protection, but we didn't care. She pushed her sweats down and unzipped my pants.

"I was only inside her for two fucking seconds before her old man came downstairs to watch the movie with us. We were mortified." Bryce paused when his friends started laughing. "So we were lying there, my cock inside her, and we watched a movie with her dad. I was too scared to come and too horny to make my cock go down. I was literally frozen. Afterward, before I went home, her dad told me if I knocked her up, he'd kill me."

Howling, Nate joked, "No wonder you two don't have kids; you're still scared of her old man."

Bryce laughed and threw his stick in the fire. "How'd you lose your virginity?" he asked Nate.

Nate winked. "You remember. Karyn Somanski."

Bryce and Chuck groaned.

"Karyn Somanski helped every guy in our class get laid," Chuck said, pulling a perfectly toasted marshmallow away from the flames.

"Even you?" Bryce asked, amazed. Karyn was so out of Chuck's league they didn't even orbit the same planet.

"Even me," Chuck confirmed, blowing on his marshmallow. "Of course, we heard the rumors, but no guy wants to think they're giving it up to the class whore. She taught me some things, though I didn't have sex after that until college. My girlfriend snuck me into her dorm room and we did it while her roommate snored in the bed next to us." He shook his head and ate the marshmallow off his stick.

"How's it feel to be with one woman your whole life?" Nate asked, then looked away into the fire, embarrassed he slipped.

Bryce took the question for what it was and took a long pull from his beer while he considered his answer. "There's a lot to regret," he admitted at last. "I didn't get the sleeping around thing out of my system, I guess. There's something . . . I don't know . . . fun, special, about fucking someone new. I didn't have that. On the other hand, you don't worry about diseases, or being embarrassed about being naked. No one night stands when you have to sneak out before she wakes up. It's . . . I don't know . . . comforting. But I've been with her for a long time, and I think I got bored. It's not a reason or an excuse to cheat, and I'm not saying that fucking around before I got married would have kept me from doing what I did. I guess I don't know what I'm saying."

It was the longest admission to his friends he'd made about his mistake. Yet he didn't consider Mandi a mistake. Maybe a wake-up call. He couldn't say he loved her, but he knew without a doubt if Alycia wasn't in the picture, he'd be with Mandi now.

"Chuck, you're gonna marry Kara. You ready for that?" Nate asked around a huge bite of burger.

Bryce was thankful his friends' attention shifted.

Chuck grinned. "Yep. It's not going to be easy with her parents, but honestly, I never thought we'd do it. I would have bet everything I had she'd buckle." Chuck flashed a shit-eating grin and stared over the fire at Kara who was talking with Crystal at one of the picnic tables.

"We're happy for you, Chuck," Bryce said sincerely. It was difficult, though, to be happy for Chuck's good fortune when his own life was such a mess. But he wouldn't trade his life for any of his buddies'.

The grass wasn't always greener.

Kara accused him of straddling a fence between two yards, Alycia on one side, Mandi on the other. All he had to do was figure out which yard wasn't disguising a pit of quicksand ready to bury him alive.

"Thanks," Chuck said, toasting another marshmallow. "But it's Kara who deserves it. She's had a pretty shitty life if you get right down to it. 'Poor little rich girl' isn't too far off."

Bryce stood. He wasn't interested in Kara. He only saw her a few times a year, and he had more pressing things on his mind than what jerks her parents were.

"Heading in?" Nate asked.

"Yeah." Bryce looked over at the pontoon where Alycia sat with Janie. He promised Mandi he'd figure this out. He would talk to Alycia, and he had a plan to finally get her alone.

❧

When Alycia had enough of the bugs swarming her, she went back to the cabin. Bryce wasn't sleeping; all the lights were blazing.

She hoped he wouldn't want to have sex again. It was only complicating matters.

Janie was right. She didn't need to wait for Bryce. She could boot him to the curb just as easily as he could tell her to fuck off.

"What are you doing?" she asked him as he knelt in front of his backpack.

"We need to talk, and Chuck keeps pulling us into these group activities like we're ten and at some sort of goddamn summer camp."

Alycia leaned against his doorjamb and crossed her arms. She didn't like the sound of this even though she knew it was necessary. "What are we going to do then?" Warily, she sat on the edge of his bed and watched him secure a sleeping bag.

"We'll take a boat to one of the islands. We'll be alone, and we'll talk."

Her heart thudded in her chest. "And if you don't like what we come up with, you'll drown me?" she asked, apprehensive. She wasn't sure they needed to be *quite* that alone to talk.

"No!" Alarmed, Bryce clutched Alycia's knees. "You scared the hell out of me today. That's not funny at all."

She thought she heard him mumble, "Grow up," under his breath, as he turned to his backpack.

He was right if he'd said it. She needed to be grown up. If they decided to divorce, they would need to do it as quickly and as easily as possible. Neither of them had money for drawn-out attorney's fees.

Disliking her train of thought, Alycia left Bryce packing his bag. She went into her bedroom and stripped off her clothes planning to get a good night's sleep. Apparently, Bryce was thinking they would spend the night out there if he was packing his backpack.

She would sleep in, then pack her bag. Alycia didn't think they had so much to talk about they needed two whole days.

She'd tell Bryce they'd leave after lunch.

She always told him what to do. Why stop now?

Alycia dreamed Bryce tried to wake her. Her dream-self told him to fuck off—she was trying to sleep. When she opened her eyes, her face buried under a pillow, she realized it wasn't a dream. Grabbing her phone, she checked the time: ten o'clock.

She made coffee, and while she waited for it to drip, ate a piece of toast.

She showered, drinking the coffee inside the shower stall. She took her time shaving her legs and conditioning her hair. Poking at the chub of her hip, she realized she *had* gained a little weight. She needed to stop wearing yoga pants. They were way too comfortable.

Sipping on coffee she dressed and packed her hiking bag.

She didn't want to forget anything just in case it did indeed take them longer than twenty-four hours to figure things out. God, she hoped not.

She grabbed chips from the kitchen on her way out the door, trusting in the time Bryce waited for her, he'd packed ample food.

She found Bryce playing horseshoes with Chuck, Nate, and Cam. The teams would be lopsided after Bryce left; they'd need to play singles.

"What the hell have you been doing?" Bryce glared at her in aggravation, chucking his horseshoe and luckily clinking the metal stake, scoring a point.

Amazement swept away his glower, and he grinned stupidly as Cam thumped him on the back. "Damn! I've been trying to do that all morning!" Bryce said, then frowned at Alycia. "Let's go now."

Alycia sighed. *Be a grownup, be a grownup*, she chanted, following him to the aluminum fishing boat. Holy hell this was going to be boring.

She couldn't remember the last time she'd spent so much time alone with her husband. Maybe two years ago when they'd been snowed in during a blizzard that had lasted several days. That hadn't been so bad. She'd hidden in the guest bedroom and read the entire time. She didn't want to know when spending time with him had become such a chore.

Crossly, she threw her backpack into the bottom of the boat then gingerly stepped in, not wanting to crush her dill pickle chips.

They would be her only light during this dark and dreary time.

Oh, stop being so dramatic, she chastised herself, sitting on a bench. This time tomorrow it'd be all done. They'd either decide to stay married and work on their relationship, or they'd go their separate ways.

Alycia couldn't think of it as Bryce leaving her for that stripper. If he'd really planned to do that to her, he would have already. No, if they went their separate ways, they would be making the decision together. She would be free to do what she liked, and so would he.

Bryce started the motor and trolled them away from the dock.

She'd been so taken with him when they were kids. Grew up together, for the most part. The only man she'd ever kissed. The only man she'd ever slept with. Thinking of dating gave her a wormy feeling in her stomach, but anticipation fizzed in her fingertips for something—someone—new.

He was so handsome. Bryce's blond hair glinted in the sun, his blue eyes flickering at her to make sure she was safe on the boat's bench.

Before Bryce opened up the motor, she nestled the bag of chips between her feet. Alycia pulled her hair into a bun at the crown of her head and slid her sunglasses onto her face.

The huge puffy white clouds in the sky were tinged with grey. She hoped it wouldn't rain. She supposed she could stand it if Bryce brought the tent, but it didn't look like he had.

She bit back a groan of impatience.

Be a grownup. Be a grownup.

Bryce was pissed Alycia made him wait. He'd tried waking her, but she mumbled something that sounded like "fuck off," and he left her alone.

Conveniently, Chuck sucked him into a game of horse-shoes which almost took his mind off things and gave him time to calm down a little.

The women had gone into town to shop the tiny boutiques that filled the equally tiny Main Street of Poplar Point. They'd wanted Alycia to go too, but he told them they had other plans.

Before they left, Bryce asked Janie how Vince was, and she said Michael's family planned a wake, a remembrance, and a scattering of the ashes, as Michael's will asked that he be cremated. Vince was going to stay for all of it and decide later if it was worth the drive to come back. If Vince stayed in the city, Janie would hitch a ride with Kara and Chuck.

To Bryce, it was just a reaffirmation that life was short.

He eyed the islands in the distance, not sure which one to choose. They were all too small to be inhabited by summer lake homes, so it wouldn't matter where they spent the night —there was no worry of trespassing.

The whole thing was a little dramatic, he had to admit. He could have just taken her on a walk but being with seven other people made finding time to be alone almost impossible, and hiking like Nate and Crystal was not his thing.

He lifted a hand, asking silently which island he should choose. She shrugged and looked away. Bryce hoped to God she wouldn't make this tough on them, but he supposed it was within her right. He was the one who cheated, so he should anticipate a little pushback.

He chose an island that looked as if it would be easy to pull the boat to shore. Bryce jumped out onto the rocks, and he steadied the boat as Alycia climbed out, bringing her bag of chips with her. He'd packed some food, and the cooler was at the bottom of the boat. He'd pull it out later when they needed to eat and set up camp.

Dragging the boat as far as he could onto the rocky slope of the shore, he shot Alycia a look. She was opening her chips and looking around.

She was still pretty. Maybe not the sparkling twenty-year-old girl she used to be, but the laugh lines around her eyes and the spattering of freckles that became more pronounced in the sun didn't lessen her looks.

Sometimes, though, he could see she was tired. Maybe tired of the day-to-day grind, maybe tired of him, tired of watching her friends have babies, or just now getting married. She could be tired of a number of things. But he'd never asked because hell, what could he do about it?

He'd done something all right.

"Well—" he began, wiping his hands on the back of his shorts.

"Can we look around first?" Alycia asked, cutting him off.

That might actually be a good idea . . . ease into spending time alone; they hadn't for so long. "Sure," he agreed, though he tried not to feel impatient. They had plenty of time now he'd gotten her away from their friends.

He drew in a deep, calming breath and lifted his face to the sky as he stretched his back. The wind smelled like water, the slightly gross smell of dead fish, crayfish, that type of thing, and trees, always trees. Bryce rubbed his hand over the back of his neck, his stomach doing queasy flip-flops. Was this how it felt at the end of a marriage? Or, if that's not what they were doing, was this how it felt to plan the next sixty years of his life?

He didn't know which he wanted less.

A cloud drifted over the sun casting a shadow, and he shivered.

Was that an omen?

Bryce snorted at the ridiculous thought. "Not too bad here, huh?" He tried to make his voice sound light, but even he could hear the underlying desperation.

Alycia licked her fingers. "I guess not." She walked along the shore, jumping over rocks or kicking them into the water that lapped along the edge of the island. She bent down to pick up a pine cone and threw it in.

Bryce watched it bob along the waves.

There were lots of trees on the little island and Bryce figured they'd find blueberry and raspberry bushes too.

The temperature dropped with the sun hiding behind a cloud bank, and Bryce was glad he'd packed a hoodie and sweatpants, just in case. He hoped it wouldn't rain. He hadn't packed a tent thinking sleeping under the stars would be romantic. And if they decided to split up, Bryce thought they wouldn't be here long enough to need it.

Alycia didn't seem inclined to talk, and he let her be. They had time, and in all the years they'd been together, he *had* learned a few things about her. One was she didn't like to feel rushed.

They wandered along the perimeter and just before they circled the whole island, Alycia veered toward the center.

A tree had fallen during a storm and she stepped on top of it, balancing along the thick log like a gymnast on a beam. "How come we never went anywhere, never took any trips?" she asked, her arms held out for balance, her chip bag hanging from one hand.

He looked up at her. The log hadn't completely fallen through the brush, so she stood at an incline, making her a few feet taller than he was. Bryce blanked at the question. "Vacation?" he asked, confused. "We came here every year."

"I know," she agreed, munching. "But we don't have any kids. We could have gone to Sandals, or taken a cruise. Maybe we couldn't have afforded Paris, London, or Rome, but we could have gone to Vegas. Hollywood. Seattle. Seen something of the world. Hell, we don't even do anything in the city unless Kara invites us to a fundraiser and she gives us free tickets. We don't see plays or go to the symphony. We never go to gallery openings, wine tastings. We're a boring old married couple. It's no wonder you cheated. You were bored with life. With me." She walked slowly to the base of the trunk where it split in the storm, sat, and wiped her nose with the back of her hand.

"I had no idea you felt like that," Bryce said, dropping to his haunches in front of her, his arms resting on his knees.

"Well, I didn't, *then*," she snapped, exasperated. "Would it have helped, do you think?"

"We had full lives, Al. We have friends, good jobs . . ." Bryce trailed off. For Christ's sake, he sounded lame. He knew he was going back and forth between tenses. Were they over, or weren't they?

"But something happened, we lost something, Bryce. The magic, the light."

Bryce stood, his calves burning from crouching, and leaned his ass against the log, shoving his thumbs into the pockets of his shorts.

He knew what she was talking about.

The dread of saying goodbye, the sweet promise of being able to see each other again. Of course, that had been when they were kids, when everything seemed so life and death. The days she was sick and he had to go to school without her. Bringing her homework to her after the day was over, just so he could see her.

He ran his fingers over the bare skin of her arm, remembering the electricity he would feel at a single touch. Bumping into her in the hall, stealing kisses in empty classrooms. "Remember when Mr. Regan caught us kissing in his classroom after school?"

Alycia giggled. "He made us clean his room before we left."

They'd swept the floor, wiped down the chalkboard, emptied the pencil sharpeners.

"He told us not to rush, that we had plenty of time."

"He was going through a divorce."

Bryce's gaze jerked to hers, but she was looking away, picking at a piece of fuzz on her shorts. "I didn't know that."

"I heard my mom talk about it after a Parent/Teacher meeting. His wife ran off with someone. I never found out who." The chip bag crinkled in her grip.

After they cleaned his classroom, they had run out of the

building, laughing, backpacks slung over their shoulders. Yeah, it had felt like they had all the time in the world, and his thirst for her had never abated. He knew the minute he wanted to marry her, had to marry her. "The night of the football game, under the bleachers . . ."

"You were out of your mind." But she said it softly, without judgment, and she rested her head on his shoulder.

"I was, I was out of my mind wanting you, wanting to protect you. He had has hands on you."

It was Homecoming, the smell of fall in the air, of popcorn and hot dogs from the vendors, the yeasty scent of beer they'd snuck into the game. Chuck was playing in the game, Vince smoking somewhere. Nate had been with this date, and Cam might have been in the marching band. Bryce couldn't remember now, not around the haze of rage that would always taint the memory.

He and Alycia and a scattering of other kids were drinking under the bleachers, and he had to take a piss. He'd gone to the restrooms inside the school, not wanting to use the portable potties that lined the field. It took him a bit longer, but he didn't mind. He'd always liked being in the school when it was empty. The sound of his sneakers squeaking on the waxed hallway floor, the lockers hanging open in the abandonment of the weekend, the Homecoming posters torn from the walls.

When he went back to find Alycia, another senior had her pinned against the bleachers, making her kiss him, groping her. Bryce couldn't see anything through the black cloud of fury. Alycia, and the police, told him later he almost killed the kid; he wouldn't have been sorry if he had.

Bryce had gone to the hospital, because the kid had broken a couple of Bryce's ribs trying to fight back. It was one of the most violent fights the school had ever seen, and Bryce had been expelled, finishing up his credits through a GED program.

Alycia had been by his side through the entire thing, and in private her father thanked him, tears in his eyes, for saving his little girl. That night, alone with Alycia in his hospital room, he told her he wanted to marry her.

She said yes.

They'd gotten married that very next summer. They hadn't even been old enough to drink at their own reception.

Bryce had never been happier.

He could still taste the cake, still feel her in his arms during their first dance, still see his future in her eyes, her love for him glowing in the light of the chandelier of the Hilton's ballroom.

Bryce made her look at him then, his fingers along her jaw, and he searched her eyes, searched for that sparkling love, but her eyes were flat.

"Remember when we got our first apartment? My parents had to co-sign on our lease." Alycia gripped Bryce's hand, and he squeezed back.

"I remember we made love in every room," he said bringing her hand to his lips.

"On the floor, because we couldn't afford furniture," Alycia murmured.

Their parents hadn't helped them with anything but the deposit. His parents said that they wanted to support their decision since they were adults, but since they were adults, they would need to act like it and pay their own bills. They slowly filled their apartment with furniture as they could afford it, and they shared one car for many years because they couldn't pay for two and car insurance on top of them.

"What happened, Bryce?" Alycia asked, turning her head to rest her forehead on his shoulder. She dropped her chip bag and wrapped her arms around his neck.

"I don't know, Al. I don't know." He returned her embrace, tucking her head under his chin.

He *didn't* know. Things had been good for so long. One

afternoon they'd made a snowman, the snow perfect for it, falling in wet globs from a hazy grey sky. They were both sitting in the yard, the wet seeping into their pants, but they didn't care. Her bright red hair had been slowly falling out of her hat, her cheeks rosy with cold. Snowflakes caught on her eyelashes, and she was the most beautiful thing he'd ever had the privilege to touch.

Autumn walks, coming out to the resort every summer. She must have forgotten—when they first started coming out here with their friends, she'd loved it. What else had she forgotten?

"Are you hungry? I didn't know how long we'd be out here so I packed quite a bit of food." Bryce led her away from the log back to the boat.

The memories of Bryce at the football game unsettled Alycia. She'd never seen Bryce like that before, and she hadn't seen him like that since. The night he'd asked her to marry him, she'd tucked herself between the bedrail of his hospital bed and his body. The nurses looked the other way when visiting hours were over. Alycia had been so scared watching Bryce and that other guy fight. The poor kid had been a transfer student and didn't know like the others she belonged to Bryce —had always belonged to Bryce.

They'd stayed in their first apartment until they bought their house. To this day, their old faded blue couch was still in their basement. How many movies had they watched while lying on that couch when they'd finally been able to buy it? How many times had they made love on it, fallen asleep on it, the two of them barely fitting, spooning?

She missed him taking her to work, having to share a car. Kissing him goodbye, him waiting for her to finish her shift, kissing her hello.

Their simple life had been enough.

When had she stopped being enough?

When had she stopped trying to be enough?

Alycia watched him grab the red and white cooler from the boat and haul it to where she stood. She sat on a rock and accepted the sandwich he handed her.

Boats motored by the island, some of the people in them waving as they flew past on the choppy water.

They had so much history, but it didn't matter. It weighed on them, pushing them down, suffocating them, but it weighed nothing, as if she could reach for all the memories and feelings and emotions and come up empty-handed.

She chewed a bite of tuna salad. It was her favorite kind. He knew so much about her, but there were days it felt like he knew nothing. "Bryce," she said. His name felt weird in her mouth. She'd say his name, in the middle of the night, when he was buried inside her, her love for him wrapped around her, twisting, until she knew she would die if they were ever apart. Fifteen years ago she would never have imagined they'd be here now on the cusp of deciding to continue their lives together or apart.

"Yeah?" He squinted in the sun.

"Do you love her?"

It took a lot for her to ask because she was so bone-scared of the answer. If he didn't love the stripper, he'd thrown their relationship away for nothing. If he loved her, this Mandi woman, he'd moved on without her. Was strong enough to move on without her.

"I don't know, Alycia. I don't want her to dance anymore. I want to be there for her and her daughter. Take care of her. If that's love, then maybe I do."

Alycia swallowed back the tears. It wasn't his words that brought the tears but the way he looked when he thought of her. It was the way he used to look at her when he thought she wasn't looking—a look of wonder, awe, a love so strong that nothing could harm it. He'd looked at her that way.

But not now. Not anymore.

"What if I said I wanted to work it out? Would you go to counseling with me? Work on our marriage? Maybe try for a baby?"

Bryce stood from the cooler and knelt in front of her. He framed her face in his hands, tangling his fingers in her hair. "I would do that for you, Alycia. If you could forgive me for what I did, if you could move on and not punish me for it anymore, I would do that for you. Counseling, a baby. Whatever you want."

"And you would stop seeing her?" Alycia searched his eyes, and at her question, a little flame snuffed out, and his hands trembled on her cheeks.

"Yes."

Alycia pushed her mouth to his and wrapped her arms around him as if he were her life preserver, and she was drowning in the middle of an ocean. She pulled him up, her sandwich falling onto the ground. She led him into the trees to hide from the passing boats. Pressing him against a tree, she slid her hands under his shirt, grazing his nipples with her fingertips. "Make love to me, Bryce. Show me you love me."

His eyes bore into hers. She knew he would never say aloud what she saw when he looked at her.

Bryce didn't love her anymore.

But because of their history, he would do what she wanted.

She could still love him for that, for willing to give up his future with . . . Mandi, because she asked.

"Let me get the sleeping bags. I don't want to do it on the ground." He smiled, but his heart wasn't in it.

Alycia waited, leaning against the tree, fought the burn in the back of her throat. She would take this one last time. He was still her husband; she felt after all they'd been through, it was her right, even if he belonged to another woman now.

She wished they would have moved right to the sex part. Now it felt contrived, set up, yet Alycia could understand. She didn't want to have sex on the ground, either. God knew what kind of plants were growing on this island. Kara and Janie had needed to see medics on this trip. She didn't want to be next for a horrible case of poison oak.

Bryce untied their sleeping bags and laid them out. He knelt on one and held out his arms. She dove into them, grateful they had this last night together.

Alycia kissed his neck, grazing his skin with her teeth. Tugging at his shirt, she kissed him, until he broke the kiss to pull his shirt over his head. He did the same for her, and the breeze that blew through the trees off the water made her nipples pebble. She laughed. "When was the last time we made love outside?"

Bryce blew out a breath, then suddenly he grinned. "We were shopping downtown. We took a wrong turn and we found ourselves in this little alley, remember? We ducked into that service door alcove. You were wearing that pretty sundress with the white flowers all over it."

Alycia *did* remember, and she felt the brick digging into her shoulder blades as he pushed her against the wall, her legs wrapped around his waist. They'd had dinner at a little Italian eatery and were window shopping, enjoying the mild evening. It was one of the last times they'd done anything together. "Yeah, I remember," she whispered.

"Hey, hey."

"What?" She'd been about to take her bra off.

"We can fix this. We can do this."

He was so adamant, she almost believed him.

She wiggled out of her denim shorts and white granny panties (God, she really had given up, hadn't she?) and lay on the sleeping bag, inviting Bryce to take her.

He finished undressing and he lay on his side next to her, his head propped on his hand, and ran his fingers over her stomach. Teasingly, he played with the hair between her legs.

A smile played on her lips, and she reached up to kiss him.

When his fingers slipped into her, she bent her knee. Alycia ran her fingers over his cock, and he pressed his body into her, closer.

It was difficult for her to stay focused with all the thoughts and emotions running through her mind. He kissed her and touched her as if he couldn't get enough, as if maybe he wasn't tired of making love to her, as if he wasn't bored of her. Passion radiated from him, from his kiss, from his touch, and she drank it in, savoring it, saving it, and suddenly she was sixteen and obsessed, petrified of even spending just one second without him.

"I need you inside of me, Bryce, please," she whispered against his mouth.

Bryce positioned himself over her and carefully filled her. There was a tenderness that hadn't been there the other times he'd made love to her on this trip. He pulled her close and whispered, "I'm sorry. I'm so sorry."

When he pulled away to look at her, there were tears on his cheeks.

She brushed them away with her thumbs. "It will be all right, sweetheart, it will be all right."

Alycia lifted her hips in sync with his thrusts, and she looked away as he came. Through the trees, the water sparkled in the late setting sun. When he rested his sweaty body on top of hers, she gave him a hug and kissed his wet cheek.

"You didn't come," he said, nuzzling her shoulder with his lips.

"It's okay." And it was. This closeness was all she needed, and it was all she was going to get. Drowsy now, she wiggled until he slid off her and spooned her from behind, his wet cock pressed against her ass. The wet spot on the sleeping bag was already cold.

With the sun warm on her skin, the bugs buzzing around, the hum of boats on the water in the distance, she fell asleep.

Bryce built a small fire, carefully building up the pit with the rocks scattered around the island. It wouldn't be a great idea to burn down the trees because of an errant spark, but it wouldn't be the stupidest thing he'd ever done.

He sat with his back against the cooler, a beer in his hand.

He'd let Alycia see him cry. And he'd apologized. What she didn't know was he wasn't apologizing for cheating on her; he was apologizing to Mandi for giving her up.

Christ, he was so weak. Why in the hell had he promised Alycia he'd try? Counseling, a baby? Five years ago, a baby would have made him the happiest guy on the planet. Now all he wanted was to give Mandi's daughter a sibling.

He'd promised his life away because Alycia asked him to.

When she'd fallen asleep, he covered her so the bugs wouldn't get at her, then built the fire. When she woke, he'd tell her they could go back to the cabin. There was no reason to stay on the island tonight. He'd agreed to stay and work on their marriage. He'd promised never to see or talk to Mandi again. There was nothing else to say.

Swallowing around the lump in his throat made it difficult to drink. He wanted to get drunk, but he needed to stay sober so he could motor them back.

Staring into the blazing orange flames, Bryce touched his neck. The noose was tight, and it would only get tighter, until one day he couldn't breathe anymore and he would be gone.

The sky was a purply-orange, the way the sky can only be in the middle of the summer in Minnesota, when the sun took its time going down. Alycia dressed and gathered the sleeping bags and when she saw Bryce sitting by the fire, she leaned against a tree and watched him.

He looked so forlorn, and she knew it was because of his promise. She'd used their trip down memory lane and his guilt to make him say what she wanted to hear. He'd promised to try at their marriage, have a baby, never to talk to Mandi again. How big a piece of his heart did she steal, making him promise her those things?

His heart wasn't hers to take, not anymore.

"Hey," she called quietly.

He looked at her and his quiet misery broke her heart.

Alycia dropped the sleeping bags near him and sat between his legs. He wrapped his arms around her and she took his beer bottle, swigging from it to moisten her mouth. She could only do this once. She'd used their history to keep him with her, and she could easily let him stay. She didn't want to be alone.

Only there wasn't much choice when your husband fell in love with another woman.

She sat for a moment, the fire crackling, Bryce's chin pushing into her shoulder.

"Bryce, I want a divorce."

"What?" he croaked.

Alycia turned on her butt so she was sitting sideways inside the V of his legs. He scooted back and the cooler scraped against the rock. Bryce stared at her, incredulity radiating from him. It would have been almost funny, except that the disbelief, the hope, and the joy that lit his features tore raggedly into her soul. "I want a divorce. You don't love me anymore."

Bryce opened his mouth, but Alycia quickly shook her head. "No. Don't bother denying it. You don't love me the way you used to. We've been together for so long, Bryce, but I can't keep you with me because of my fear. The look on your face when I asked you to work on our marriage, to have a baby with me . . . to stop seeing her." Alycia's voice shook and started to squeak around the tears. "I can't do that to you."

"I don't know what to say."

"There's nothing to say, really. Go back to the city. Call . . . her . . . to come get you. I'm going to finish the rest of our vacation, and I hope when I get back you'll be out of the house. I'll get an attorney and we'll figure out . . ." She couldn't continue.

Bryce took her face in his hands. It was difficult for Alycia to meet his gaze. There was so much . . . life in them now. Joy, happiness. A future full of possibilities. It had been how he looked at her when they were dancing at their wedding reception. She tried to look away, but he wouldn't let her, his grip firm. "You don't have to do this. We don't have to do this. We can work it out. Start a family. I'll do the counseling, and we'll go on family vacations, and—"

Alycia shook her head. "And grow more and more miserable as the years go on, and in ten years really *do* get divorced when we have children depending on us?" She placed her hands on his. "Take what I'm offering you. You want it, take it."

He pulled her into his embrace, and his heart pounded under her ear. "Thank you."

She might have held it together if he hadn't said those words, but thanking her was her undoing and she burst into wracking sobs as she mourned the ending of her marriage. Twenty years of her life, so many years, so much pain, happiness, love, with this man she'd called her husband, the love of her life. Alycia might have blamed Mandi, but she'd lost him, lost her marriage, long before Bryce had gone to that bachelor party.

He held her as she cried, and if he cried with her, she couldn't tell. Her keening consumed her, her agony echoing off the water, eerily bouncing through the air and against the trees and stones. Bryce rocked her as he would the babies they'd never have. He ran his fingers through her hair and rubbed her back.

Finally, she pulled away and wiped her face with her hands. The beer bottle was wedged between her legs and she was surprised she hadn't toppled it while she was crying. Grateful, she drained the bottle, the flat liquid soothing her raw throat.

"I can finish out the vacation," Bryce offered, turning to the cooler and grabbing two more beers from the ice. The bottles dripped cold water onto her skin, and she shivered.

"No. A . . . a clean break would probably be best." If he hung around, she would be tempted to try keeping him, and that wouldn't do anything but hurt her and Bryce. She was tired of hurting.

"Do you want to go back to the cabin tonight?" He unscrewed the tops, protecting his hands by using his t-shirt for grip.

"Not unless you want to. The fire is nice and sleeping out here will be okay." Alycia took the beer and guzzled it. She needed the buzz. Her head was pounding, but she felt numb. She doubted she would feel anything for a long time.

Attempting a smile, she met his eyes. "One more night?"

Bryce returned her smile, his relief evident. "One more night."

❧

Bryce slowly opened his eyes. The fire had gone out long before. Though the air was cool now and the sun was barely peeking over the horizon, the day had potential to be a scorcher. He wished it could warm the icy feeling in his heart.

Alycia had given him want he wanted, but the old adage, "be careful what you wish for, you might just get it," floated through his mind. Only, the way he'd felt promising her the rest of his life threatened to cut off his air supply, and he knew no matter how difficult this would be, this leaving, this starting over, would be worth it in the end.

He sat up and ran his fingers through his hair. His mouth tasted like shit because he hadn't brushed his teeth the night before.

Alycia was still sleeping, her cheeks and eyes crusty from crying.

He'd lain awake last night stunned and grateful. He would have done the honorable thing, staying, if she truly had wanted that. He would have given it his best shot. He'd like to believe he would have. But Alycia was right. When they had kids who depended on him, maybe a bigger house, newer cars, that wouldn't be the time to cut and run. To do it now, when the split would be mostly amicable and far easier than he had any right for it to be, would be best.

He unzipped his sleeping bag and groaned as he stood up. Sleeping on the hard ground wasn't easy. Bryce stretched and slipped on his flip-flops to walk into the trees to piss.

He pushed his pants down just low enough to pull his cock out. Elastic was a man's best friend. He shook off the droplets before pulling up his pants. He couldn't believe Alycia let him off the hook. Here he'd been all prepared to . . . well, he didn't want to think about it. He'd been in a pretty bad way when Alycia found him by the fire. He must have looked it.

She was just stirring when he stepped into the clearing near the shore.

He wanted to boat back to the cabin as quickly as he could, so he could call Mandi. He wanted to give her time to pick him up before her shift, but it was a three-hour drive from the city, then she'd need to drive them back. At least he could stay with her daughter tonight; she could let her sitter go. That'd save her some money, too.

If Alycia didn't turn bitchy and demand an unreasonable alimony, Bryce could ask Mandi again to quit. She could work somewhere else during the day part-time while she went to school.

The sale of their house would help; the mortgage payment took a huge chunk out of his paychecks every month.

Where the hell was it?

Bryce looked frantically for their boat. It wasn't on the shore where he'd pulled it up yesterday. Squinting, he searched the water as far as he could see.

Nothing.

"Bryce?" Alycia mumbled, sitting up and rubbing her eyes.

"The boat is gone," Bryce growled.

"What? How?" Alycia scrambled out of her sleeping bag, wincing as the little rocks bit into her feet. She slid on her sandals and adjusted her twisted clothes. "Where'd it go?"

"How should I know? If I could see it, I'd swim out and get it. Son of a bitch." His wish of getting back to the city today went up in smoke. Who the hell knew how long they'd be stuck out here. "I'm going to walk around the island and look for it."

He stalked away, his flip flops slapping angrily at his heels with every step.

When he made his way back to Alycia, she was standing near the water shivering in her shorts and tank top. The morning air was cool and a white hazy mist hung over the water.

Of course, their backpacks were at the bottom of the boat.

"Nothing?"

"Nope," he said tersely. He pulled a sleeping bag from the ground and wrapped it around her shoulders.

"I'm sorry. I suppose you wanted to take off as fast as you could," she said, clutching the sleeping bag closer to her.

Bryce sat, his arms resting on bent knees. He stared into the horizon, his shoulders tight.

Alycia unzipped the sleeping bag and covered them both as she sat next to him.

In the distance a boat floated by, but they were too far away for anyone to see them.

"Thanks," he said, then relaxed when Alycia leaned into him. "I had thought maybe if Mandi could come and get me, we could make it back before her shift."

"You can take the car," Alycia offered. "Bailey and Cam will take me home."

Bryce chuckled under his breath. "You've been real good about this, Al. I don't deserve it."

"You don't," Alycia agreed, but she took his hand and squeezed. "You cheated on me, and we never talked about it for four months."

Bryce opened his mouth to object. Like hell they hadn't talked. All they'd been doing lately was talk, since the second he told her.

"No, I mean, *talk*. We did plenty of screaming at each other, but we never talked. I was too scared you were going to say you wanted to leave me."

"So what was last night then? I gave you what you wanted."

"That's why I did it. Because you were willing to give her up. I guess in the end I couldn't let you do that. I didn't know you had feelings for her. I'd been thinking all along she'd been some quick drunken lay, but last night I saw her as a person, someone you cared about. If you can make it work with her, well. I'm trying to be a grownup. Give you the understanding I would want if it'd been me who met someone."

Bryce's jaw tightened. After four months of Alycia yelling

at him, her quiet admission of compassion left him puzzled and thankful.

"Plus, I plan on taking you to the cleaners in court."

Bryce bristled until he saw the twinkle in her eyes, and her lips pressed together in suppressed laughter. "Brat."

"Well, I should get something for my pain and suffering," Alycia jokingly griped.

"Oh, hey, I brought you something." Bryce got up and trotted over to the cooler. Grabbing a soggy box from the melting ice, he shook it, and then brought it to her, throwing the wet box into her lap.

"Twinkies!" Alycia squealed. "You do love me." Embarrassed, she looked away and opened the box.

Bryce sat next to her and wrapped an arm around her. "I do love you, Alycia. I always will. You've been a part of my life too long to throw that all away."

"I know," she sighed. "You're lucky to be the first to find someone. To move on with someone wouldn't be so scary. I've always had you with me. Being on my own will be . . . different. But a good different, I think."

"You know I'll always be around for you, Al. Whatever you need, I'll be there."

Alycia crumpled the cellophane between her fingers and took a big bite of Twinkie.

Suddenly, Bryce was worried how she would live without him. Where would she go? Their house wasn't paid for; they'd have to sell it because she wouldn't be able to afford the mortgage on her own. Who would she talk to at night when she couldn't sleep? He pictured her eating TV dinners alone at the kitchen table, while he shared dinner with Mandi and Lindsay.

Bryce rubbed his aching heart. "Maybe this isn't such a good idea." He made her look at him, this woman by his side who'd been his wife, his best friend since sixth grade, his first and only lover until Mandi. She had a dab of white filling on her lip, and he smeared it with the pad of his thumb.

Licking her lip, Alycia shook her head. "That's too little, too late. I still haven't worked through what you did to me. If you really wanted to leave me, before Mandi, before all our fighting about her, you should have told me. If you were unhappy, you should have told me. I should have told you, too." She took another bite of Twinkie, chewed, and swallowed. "I was scared, and probably so were you. But now that it's out in the open, Mandi, these feelings, we can't go back. I don't want to go back."

Bryce heard the quiet resolved in her voice. Maybe she would be okay, after all. He could promise to always be around. He'd help her if she needed it, no matter what.

Not that she'd ask. He realized now, paying the bills, moving up in her job, doing all the housework, she'd always in some way, been on her own, been in control.

They sat in comfortable silence as the sun came up.

"You don't have your cell on you?"

Alycia shook her head. "I left it in the cabin. I didn't think I'd need it, or want it. You wanted to get this resolved, and I knew we needed to. I'd been hiding my anger, blocking you out. You?"

Bryce shook his head. "It's in the boat. Not that it would have done us much good."

Alycia rested her chin on her knees, done with her sugary breakfast. "Do you remember your Uncle Bob at our wedding? He got drunk and started preaching at us we were too young to be married."

Bryce laughed. "I never told you, but my mom, when she had those disposable cameras developed from our reception? One of them had dick pics on it. She always thought it was Bob."

Alycia swatted at him, laughing. "No! Why didn't you tell me?"

"My mom didn't want the rumor to go around. Everyone knew her brother was a dumbass. She didn't want to make it worse. He still is. He was picked up for a drunk and disorderly a couple months ago."

"Ugh. Then one of my bridesmaids and one of your groomsmen, skinny-dipping in the courtyard's fountain. My mom was so mad."

"That was Patrick because Chuck was moving into the dorms to get away from his parents, and he was too busy to get away."

"That's right," Alycia murmured. "And the bridesmaid was my cousin. My mother insisted her brother's family would've been mortally offended and never talk to us again if she wasn't included. I don't know how that would have been bad."

A mama mallard duck and her ducklings floated by, little brown blobs bobbing on the gentle waves.

"When will someone find our boat and look for us?" Alycia asked, watching the ducks drift away. "I want to shower and take a nap. I slept like shit. I'm never camping again. And you . . . have . . . things . . ."

Bryce shrugged and stood, his ass numb from sitting on the rocky ground. He was starving, and he pulled out a massive bag of trail mix from the cooler. He was shoving handfuls into his mouth and pacing when Chuck cruised by in the speed boat they used to go tubing.

Alycia jumped up and started waving her hands, screaming.

The screaming was useless—Chuck wouldn't be able to hear her, but Bryce followed suit, flinging trail mix all over the ground.

Their movements must have caught Chuck's eye, because to Bryce's immense relief, Chuck swung the boat around in a wide arc and cruised by the island. He pumped a fist in the air, looking pleased he'd found them, then cut the engine.

"What the hell?" he hollered good-naturedly, pulling a paddle from the boat's floor and guiding the boat toward the rocky shore.

"How did you find us?" Alycia asked, jumping into the boat.

Bryce grabbed the cooler and the other sleeping bag. He looked over his shoulder as Chuck took the cooler. This was the last place he would ever make love with Alycia, the last place where they would have any meaningful conversation. The place where they had decided to dissolve their marriage. He would always remember Alycia with Twinkie filling on her lips, the sad yet teasing glint in her eyes when she joked about cleaning him out in court.

There would never be anything that would make him forget those moments.

"Are you coming, or did you want me to leave you here?" Chuck asked, the boat bumping against the rocks.

"I'm coming," Bryce murmured, turning to the boat, but seeing the trees, the fire's ashes. The ashes were a symbol of their relationship. Once they burned hot and steady, but now they were cooling, like the dying embers of a fire. The only thing left was the grey soot of what once was.

He climbed into the boat.

Chuck pushed them away from the rocky bank. "Some kids found your boat early this morning. They were on a pontoon and hadn't gone to bed yet. They hauled it to the main docks of the resort—away from us—and the office guy tried to call Kara on her cell. He didn't get anywhere, of course, being her phone is at the bottom of the lake. Anyway, the guy ran to our cabin hell bent for leather, practically having a seizure at Janie's door. We split up to look for you. Nate and Cam took the Jet Skis, and the women took the pontoon and binoculars."

"How did the boys know the boat belonged to the resort?" Alycia asked, throwing the box of Twinkies into the cooler and grabbing a bottle of water before sitting, the sleeping bag still wrapped around her.

"The name of the resort is spray-painted onto the side of the boat." Chuck started the engine. "You must have kissed and made up?" he asked over the growling of the motor.

Bryce met Chuck's eyes, but he didn't try to offer an explanation. He was focused on getting back. He wanted to leave, thought it was best. They needed a clean break and little by little maybe they could go back to being friends. Maybe. Divorces could get messy, even amongst the friendliest of couples. Bryce could only hope they would come out the other side unscathed.

He looked at Alycia who was huddled under the blue sleeping bag, her eyes closed, her head resting against the back of the chair.

Bryce would remember her this way, her hair blazing in the sun, and maybe, maybe, a faint smile on her lips.

Or maybe he was only seeing what he wanted to see.

Alycia bolted the moment her feet hit the dock. She wanted a cup of coffee and a shower, but mostly she didn't want to be around Bryce when he made "the call." The call to tell Mandi he was free, that if she could, to pick him up. She didn't want to be around when he packed his bags, didn't want to wait with him while Mandi drove from the city.

She was debating caffeine or a shower when Bailey burst into the cabin without knocking. "You're okay!" she cried.

Define okay, Alycia thought, but simply nodded instead, knowing Bailey was referring to the missing boat and not to Alycia's broken heart. Only, maybe it wasn't that broken.

She filled the carafe to start coffee.

"What happened?" Bailey asked, giving her a sideways

hug because Alycia was filling the back of the coffeemaker with water.

"Sometime during the night the boat drifted away. It's not a big deal."

"Did you get everything worked out?" Bailey asked, sitting at the table.

Alycia wished Bailey would leave her alone. "In a manner of speaking," she allowed, measuring coffee grounds into the filter.

"Oh, good!" her friend said, breathing a sigh of relief. "I never thought you two should break up. You guys were meant for each other."

Alycia turned on the coffeemaker and leaned against the counter. She felt old, and dirty, and tired. Camping did not agree with her. "We're getting a divorce." With that, she let the tears come and cried into Bailey's shoulder, who was suddenly there, wrapping her in a comforting embrace.

"Oh, baby," Bailey crooned into Alycia's ear.

She cried while the coffee dripped behind her. She cried for the loss of her best friend, her husband, all the years behind them.

"What happened?"

Alycia wiped her eyes and tried to control her sobs. Crying wouldn't help now. "We decided it was best. He would have stayed with me, gone to counseling, tried for a

baby—" She caught Bailey's eye and winced, but continued, "—the whole thing. But as we talked, I realized he cares about this other woman, and he wants to be with her. I can't keep him from her. He'd be miserable, and so would I. I don't even know where he is. Calling her, probably, to come get him. We thought it was best for him to leave. I'll finish out the vacation and drive back alone."

"I can't believe it," Bailey breathed, accepting the mug Alycia handed to her.

"We might have been able to fix it if it had been a one-night stand. But Bryce loves her. I couldn't stand in the way of that."

"That's really brave," Bailey said, then took a sip of coffee.

Alycia studied at her friend. Bailey looked cool and breezy, dressed in a white gauzy sundress, her hair pinned in some curly updo. She looked ready for a garden party, not an afternoon at a lake resort. But despite what Bailey said, she exuded a quiet bravery that Alycia would never have.

It took courage not to run away.

"I'm sorry, but I need—"

"Oh, of course," Bailey interrupted, setting her coffee mug on the table with a little too much force. "You sure you want to stay here?"

"I think so." Alycia chugged most of her coffee. "I'll need the time to process what happened. I'll need Kara to recommend someone. But for now, I can only think of a shower and a nap."

Bailey gave her another hug Alycia returned only half-heartedly. "We're glad you're okay," Bailey whispered. "If you need to talk, I'll be around."

After Bailey let herself out, Alycia refilled her mug and ran the shower. She stood under the hot water, washing away the dirt, sweat, and bug spray. It was too bad she couldn't wash the pain away too. How long would she feel this hollowness?

Alycia dressed in draw-string shorts and a plain tank top, skipping her bra. As she lay in bed, praying for sleep to come, a tear slipped down her cheek and soaked into her pillow.

⁊ฺ

Voices woke her, a vehicle engine shutting off outside her open window.

Her head felt stuffy with cotton and her throat was sore and dry from holding back tears.

"I'm ready to go."

Bryce's voice floated to her through the screen, and Alycia scrambled for her phone, running wildly into the living room to find it.

Frantically pushing the buttons to bring her phone alive, she saw she'd slept for almost four hours. She ran back to her room and peeked out the window, hiding behind the sheer curtains.

A tall, coppery redheaded woman stood near a white compact car, and she was speaking with Bryce, a smile lighting her features.

She watched Bryce throw his backpack into the backseat and the woman walk toward the driver's side.

Realizing this would be the last time she would see Bryce without lawyers involved, she ran from the cabin, her hair flying behind her, over the grass. "Bryce!" she yelled as she rounded the cabin's corner and onto the gravel lot where they parked their cars.

Bryce looked up from the car, a shadow crossing his face. "Alycia, don't—"

Alycia skidded to a stop in the middle of the small lot, the crushed rock and small sticks poking into her bare feet. She stared at the woman.

Mandi was at least a foot taller than Alycia. Her feet were clad in white sandals, her legs longer than a giraffe's. She wore denim shorts accented with patches of lace, and a white lacy top which showcased her magnificent breasts, that were, to Alycia's eye, real. Mandi's eyes blazed a hot golden brown, and her hair was like a brand-new penny, shot with strands of blonde, matching Bryce's almost-white hue.

Did Bryce realize? Alycia blinked furiously. Did he realize he truly had traded her in for a newer model?

She lifted her chin. "Bryce and I, we've been together for a long time," she started but had to stop and clear her throat, her voice sounding foreign through the blood rushing in her ears. "Since we were kids, he's been my best friend."

"Alycia—" Bryce tried again.

"No, let her speak," Mandi said, holding a hand up to Bryce and nodded for Alycia to continue.

Alycia's chin wobbled. "Thank you. We've been friends . . . for a long time. The only man I've ever loved, the only man I've ever slept with. We've had many firsts, and I'm not going to lie, this hurts. A lot." She twisted the bands on the ring finger of her left hand. "But sometimes, things happen, and I've tried really hard not to hate you, blame you, for this." Tentatively, she took the few remaining steps needed to be close enough to touch her.

She pulled the rings from her finger and reached for Mandi's hand.

Alycia pressed the rings into Mandi's palm. "These are a symbol of the past twenty years of my life. I heard once, rings are supposed to represent an unbreakable love, an unbreakable circle. Bryce and I . . ." her eyes flicked to him, then back to Mandi's face,

". . . we still love each other, we always will. But I know we're not in love with each other anymore, and it's time to move on." Alycia folded Mandi's fingers around what used to be her whole life. "He's moved on to you." She blinked back tears. "Take care of my best friend, please."

Mandi nodded. "I will."

Alycia wiped her cheeks, offered Bryce a small wave goodbye, then ran across the parking lot, away from her old life . . . away from everything she ever knew.

Summer Secrets Novellas 4 - 6 are available now. Don't miss what happens next!

ACKNOWLEDGMENTS

Thank you to Jewel E. Leonard
(http://www.jeweleleonard.com) for editing Summer Secrets.
You made them sound fabulous!

Thank you to my beta readers—your feedback is priceless

ABOUT THE AUTHOR

Vania Rheault has lived in Minnesota all her life. In 2003, she graduated with a BA in English with a concentration in creative writing from Minnesota State University, Moorhead. When she's not writing, she's reading, playing with one of her three cats, or going to movie night with her sister. All of Nothing is her fifth Contemporary Romance.

Find Vania at www.vaniamargene.com and these other social media outlets: